Big Chocolate Cookies

BIG CHOCOLATE COOKIES

a novel by

E.S. Goldman

JOHN DANIEL PUBLISHER · SANTA BARBARA · 1988

PRINTED IN THE UNITED STATES OF AMERICA.

LIBRARY OF CONGRESS CATALOGING-IN-PUBLICATION DATA
Goldman, E.S.
I. Title.
PS3570.U3985 1988 813′.54 87-30306
ISBN 0-936784-49-0

Published by
JOHN DANIEL, PUBLISHER
Post Office Box 21922
Santa Barbara, California 93121

The characters in this story are imaginary;
like most people.

One

EDNA'S SQUARE-GRAND PIANO

1

NUMBERS ALWAYS came natural to me, were always something I could do. I liked going into that class in school. I picked up on the numbers part when I got into business. It wasn't till I used up most of my life—already had all this money and my picture on the cover of your friend Malcolm's magazine—that I found out numbers were built into me the same as lungs.

Ten twelve years ago when those Nautilus exercise machines were coming in I got interested in doing workouts. Get the belly down. Get the bacon off the shoulder. I was sixty and decided like everybody thirty was a better number. I went in for a checkup before taking that on and my doctor gave me the works. Breathing. Stretching. Running on the treadmill. Lifting. Listened all over me. Felt all over me. Laid me down, taped on those cold buttons and wired me to that KGB machine that reads you on the graph paper. Shows the tribulations of your heart. Looked important.

I asked him how I was.

"I'm sorry to tell you you won't live to be more than a hundred and forty years of age. Take a look at this KGB for a man his age" he said to his nurse and she admired it too.

"If it's all that great" I said "make me a copy and I'll give it to Edna for her birthday coming up. I never gave her a present like that before."

I gave it to Edna in a pocketbook I bought her at Saks and we admired it some more and I made her promise to see the doctor and get me one of herself for my birthday. I wouldn't have that much interest in going to a hundred and forty without her there.

While we were looking at it I said to myself Hey I've seen that chart before. That's a stock chart. That's the chart of a stock I know.

Zap! I got that zap experience of discovering something. How you get when you see something nobody else sees. Buzz comes on your skin like a fly in a blue light. Zap!

Say you're walking down the street and there's a saint's face plain as day looking at you from a church wall. Those things happen mostly in Italy. Street's full of people, but you're the only one sees that particular thing. You have to be a certain kind of a person, your nerves have to be connected in a certain way. Those 3D movies with airplanes coming at you, they make you duck in your seat if you're wearing the special glasses. If you don't have the glasses on you just came for the popcorn. I had on my 3D's for that KGB.

I want you to know I was in a high state of excitement. I kept taking that chart out and looking at it. I was sure as I was alive I knew that chart. Next morning I went in to Greg Wyman's first thing and closed the door on his office.

"What do you think this is?" I asked him. Cool.

He looked it over. No zap. "What am I supposed to think?"

"You're supposed to think it's a chart."

"That's what I'm thinking."

"Yeah but of what?"

"I don't know. Okay, I got it, that's one of those heart things. I had one of them last year. Is that you? Is it good or bad?"

"What else is it? Go on look at it good."

He couldn't get it so I gave him a clue. "Let's say it's a stock. What stock would it be?"

Dug down deeper into his attention. Still couldn't get it. "I don't know. What am I supposed to say?"

Goddamit. "Think about it. What stock is it? Call me if you come up with it."

"Do I get a prize?"

"You get the commissions."

By then Greg knew I wasn't somebody's uncle Nut, I was a serious investor. I was the biggest customer he had. Must be something on my mind. In a couple hours I got the call. It wasn't any stock. It was the Dow Jones Industrial Average for the month ending February 28.

March first was the day I had the checkup.

"You're sure of that?"

"I'm looking at them. What's up?"

"I'm coming over."

Holy sweat! Can you imagine? I was wired to the Dow. Take me about one week to own the whole world.

Being as I say a rich man already long before, I had everything I could think to want. I was used to thinking in millions. I went on up to billions. I was going do things like buy up General Motors and fire the president because of a Nova car they sold me, first car I ever owned, miserable damn car, and they wouldn't talk it over. That's one of the things brought on Ralph Raider, that type company being too important to pay attention. You're fired. I was going buy all the wheat and corn stashed in those silos and ship it out to hungry people. Makes no sense having all this food here and all those people starving there. All those hardluck stories in the papers, people with sick kids can't pay the doctor, people lost their pocketbooks on the way to the bank to pay off the mortgages. Cancer research. You just tell me how much. Arsdur U. Stiff was going take care of all those problems. Wired to the Dow! Man! Wired to the Dow!

Turned out to be only one hitch. The Dow is something that already happened. You can't make any money on something that already happened. Never found a way. You can't get any bets down on yesterday's ball game, people aren't interested in but one side.

I hired a Harvard professor and gave him the problem. Told him he didn't have to wait on any grants, I'd put up what he needed to get the job done. They tried hooking up different parts of my body to get different readouts. They put me to sleep, looking for brain waves that get into the future while I'm sleeping. They tried setting my clocks ahead, printed a calendar just for me beginning next month. Supposed to put me in next month's mood. I talked to various fortune tellers. With this input, how are we going find out what the Dow is next week?

Okay not next week. How about tomorrow?

Okay give me a five minute start, I'll settle for that.

Never could find a way. I don't have anything to show for it but a parlor trick. Wire me up and I print out the Industrials going back thirty forty days. Big deal. You can open the Journal and see that. That's no better than being able to wiggle your ears. One thing though, it does tell you the stock market was a natural built-in thing with me. It's how I'm made like some people see saints. You wouldn't know that unless I told you.

Malcolm never heard about the KGB. You tell him if he doesn't believe it he can talk to Greg Wyman.

2

Now how are we going do this. Most important thing in my life is Edna. Let's start off with her. Get back to me after.

Around Thanksgiving, just before hours, the door was open airing out the room and I was going over stock behind the bar playing Ronrico, Johnny Walker, Turkey, Gordon's Gin. Glass organ was my idea, playing along here at a glass organ. Musical ideas always coming going in my head. I play a little piano—I mean I play a regular piano but not too good. Blew a cornet in high school and thought about making the band but lost interest, took too long. Found a whole gang of things to like but I was never one to do any particular thing that didn't come naturally.

Took to the piano in Reverend Multrie's church, a little school type upright in the cement room, the new-built part of the church where they had Sunday School. That piano was kept up, only two three keys if you hit there was nothing there. Hitting a piano key that doesn't answer back, that's a jolt even if you know ahead that's the way it is. When I was a kid I slid into second base and came up with a dead nerve in this hip. Doesn't bother me at all till I touch it, say drying off after a shower. I can feel that hip on my finger but it never heard of me, might as well touch a table. That hip still gives me the same Hey what's going on feeling I got sixty more years ago till I remember I'm part dead there.

The first part of me dead and I was only nine ten years old. When you hear somebody say Time flies you want to think what that means. You want to think of some part of you flying off and being gone—gone, you understand that? That time's gone, never coming back, instead of like you think hanging around like a dog waiting on you take him for a walk.

What are we going do about whether we say Or her as we go along? I want to do things right. You can say dog Or bitch if you want and you can say him and add on Or her. You do it, I'm not going bother with it. I learned in school if you said him it meant her too and that's good enough for me. Just don't have me saying Them if it's only one of them because I know better than that. I learned plurals in school. Arithmetic was my best subject, maybe that's why I picked up on the plurals. You can't say you're taking Them for a walk if there's only one of them.

I'll leave that up to you, but it would be embarrassing for a man in my position for people to think I can't count.

Standing by that piano watching how Moses Leach did things gave me the principles. Ten minutes now and then fooling around on my own got me up to one-finger melody lines, blues chords and bends, two-hand slam-dunk sevens, things like that. Make you expect something is going happen but you already heard it. I hear arrangements in my head make Strayhorn rise out of his grave like that big stone statue in the Mexican museum if it had on aviator glasses. Strays rises up prickling Stiffy where in hell you find that last chorus on Birmingham Breakdown?

Jazz is something I was always into. Music and numbers go together in some people, working along the same nerves, like some foods go with other foods you can't say just why. A piece of apple pie sits there waiting for ice cream. You can't say the same for a lemon pie. I don't mind telling you jazz played right on the piano or guitar's about the only thing can make me cry. Maybe not cry. Eyes fizz like humming into toilet paper on a comb is more like it. Lemme hear chords and breaks nobody ever thought of before in that particular tune and keep on doing them so I say Yeah that's the best anybody could think to do with that right now. I appreciate it.

There's the doers and there's the appreciators. Then there's the rest you have to keep an eye on just using up the earth.

Piano's the best because it's got the tune, got the beat. Chords. Breaks. Got it all. Maybe—I said maybe—it can use a string bass under like Edna says and she's sitting there but that's just her view. Could do without it myself because if there's a bass you have to throw him a solo now and then. You're an intelligent person, must be doing your kind of work—if God meant the string bass to solo wouldn't He make people want to hear it more than one number at a time? You ever hear anybody ask for a string bass encore? Maybe the man's mother. The most surprised people in the world would be you give Ming a big hand and have him turn around and show his gratitude with an encore. Like telling him when a fella is nice enough to ask How are you. The bass is a band instrument, there to move the band. Wasn't ever any bass going move Edna around anyhow. All the bass did for Edna was let her rest in a long set. That's my view.

Since I opened up always had the idea to put music in the place. Got the piano early, gave up four tables to put it in the corner come the day I could afford fifty seventy a week for somebody to play it.

I saw this auction ad in the paper for this estate, disposing of this estate including a dining room, two sitting rooms, fourteen beds and fourteen dressing tables, all this stuff, and this special Henry J. Miller Square-Grand piano. I remember about the fourteen beds and fourteen dressing tables because I said to Sid "That's a big house, rich people, bound to be a good box." Couldn't let that piano go by.

Believe me it was big. We got it over in the apartment now. That's Edna's personal piano. We used it here till we took in the next room and put in the two matched Falcone grands. We were the only place with two good pianos. Okay, Cafe Society had three but we had these Falcone grands.

Edna never used them for piano battles. She never believed in that challenge stuff, making people look bad. She plays as fast as Tatum or any of them but she likes playing with other people, not making them look bad. Shearing, Nat Cole, Monk, Dave McKenna, Billy Marcus, Oscar, Bud Powell. You name them, all the real piano players in their day come in here to play two piano with Edna and no shoot-outs, just jazz.

Cleaned that piano up after it got in here from the auction and after we made some money cleaned it up again, second time cost as much as a Cadillac. Painted blue when it came in here. Scratched. Wood bruised along the key cover like a hungry dog heard there were eighty-eight bones in there. The main thing is it sounded good—big tone—none of that church bell clang you never get out. I liked it soon as I laid hands on it. Rolled two-hand majors all the way up the keyboard, people on the street probably thought it was Garner. Bid it in for $230 and I'd pay to move it from the auction house. That was the thing about pianos in those days, could you move them. I had six buddies came down with a truck and carry it off.

Awhile after it got in here this old-fashion type gentleman drinking at the bar noticed it. Quality type gentleman. Little bit of mouse hair split down the middle. Gold rims on his eyeglasses. Gold cuff-links with wedding invitation initials came down from granddaddy. This old gentleman got off the stool and went over to the piano and he looked at it real careful.

The man knows I told Sid. You can see the man knows. Got me something in that piano.

He comes back to his seat, nodding his head. Yeah something.

"Say, Stiffy" he says "I see you got Franny Dillingham's piano. Too bad they closed her. That was a classy house."

Yeah well. You never know looking at a man what he knows.

3

A few years back I got to thinking about people who did for me, people I owed without their knowing. Like this big kid we called Bums watching me pitch a baseball came over and showed me how it's all in the wrist. You gotta cock your wrist, then you unwind and it goes. Man, do you know how much mileage you get out of an idea like that? That's good information for every man's game there is and I was a player. Baseball. Basketball. Tennis. Football. Golf. It isn't that important in football except for the passer.

I had a teacher in the sixth grade, Miss Phillips. Art teacher. I made this drawing of an aunt I had showed every mole and bump and curl hair on her face. Not much of a drawing, I can't draw worth a dime, but I got it all in. Miss Phillips told me "Arsdur you see things better than most people."

Never forgot Miss Phillips. Couldn't draw but I could see, and better than most. Didn't even know I was looking before that, been looking ever since. Couldn't play but I could hear. That's me, your basic appreciator.

Things somebody like old Phillips does for you lasts and she didn't even know she did it. Comes free, not something you pay back with a present or taking you out to dinner. I was thinking along those lines when the V Squad came in looking for a donation. Big Brothers. Camp. Annual Ball. One of those things they do.

"Here's a special hundred for the piano" I told him.

"I'm taking it. What's about the piano?"

"If it wasn't for you fellas Frannie Dillingham would still have it. If I don't have it I don't ask Charlie Duvall to find somebody to play it for me. He'd send Edna some place else. She'd be playing a beatup Chickering at Joe's Chicken Shack."

Fact is you never know who's going do you the biggest favor ever happened to you and he doesn't even know he did it.

All right. I'm behind the bar playing head tunes on the bottles and I hear this good solid woman voice asking if I'm the owner. Wasn't one of those voices afraid what the answer's going be. Some people are scared to death you're going say yes when they ask for you. They'd rather go back and say He wasn't there or they call on the telephone and give it two rings and hang up. He don't answer. That way it isn't settled nobody paid attention. Not paying attention to somebody is worse than stealing from them. I admitted I owned the place.

"I hear you're asking around for a piano player. Would you listen to me? I got a card."

Turned around and saw it wasn't a woman at all, more of a high school girl. Just about old enough so you notice she's not too good looking. That's the first thing you think about, that's how it is. Figure on the chunky side not organized yet for a girl cut off that low. Take a couple years growing to get that done. Wide and slow across the eyes like an Indian, the chief, not one of the maidens you take out in a canoe. Hair flat as a wet paint brush pushed back plain to get it out the way. Plain. Neat. Brown sweater. Brown skirt. Big brown saddlebag hung on the shoulder of her brown coat. Brown girl with no flash. Sisterly. Not somebody you want to try for right off. See all that in an eye blink.

I thought she was showing me a union card. No it was Charlie Duvall's. I mentioned to Charlie I might be in the market for a piano player some day but I wasn't too serious right then, still paying off investment. Charlie knew that but the way he ran his business was if there was a chance you might want somebody he wrote your name on a card and sent the talent around. Law of averages might make somebody stick.

Listen to Edna Bundige. Real good. Kenny Clarke say so.

You don't have to see his name to know it's Duvall's card.

"I told Duvall a combo." Putting on some big shot for this little gal. I couldn't afford any combo just then.

"I'm a combo. I do piano and sing." Spoke up, not arguing, just telling you how it is. Laid that Indian Chief face right on you. Her eyes taking you in. Eyes move like your camera on the slow mark and you're surprised how long a second is holding still for the click. You'd like a nurse in the hospital to look at you like that. Seeing you, not seeing only what's in her own head like most people.

"That's no combo, but anyhow you're here. You good like Kenny Klook says?"

"Listen is all I ask." She didn't stand still for more talk—jumped me like in checkers, and went to the piano. Had a couple chairs upside down on it put there by the cleaners to get off the floor. She handed them down like she was used to it. Lifted the top, went around to the keyboard. Touched down some notes, a couple chords. Nothing showy, let it die. Me, I'da hit all the chords I knew, showed you the main parts of my repertory.

"Nice sounding piano" she said.

"Got it from a millionaire's estate. Give you some more light." Switched on the bank.

"I can play in the dark but I like to see for a tune-up. You mind if I tune it some? It isn't far off."

Don't mind. How was she going do it?

She opened her pocketbook and took out a spanner and went at slurring the wires. That's pretty good, never mind if she can play, I get a free piano tune out of it if she knows what she's doing. There's a feeling you get when you find something that it's a reward from a saint who's watching out for you. You don't know what you did to deserve it, but hey. Made me more sociable to her.

"Where you from?"

"Pittsburgh."

"You know Klook from there?"

"Sure did."

"How long you been in New York?"

Tuning. Not listening to me too hard. "A week."

"We gotta lotta Pittsburghs in town. You know Garner? You know Mary Lou Williams? Lena Horne?"

"Sure do. They all worked one time or another at Moonrow's. I looked up Klook when I got here."

"He's some kinda drummer he is. Did he tell you places to go?"

"Some."

End of being sociable. Basically she was listening to the wires so I shutup and let her do what she wanted. Didn't take long before the spanner went back in the saddlebag and we had another problem. When she sat down she was drowning and looking for a lift in your rowboat. Maybe not that bad. Edna's used to being kidded about being short, that's the main thing the saddlebag was for. She slid it under and raised up a couple inches.

"Is there some particular song you would like to hear?"

"Whatever. They play Dixie piano in Pittsburgh?"

Her eyes closed down enough to let me know she wasn't too keen on it.

"I can play Dixie."

"You don't have to play any that for me, I was only asking. Not too much into that rinkytink myself. This is New York. New Orleans is kind of old timey for us." Now don't get that New Orleans crowd down on me either, just say my idea is when Dixie gets driving it's fast forward on your tape. You don't have to say I think that's good or bad.

"I do my own style. See how you like it." Working down into the saddlebag. "You like a song like Georgia Brown? Blue Skies?"

She was mentioning what I call downtown songs, standards, the songs I liked at that time. Still do. Even while I was a kid cleaning up and busing in Harlem jazz joints, while they were still speaks, I was getting away from repeat blues, those word type songs about Pigs Feet and Get Outa My Bed. Bessie Smiths you might say. I was into Waller type songs like Honeysuckle. Ellington. Fletcher Henderson doing Your Lover Has Gone sent me. Seemed better music to me, that's all. Didn't need words.

That sounds like a white type statement favoring those songs over real race songs. Let's see if I know what I'm talking about. Sometimes I don't, you have to watch for that. Just because I have money in the bank and say something doesn't have to mean that's it. If you have to watch out for it in the president of the USA who has all those people checking up for him you sure as hell better watch out for it in somebody you shook hands with the first time twenty minutes ago.

Those old songs, words were the main thing. They had blues and shouts on real topics like what are you going eat, where you going sleep and who with. Doing time. Being on the road. Lynchings. Real sex going on in the room, never mind if it wasn't June and no moon. Music was nothing special. A blues piano player like Deever at Larry's Door could make a living on three chords in three keys. If he had to take a solo he'd just lift his arms higher and kick the floor and swing his body around to make action. Put in some James P. Johnson rhythms. Same three chords and a couple peggios. A singer would say to him You know Hot Handle? He'd say Give me a line and he'd find where to put his three chords.

When Deever learned sixes it was like he graduated from Julliard.

He'd do songs with nothing but sixes. Fives minors and sevens were beneath him. Listen to this dirt he'd say and give you a six. Hot damn.

Then we had the Avon Guard come in putting chords down there on the keys it used to take the whole Henderson band to do. We had augments and twelves, flats moving on each other. They would have been mistakes a few years back. Songs ending on flats people would have hooted at. Used to be they changed the chord once a bar, once a phrase. Got to be if you didn't move with the halfnote somebody looked over to see if you're on the doze. Change key on the bridge. Musicians playing like that looked around for tunes, man, tunes. Changes. Never mind the words.

Take a great jazz song like Satin Doll, you could make it about any topic. Didn't have to be about a lady, could be about say New Jersey.

Wearing my short sleeve new jersey
Going to Newark New Jersey

Take it from there. Mercer wrote good words but he didn't have to write so many. All he had to do was put down Satin Doll so the trombone can find it when the leader calls Satin Doll. Tune by Ellington, title by Mercer. That's nothing against Mercer. He's there basically so singers can make a living, same as the instruments. Everybody's entitled to make a living the best way he can. We're not here to starve to death. That goes for string bass players too.

You'd think with the Depression they would go in more for word songs telling about all those troubles. Instead we got these great standards for the tunes and the changes. As far as words, they traded in real songs mostly for moonjune and putting turkey with Albuquerque. Funny stuff.

Could be we'd be better off if jazz songs let everybody know about real problems instead of Satin Dolls. Would be all right with me as long as we don't have to give up the music. They almost took the music away too when Coltrane and Davis and those fellas kept on going after bop, missed the turn and fell off the jazz road into stream music. Tyner. You don't know where you are in that less you're the one playing it. Most of these songs don't have any words at all, no place to put them. Edna still plays with those fellas when they come in. Ornette, Braxton, Kenny Wheeler. Now and then I give it a listen, trying to get the idea. Mostly I go visit one of the clubs, come back and get her later.

You putting down all I said? What makes you think I told you anything? What makes you think it's all just not something that sounds good, makes me a big shot with opinions on this and that making you feel good that now you know something too? Like those fellas in Malcolm's magazine telling you about stocks to buy. You're a young fella, you want to watch out for that. The next fella you talk to may not be as reliable as me.

"You play anything you want" I told her. "Georgia. Got it Bad. Blue Skies. You're on."

4

She started on an easy vamp, could go anywhere. Something I could learn to do. Progresses. You know. Over the vamp she put down two notes like silver dollars said what the song was going be.

Yeah, Blue Skies is a song you can hardly ruin. Plays in your head if the piano gives you something now and then.

Put down those two silver dollars again. Looked into outer space and began pumping back and forth, working an old church organ. Pumping away, pumping away, played a couple bars in a slow stride right on the beat. Made me think right away of somebody learned to play from sheet music, a professor sitting alongside with his hand going up and down, up and down.

We were coming up on eleven o'clock opening. Sid Callis, my bar backup, was clearing fruit slices off his cutting board, listening to what's going on. I'd like to get something about Sid in here. Sid was the best bar manager in New York. He retired three years ago. Sid lives in Florida, lives good. Has a thirty-four foot fishing boat and a condo on a marina. Earned it all right here, never took a dime from the register.

One thing I want to say about Sid is that except for hurricanes and a foot of snow nobody can help, Sid was always on time. I give a lotta credit to a man being on time. Lets people know you're in business to take care of them, you wouldn't rather be doing something else like sleeping late or counting bottles. Hang out there, we'll get open in about ten minutes, maybe fifteen, attitudes like that. Show me a place that opens later than it says on the door, I'll show you a place that's faking it about how the customer comes first and this and that.

Take a man that locks his door and puts a sign on Back in an Hour. You come to see him. How do you know where in the hour you are? An hour from when? What's the starting place? You don't know, and that man doesn't care all that much if you do or you don't, he's thinking about his time not yours. A place like that and a place that opens late, take your business some place else is my advice. Sid thought the same way as I do about how you treat people. Never was any color between Sid and me. We had the same ideas. Same time I raised my eyes to him he raised his to me. Amateur Night.

I was that sorry about it too. The way she laid down the two-note bet made you think she might have a hand. Now I had to think of a nice way to tell her No.

She drifted off the beat, started ringing in extra chords. Different sounding progresses. Nothing sensational but it was coming out jazz all right. Still in an easy ballad beat. Good enough to count stock by and getting better. In about two bars she went past anything I could do. Pumped away, digging her can into the saddlebag the way a batter makes a take-off hole for the foot he hits off.

Yeah I'll listen. Sid was listening.

Basically she listened too, never looked at the keys. Second chorus she let the tune out on a string in the breeze, let it bob around out there, tugged it now and then to remind where it came from. Hands began running those Edna-peggios on each other's back. Raised the stakes on the harmony, shuffled chords, dealt them around two to a bar—then I was hearing four—everybody had winners. Felt good. All that going on and still in ballad tempo. Just a kid and not a bit nervous, not pushing the tempo at all.

Then she began playing piano. Upped the tempo. Went at it like house-cleaning, changed the key, scraped off music never heard of before, trying to get down under the ivory to the wood. Bad as the dog ate the key cover. Talking to herself, has this way of talking to herself, throws her jaw off to the side like you try to open your ears on an airplane, possessed by what's in that song she's going get at.

I don't know why I was surprised. Piano players come all sizes, shapes and colors. Donegan, Mary Lou and Hazel had been around some years. Dot Moore was the house piano when I was a bus at Monette's. I knew a black girl could handle a piano, no doubt about that, but you always think the next one can't.

Forgot about she's suppose to sing too till she was in another chorus on Never saw the sun. Said it to herself, just thinking about it, *Never saw the sun*. Middle of the next phrase says *Never*—just *Never*—out of nowhere, telling you she found this great thing. Unique, you got to believe.

That's all the singing till she let go like a wild woman *When you're in love my how they fly how they fly how they flyy-y* and added four measures to the song right there, same as on the Columbia sleeve with Vance Addison on bass behind her. That was it for the lyric, but you knew you heard that song. All that coming from this high school type kid.

Sid opened his eyes, looking for a word. "Kid has style."

She drove on, talking to herself, rocking, sliding the beat on her shoe. We get another Depression Edna can make a good living stomping cockroaches. Hardly looked at the keys. Had the notes on the ends of her fingers, she could put them down where she wanted. She can play a dead tree if that's all there is.

She didn't have it all down her own way yet. Still doing that Tatum lace work in the high scales. The top musicians then were marines proving they could do the Tatums. I knew something was wrong with that, never knew what it was till later she pinned it down herself and told me it broke the song up into little stunts instead of it being one nine inning game. Sat there looking at the keyboard, talking to herself.

"I'm trying to get my work done. I want my hands to pay attention to what they're doing. Instead they're running off answering the door.''

That was her style she was working out. Ten tight on the keys, holding the big chord in the middle. Hands moving around together like a big insect eating music. Carried the melody in her left thumb and right pinkie and riffing out left and right but always knowing where home was. You name me who else can riff a left hand like Edna. McKenna has a great left hand yeah, but he walks it. Dave would be the first to tell you.

5

Meantime this fella's been going along the street, heard the piano, saw the door open and came in. I knew him but I didn't, loner kind of guy, came in three four times around midnight I remembered, sat at the end of the bar against the wall if the seat was open. Big good-looking guy, smooth dresser, just this side of sharp. Pin in his tie. Homburg hat. Velvet collar coat. Sometime a female with him but basically by himself. Fellas seem to know him, came up talking inside stuff in his ear. He just sit there looking at his drink, say a couple words. Wrong face wrong color for numbers. Irish. Could be track. Man looked like track.

''Who she?''

I had to look at the card.

''Edna Bundige.''

''Great piano player.'' Walked out. God kind of a man expected you to believe anything he said. Worked too, wished I knew how, save a lot of discussion. You have a hard time not believing that kind of fella even if you know more what he's talking about than he does. Hitler had some of that juice. Same as looking out a window high up in the Empire State, you want to jump out and you have absolutely no reason. The man just draws on you. You don't even have to know him, just seeing him on a street draws you.

I didn't know it then—wouldn't have made a difference, it was a few years before he got to be known—he was Al McGarvey.

I see I'm not making any impression on you. If you don't know who Allen J. McGarvey was you're born too late. Think of the biggest rock star you can name—Jagger, any of them—that's Al McGarvey on Wall Street later on, not too long. If word got out McGarvey was in or out of a stock it was good for five ten points before you could get an order in. Crashed the whole market one day when Dorothy's column said McGarvey's Market Letter's coming out tomorrow hollering Everybody Out! Everybody Out! McGarvey wouldn't say yes or no when the reporters asked if it was so. No comment. Tight-mouth. Sphinct of Egypt type fella.

Wasn't only stocks. Hats. One of the columns said McGarvey bought his hats from Overton, fella with a little business making hats to order on the second floor over on 48th. Maybe owned a stable of beavers, hard to say how a man gets into the business of providing hats. Overton had to move up to a real big store to take care of business after it got out he sold hats to McGarvey. He was famous. Used to see his name in the columns all the time giving big parties with Henry Kissinger there, that crowd. Most of them my customers. Never hear of Overton any more. Maybe he went broke. Maybe he added it up, decided he had it all, moved out on the Island where it's quiet, like Mr Berlin. All on account of McGarvey buying a hat. Changed the man's life.

Any kind of rumor you can name, they put McGarvey's name on it and it made the columns. Item in Billboard said he was head of the syndicate owned Edna. Nothing to it, nothing at all, he wasn't even a partner, just a customer here like everybody else. Nobody could make a dime out of a rumor like that but people just liked to say his name and stroke it, made you feel good, part of your luck.

Mention his name to Malcolm. Malcolm'll know McGarvey.

You putting this down like I'm saying? That's okay. I can talk as good as you if I want but I have to think it out first and it slows me down. I bet I'm better on numbers than you are in English. Comes natural to me. Uncle Cousin Foss put me into real English. I was talking to Uncle Cuz when I was getting ready to go into business. Answering him on something I said

"I knowed that."

"Ar sdur" he told me—he talked like that. Ar sdur. Broke the words in pieces and fed them to you one at a time. You could be a pigeon. You could be deaf, he didn't take a chance on you missing something. Made everything seem twice as important.

"Ar sdur if you plan to be a bu siness man it would be a good i dea to speak English as you learned in school. A knowed is a pim ple on the end of your nose."

That's in my mind but I get out and around and like the preacher says I get lapsed.

I remember Edna's whole set. Blue Skies. Idled down into Georgia Brown, came off Georgia into Making Whoopee. Tell you the truth Whoopee wasn't my idea of a jazz song till I heard her do it on a long slow line and that special sound she had I never heard before. I went over behind her to see how she was getting it. Her hands were moving like they were locked together inside about an octave octave and a half with her right pinkie running a split end like I told you. Changing four to the bar. I'm not saying Milt Buckner and Shearing got that from her. I'm just saying I never heard it before.

After Tatum any good piano player knew there was chocolate icing the cook left inside that bowl. That's the main thing Tatum did for the piano. Showed the possibilities. Ran the first four minute mile. Wasn't much left though after Edna scooped her fingers around in there. If there ever was any better jazz piano record made than Bundige and Buckner Locked In call me up any time to hear, I'll be right over.

She scrambled Whoopee into Mean To Me, played Mean To Me and sang Whoopee over it and in general went to war with the piano and the two songs. Shot down everything in sight.

I hired her right then and there, none of this Come back and see me. The partners thought I was moving a little too fast. Hadn't got over yet that I put the piano in and took out four tables before I had anybody to play it. Two more came out when she came in.

Standing behind her watching her make those chords I told her "You got the job."

She shifted off the seat and turned around with the corner of the piano between her and me. Looked at me straight on awhile before she said "All right, I sure do need it. Only one thing. Do I have to do anything else?''

''Like what?''

Studied me some more. I studied her too. Unusual looking girl. Lotta face to look at for that size woman. You don't just pass that face by once you look at it good. Long space under her nose before the mouth. Mouth caught up thinking about whistling, just thinking about it. Chin out in a wind you don't know about blowing her hair back. Indian eyes. Lie to me if you want, fella, that's on you, I'm not lying back. That's what Edna's face tells you. If it aint straight she won't truck with it. Life's too short. Wouldn't even tell a judge once I was going twenty-five. Hell I wasn't going over forty. Hick town in New Jersey.

''Like tricks or anything.''

''You play the piano. Sing your style. That's it.''

''That's okay, that's all I do.''

6

I found out later what Edna was saying to me from Eunice Cole the gal she came from Pittsburgh with. They stayed with Eunice's aunt while Eunice went around looking for beauty shop work same time Edna made the rounds of the jazz places.

Edna didn't ask to try out anywhere, just went around looking and talking to find out what places were like—Nully's, Swingers, Wells', Jerry's Tap-a-tap, Three Eye Club, No Saint's. Bands were man's work, no woman played in a band. In a band the girl sings and goes off and sits till she's on again. That part was all right because Edna was used to being the house piano and doing the single she did in Pittsburgh and looked to do the same in New York.

I guess she would have taken up with a band if it offered, but to be truthful the clubs didn't look too good to her no matter what. Dark places, smoked up. Lots of traffic—you know, traffic. Till she walked in here it didn't seem like she was going be any better off than in Pittsburgh.

''Better off than what?'' I asked Eunice.

Eunice told me about the jazz place run by Moonrow Fargason on the Hill in Pittsburgh. That was the main place for club jazz, singles and groups. The big bands booked into the Savoy or the hotels, anyhow those still making it after the war tax against dancing that was still hanging on the way taxes do. Moonrow let her be one of the kids who played for throw money and hat money before the real acts went on, what he didn't hold out for himself. Same way in Harlem, people think the quarter they threw on the floor went to the talent. Yeah. Same way the dollar you give the hatcheck belongs to her. Fat chance.

After school she practised and listened to blues and jazz records. Slowed her old hand-crank grammarphone down to hear the changes separate. Tried that out on a little four octave keyboard they had at home. Maybe that put the idea of the tight ten on the keys in her hands. After supper, over to Moonrow's for a chance on a good piano and some of the floor money. Got so she pulled ahead of the other kids, and like in the Bible when they're heading for trouble Moonrow favored her, let her be the house piano when visiting stars weren't too important. Let her single now and then. Fill the breaks.

Sonofabitch Moonrow Fargason was a gambler always this far from broke. Had this idea for a money act, looked around and figured Edna could do it for him cheap.

She's supposed to come off the piano singing Take Me Out To The Ball Game like a come on song. She's supposed to lift her skirt and show herself with nothing under. She's supposed to grind around amongst the tables and the customers. The customer's supposed to get the idea to take a green bill and fold it like a tent and hang it off the edge of the table and Edna's supposed to grind it off.

"It's your idea you do it" Edna told him.

"Don't you be cute with me, I want you to do it" says Moonrow. "There's real money in it. They'll come from all over to see the gig."

"They won't see me doing it."

"Your mother can use the money if you don't want it."

"She'll be glad to hear you're thinking of her."

He tells her he saw the act in Chicago and his idea cleans it up. In

Chicago the man tucks the bill in his fly and the act grinds it off. For a $5 bill they make the change in a room off the kitchen. Tell that to the Board of Health Inspector if he wants to know what goes on in kitchens some parts of this country. Giving you this and that about one cockroach in New York City. No matter what problems people have, no matter how puny, somebody makes a living off it in New York City.

When Moonrow sees he's not getting anywhere with Edna he tells her she can wear a string. Tells this sixteen year old kid she can wear a string.

"You too" she says. That's it for Pittsburgh.

Should have added Moonrow Fargason's name in when I told you about all those good people who did for me without they ever knew it. Should have sent at least a fifty to Moonrow's favorite charity right then and there instead of just thinking about it.

Lucky for her, before she had it out with Moonrow, Tatum came in for a two night gig. Lotta young people hearing Tatum got so scared they gave up on the piano, got into another instrument. Drums. Woolworth's. Took Edna like being in love the worst way. She went to bed playing Tatum breaks, woke up playing Tatum changes. She cut school, wasn't going be any good in school with her mind on Tatum. Teacher going on about the War of 1812 or so and she's on Sweet Lorraine.

They had this armory type building on the classy side of the Hill from Moonrow's called Syrian Hall. I don't know why, I didn't name it. Has nothing to do with the story, could have been named something else just as easy. Mostly they had nothing going on and Edna knew there was a piano in there. Walking to the library she'd heard it from the street. Piano just sitting there and you didn't see even a parked automobile showing somebody inside. Why not try for it? Taking Eunice along for whatever, they went over to see if there was some way she could get at that piano.

They push the service door open and they're in this auditorium. Dark. Empty. Inside the earth. They know the janitor from the neighborhood and start calling his name. Mr Fanning. Mr Fanning you there? Inching around in there in storage rooms and down scary hallways. He must be in there if the door was open. Finally turn him up in the basement.

"What you kids doing in here?"

Well she couldn't lie. I don't know, something inefficient in her upbringing. Not enough milk. Something like that. She can't even fib without half her face falling off. You can't have a surprise party with Edna in on it. She has to walk around those things when necessary. Told him she was getting ready for a big concert. Didn't have to say where or what year. Just getting ready. It got past him. Probably too dark in there to see her face.

"That's a good purpose but I don't know. What gave you the idea to come here?

"They said so in school" Eunice butt in. She didn't have the same inefficiencies Edna had. Always good to have somebody like that with you. They thrashed at it.

"It's not mine to say."

"Could I use it just today? Then you could ask somebody."

"Well I don't know about anything like that."

"Let me play for an hour?"

"I got bosses I have to explain to."

Edna played Tatum on that piano every day all day for five six months except one week when they booked a circus and Fanning only let her come in until noon. At the end of that time she knew she wasn't all that much in love with Tatum any more, but no bad memories, no hard feelings, she'd keep a place for him. No more running all over the piano every time he whistled. Only sometimes. You don't get over being in love all at once.

She got as much of him as she wanted to keep inside that little four octave box at home. Put him in there with Hines and Garner. Packed them all in her head and came to New York.

7

After going around the jazz scene in Harlem she decided to see if that older fella who played drums at Moonrow's and now was making himself famous at bop headquarters might remember her enough to say something good like Play here. When you're real young you basically don't think older people—say five years—have time for you. Makes some kids mumble. Not Edna. She walked in on Klook at Minton's saying her name and telling him where he knew her from so he won't say to himself Who's this?

Oh yeah he says, thinking this is the kid with the heavy stride left hand sounds like taking peanuts out of one jar and putting them in another for piece wages. What's she doing here? He was on the stand by himself tuning his skins.

He didn't know about Tatum and her putting in that time in Syrian Hall making herself a genius. He's in with the real genius musicians holding the fort at Minton's. Gillespie. Bud Powell. Monk. Parker. Those fellas thought they had it all. While your daddy was thinking how great that King of Jazz Paul Whiteman was, these cats were laughing on the side that anybody mistook that for jazz music. Mostly they did in the other instruments what Tatum did on the piano, except instead of interrupting the tunes with the fast riffs they let the tunes go and played only riffs. Got rid of the interruptions that way. Some kinda musicians they were but that's what it amounted to, sixteen cylinder hundred mile an hour interruptions in the high octaves. It was Edna and Erroll built the riffs back into the tunes like new melodies on the chords. Made them new ways to hear those songs.

This small girl peanut counter from Pittsburgh with small hands tells Klook she's looking to make it in New York and Klook's looking across the room at Bud Powell at the bar. If he lets this peanut counter near Bud's piano he'll come over and destroy her. Bud hates anybody who doesn't play good music. I mean hates them. He'll drop the cover on her hands. He doesn't care if she is a female. Bud was into the him Or her before it got so popular. He didn't like the left hand to begin with and if he heard a stride left hand like hers on his piano he'll break her hands. She's asking Klook will he listen and he's looking at Bud and saying Sure sure you don't have to play for me I know how good you play.

The absolutely main thing Klook saw to do was get her back

home. Nothing as wrapped up in what he's doing as a man doing a righteous deed. You don't get that many chances, at least that interest you, and nothing makes you feel better than giving somebody good advice. Better even than getting it, which is upside down but what isn't.

"No no gal you don't want to be here just yet. This scene is real real sour. We have ace sidemen trying to get by on ten bucks twice a week—ten bucks twice a week in a big week. Good sidemen going back to Chicago and K.C. and Philly. Even going back to Philly. It's even worse on gals. Worse for you. Gals that never thought they'd do anything like that puttin out for a place to sleep. Puttin out for alcohol. Tea. Horse. All that junk. What do you want with that. They got pianos in Pittsburgh and you got a momma and daddy to go home to. Come on child, get away from this scene. It don't make any difference how good you play. No difference. You hearing me?"

"I hear what you're saying. I have a place to stay. No way am I getting into what you're talking about."

"You don't have to get into it, it gets into you. Just stand there you'll catch it. You're just a kid now, you don't even know—don't even know, you hearing me?—what I'm talking about. Go on home. Take some lessons. Practise more. Come back when you can handle it. You got time that way. You stay on this scene they don't give you any time at all."

"I'm not going back unless I don't make it here."

When she says "here" she may mean New York City but he thinks mostly about right there at Minton's. He knows that aint going be. Klook Clarke's not going be the one that sits this child at Bud Powell's piano. If you think he won't bang the piano on your hands, sit down there and play a bad piano on one of his bad days but get your hands out the way fast when you see him coming. That's how he was.

"Okay you say you're listening but that's not the same as doing it. I'll give you a man to see."

He sent her to Charlie Duvall and told Charlie to treat her right, her folks knew his in Pittsburgh. Told him she could get by in a downtown honky piano bar if he knew one to send her to, they wouldn't know any better. Keep her off 52nd, be wasting her time. Promised to kill him personally if he sent her to any those tough places on the docks. Klook didn't think about me, I wasn't doing music at the time yet, but Charlie knew of my interests.

After she worked for me five six weeks Klook came in asking about her. Hanging on his conscience I guess. First time he'd been in my bar and no reason to before. In those days we didn't have any black trade downtown, especially a bar without music.

I knew him from Minton's. Knew all those fellas at Minton's. Monette Moore's. All those places. Used to drop in on my way home after my place shut. Told Klook once when I was there how I appreciated him sending me that good girl piano.

"Oh yeah, she's a hard worker" he said. I didn't get to him. He thought I was being polite or I didn't know better. Now he heard.

We got going earlier than the Harlem joints and Edna was in her first set. You heard of the word stunned. Like you hit a cow in the head. Stunned. Kenny could hardly stand up long enough to steady himself on the bar. Stood there with these three big holes in his face at the music coming off that piano. "I told you" I told him.

"Show me those hands" he said when she came over after the set. "Like I thought, different hands. You used those small hands in Pittsburgh. Makes some difference. Come up to Min's and have jam with us sometime. Make it soon."

"Sure would like to. Thanks for the invitation."

"I told Duvall you weren't too much of a piano but if he got you in some piano bar downtown you'd get by okay. I told him you were clean and if he got you mixed up with any junkman I'd personally take him down."

"Duvall sent me to the right man" she said laying a hand on my sleeve "I couldn't make up a better place to be."

Some fellas deserve it more than me and go through their whole life without hearing a compliment like that but I'll take it. How much money you got can buy that? I mean you can buy the words from some people but you couldn't buy them from Edna.

Two

BIG CHOCOLATE COOKIES

1

MOST OF THE TIME you get a good idea and tell it they tell you it won't work. Costs too much. Somebody else doing the same thing first, only it's not the same thing no way just a little bit like. Ten years later somebody does your idea and makes a million dollars and everybody says Hey that man's thinking. Supermarkets. Big chocolate cookies.

I told momma the idea about big chocolate cookies before Famous Amos was born. I told her she could make them and I'd put them in a bag and sell them around.

"Yeah." That didn't mean she'd do it. She was just saying she heard me while she counted out the groceries she brought home from the store.

"I'm not talking about just a little bit bigger like you look for on a plate when they pass around. I'm talking about a cookie big as the whole plate. Big as the Oh Joy lollipop. People give you a nickel for a chocolate cookie that big."

"Yeah and it makes you sick. That's four cookies. Five." Counting groceries and I'm nagging chocolate cookies at her.

"You don't have to eat it all at once. You can give somebody a piece. It's the idea. They're selling soft pretzels for a nickel. They's nothing cheerful about a soft pretzel like a big chocolate cookie. Make me up some, momma. You'll see."

"I don't need to see. I see already. I got good eyes. You see these here groceries. That's three dollars worth and no meat yet and it won't last the week. Can't be fooling around making chocolate cookies they'll take off you and eat.'' Momma talked in jabs, same as I do. Comping like Monk and Basie. Things like that run in a family. Comes from having an active mind, sees the next thing before the last is finished. Gets there ahead. ''I got enough to do without feeding the street cookies.''

''You make the best chocolate cookies of anybody. If they don't pay me this time there's no next time. Then what they going do if they want a big chocolate cookie?''

''Yeah well. You give me an idea. Not going make no more chocolate cookies for nobody. Too popular. Cost too much. Going make soft pretzels instead. Now you go on and let me get supper.''

There was a time they're going up and down 125th painting on store windows. Snakes. Stars. Piss on you. Leroy and Betty do it. German Swastikas. That was even before the war, before they put the paint in a can, blew it out, made it easier. I never messed much with that stuff, I was a watcher, but I knew the man can't appreciate his windows marked up like that. Say I get a bottle of gasoline or whatever and a rag and go to the man and tell him for a dime a quarter I'll clean off your windows. I'm right there. He doesn't have to call anybody up. I could make a dollar two a day easy and then the guys could do the windows again that night if they wanted and I could make another dollar two.

''What do you think of that idea Leroy?''

''That no idea at all. What the man going do is call the cops and the cops be after you like they be after the gangs selling protection.''

''Yeah but it aint the same thing. I don't do windows. I'm the cleaner.''

''No matter. You on the street you in it some way and the cops going take you to the station and beat you ass till you give everybody's name and everybody's going beat you ass when you get out for giving names.''

''I wouldn't give no names.''

Leroy started talking loud and flapping his arms and legs like he got when he was teed off. Big skinny fella, arms and legs shooting out every which way like he was made of those party snakes you blow in they wrap out.

"You say. What you know. You just a kid. What I'm going do is beat you ass first before you going any stores making any window washering deals end up telling the cops Leroy Haynes painted them. How that sound? Hey? How that sound? You tell me how that sound?"

Probably wouldn't happen the way Leroy said if I'd gone and done it. That was the best idea I ever had to make money when I was a little kid.

Along that line, you read that story in the paper lately about that fella with the windshield business got himself arrested for going around the neighborhood nights banging on windshields with an iron pipe. Left his card so the party would know where to go for a good repair job. If you want a lesson on how not to run a business he's it. He can't delegate. You can hire all the minimum wage labor you want to go around hitting windshields with an iron pipe. Kids would do the job for nothing, for the job training. He should be making time to read up on his business. Go to night school. Spend time with his family. Instead he can't think of a blessed thing to do with his time except take jobs away from kids.

Even if you delegate you can't keep banging up windshields in your own neighborhood night after night and leaving your card without people catching on. People don't care about your car getting it but how long before they begin to think It's running on this block, I could be next?

The I could be next part is the main thing. Pretty soon everybody's looking right at him. That's called cui bono. Which dog has the bone? I heard about that at the 92nd Street Y. Those old Latinos thought up just about every idea there is and I'll bet you a dollar none of them smart-mouthed their teachers. If this smartass windshield guy had picked up on cui bono he would see right off it wouldn't upset people that much if he branched into other neighborhoods, spread the action, made it more the usual thing.

People don't think they have as much trouble if it's shared out. If everybody woke up every morning and had to buy a new windshield nobody would think anything of it. It would be tributed to the cost of living. Bread. Milk. Windshields. If the Harvard B asks me back I'm going build my whole talk on that man's mistakes.

Another idea I had after that was about horse racing. I was in the barber shop, two three fellas ahead of me. You know how in a barber shop you pick up whatever is there and you read it. Sport magazines. Life. Ebony. Fortune. Health. I was one to read all the time, still do, it just came natural to me. All that was there was the Daily News sport pages from last week one day but I read it anyhow. I read about the ball game and the standings and the averages and it's still not my turn. I got to horse racing.

I didn't know much about horse racing except they line up in a row behind a gate with the jockeys up high to stay clear of the saddle. That's the style of the event, like dogs at a dog show have to hold their tails a certain way. They put tacks in the saddle to be sure he stays up there. They have jockey stores that specialize in tacks, it's in the ads, anybody can make a living in this country, all you need is an idea. No I don't know why they decided to do it that way any more than I know why the Chinese used to squeeze the feet of the ladies into shoes two sizes small. I don't know why they put lapels on suits. It's style, it's how people do things. We have nine innings in baseball and four quarters in basketball. That's how they decided to do it. That's how they decided to do horse racing.

All I knew about horse racing was win place and show. I knew post position but I didn't know if it was numbered from inside or outside. I never played horse racing so I didn't know it like I knew real sports. Football. Baseball. Track. Basketball. Still don't. Got enough to do taking care of this place and the oil company and the franchises and boards and all. I don't need horses.

I sat there trying to figure those numbers in the lists. One two three four five in this column. One two three four five in that column. Six one. Fourteen three. Must mean something. When I see numbers I try to figure out what they mean. I was always like that.

Sure enough, pretty soon those numbers reach up and grab me Zap! Looka that! See what's going on there! Some people study at something all their lives and never get that feeling and somebody else never studied at all sees it right off. Like Edna on the piano. Six years old, doesn't know E flat from canned peas and zap she's picking out tunes. Einstein.

I didn't wait to be barbered—Hey I just remember something, be back—and headed over to the old St Nicholas Hospital where Mubbles Thompson had a book under the overhang by the iron door out back. Mubbles was the one I knew could use the idea.

"Listen to my idea" I told him. "There's the favorites one two three. Then there's the line up numbers one two three four on up. Now listen to my idea. At Adequate race track last Tuesday the favorite or the second wins every race he's in position one two up to five. How about you bet the favorite or the second every time he's in one of the first five gates? You win every time."

Mubbles was like most everybody you bring a big idea to. What's so great, you know, What's so great about that idea? Like they said to Newton What's so great about apples falling off a tree? Stick to something you know, man, like Fig Newtons. Nobody thinks an apple's going fall up or just hang there.

I'm not that way. A man comes to me with an idea, it may be a terrible idea, I pinch up my eyes like I'm listening real good and I ask questions and I tell him I'm going think about it, and the next time we get together I don't wait for him to ask what I think, I tell him I been thinking and to prove it I ask him more questions. Then I say no. A man wants to know you're giving it a try to say yes before you say no. That way people keep on being your customers. Write that down.

"What you know about horse racing?" His idea of a question.

"Nothing but I can read."

"You want to be real careful having good ideas on another man's business. If there's any good ideas you can be sure the people in that business has them."

"Has anybody got this idea?"

"If anybody has it he's too broke to use it. You telling me last week at Adequate. I'm telling you yesterday at Adequate the favorite win only one race and he posted number nine. You want to bet your system I got a book."

He flashes his double-b open and shows me his white shirt with the wide red stripes like he pushed up against a painted cage Lemme out. Showed off the ring he got from the hock and aimed at his pocket where the slips of the book stuck up. What he really was showing me is it was no dollar-down, the label says Kollmer-Marcus.

I didn't have a dollar to spare, all I had was this idea somebody with eyes to see could use. Maybe didn't work every day on every race but hell you don't have to win every race.

I was up to waiting tables at Cecil's on Columbus. Any extra money I had went to momma where I was living. My daddy had a bad hurt back from a foundation he was digging caved in on him. Momma cleaned for people in apartments on 5th Avenue. Eight dollars a week is the price I remember. I had two little sisters. You don't have any investment money in those circumstances. I don't know, maybe I just didn't have the confidence then. People always have ideas for other people to put money on. I didn't have that Allen McGarvey juice I say it you do it.

That was my last good idea before the war. I read lately a college professor has the same idea I had fifty years ago but I don't need horses any more. Different times in your life you need different things.

One other good idea I had I forgot to mention. On the radio those days if you played it on a record you had to say By Transcription. I don't know why they didn't say It's on a record but they didn't. Made it sound better I guess. Lawyer type thing so they don't break the law but you don't understand it either. All day and on to midnight the announcers were telling you Buy Transcription and you couldn't buy one anywhere. I took the idea to Mubbles.

Isn't this some way to make money, I said. You could have a candy bar and name it Transcription. Peppermint patty would be the right shape, look like a record. People see in in the store say It must be a good product with all that advertising, give it a try. If peppermint wasn't too popular you could use the idea for any candy bar. O Henry. Baby Ruth. Just change the name to Transcription. It didn't even have to be candy. It could be toothpaste. Babyfood. Dogfood.

Like you can call anything Cadillac, it doesn't have to be an automobile. I had it all worked out. The free advertising was the thing.

Mubbles couldn't see it. Couldn't see it at all. I didn't know anybody else to take the idea to. The main shortage in the world isn't good ideas but people who can use them.

I went in the navy.

2

I was twenty-two years old when I went in but most ways, except knowing how to fool around with girls, I was still a boy. Had no sure thing to do. After a couple years washing dishes and busing I got to waitering and that's as high as I could see. What you don't see you don't grab onto, less you're just flailing around and catch something going by. Most people hang on there the rest of their days, go the same way it goes. People live like getting on a train and then asking.

I waitered where I was. Stayed in the neighborhood, couldn't even see waitering downtown. I liked the idea being near home, taking care of momma and the family as best I could, helping out in my daddy's place who couldn't work at all. Bent over. Had operations later, the best that could be done and it didn't make a bit of difference. If I'd thought about it I could have found something for him to do at home with his hands like repairing broken lamps for the hardware store. Things like that. I didn't think along those lines. Had my head down, doing what was in front of me. Nobody told me to look up. I didn't have the idea of looking up in my head at all.

With me the few ideas I had about ways to make some money, seemed like thinking of them was the same as doing them. Think of it, talk it up some, forget it, you did it. Think of something else. Easy to talk me out of things. If you didn't do it I'd do it myself. Like if it was supposed to be it happened. If it didn't happen it wasn't supposed to.

It was like now, no jobs for black kids. I went around asking. Nothing till I got to the Gold Plate. Nine dollars a week dishwashering, not bad considering the minimum is fourteen in the newspaper. End of the week I'm looking to get paid and he acts like that's something he's not used to. He's busy. He says over his shoulder like it's something everybody knows "Pay's Tuesday."

We don't get to Tuesday. Monday morning the sheriff put a sign on the door.

Got another job busing at Frank's Grill, same money, only this time I got it. Bused and dishwashered and swept up at Nully's. Same at Jennie's where the boutique is now. Worked lots of places, jazz places, speakeasies. Mostly places you got a hot dog or hamburger for a dime, a beer for a nickel, Scotch for a dime. Fifteen cents if it was imported. Gin was the big thing, a dime of gin could kill you.

Some of them were mostly whore houses. Didi Temple's was a whore house. She had a bar and backroom jazz at the walk-down level off the street and rooms for the girls upstairs. I worked there. I never got upstairs. Too young and too poor. Bad combination for access but seeing the girls and knowing what's going on is something for putting ideas in your head.

We had those places in brownstones downstairs with rooms up but they weren't all whorehouses. Most had church-going families like mine upstairs trying to keep their kids clean with all that going on in the street. If you had a cabaret downstairs of one of those family houses you had to keep the music quiet or they called the cops. They pushed handkerchiefs in the horns. You never heard a real two four. At a place like Monette's they could open the stops because it was a legitimate cabaret cafe.

Place named Cecil's opened on Broadway let out it was hiring colored waiters. I run right over, got my first real job there. I was nineteen years old, made thirty thirty-five a week with tips, and hadn't there come the war I never would have looked up, probably still be waitering at Cecil's or some other uptown place.

Yeah, you can say that, easy enough to say, but first it has to happen. You just don't think to look around. You wish some but you don't think. Something's got to turn your head around or you keep on looking in the same place, don't have the idea those other places are for you.

Having a steady girl, wanting to get married turns some guys around, sometimes the gal pushes him. Nothing like that happened to me, never had the idea of getting married then. Looked too tightening. Didn't see any need for kids. Less you know you're going need them to give you shade in your old age no use planting them, giving all that care and turning out weeds when they're needed. Kids never appealed to me as something you just have around for no particular reason.

Only other use I could see for a wife was somebody there to cook and do the other usual things on a steady basis. Couldn't see it, couldn't see it at all. Had everything at home except the steady basis part and that's out there to be had. Only problem about that we had a flat just big enough for us and there was no place to do it, especially you couldn't bring it into a Bible-study home like mine. Wasn't any easier to bring it to where the girls lived, not any girl you liked on a steady basis. Same Bible.

Big problem, no place to take things up with her. You tell me the solution, see if you're as smart as we were.

Yeah we tried that but there's drawbacks.

Something else we tried was giving Sam Heatter a dime every time to leave his firescape door open. Opened into a room exactly the size of a cotbed somebody shoved in there, closed the door on, and forgot about because they built a closet in front of the door. Cotbed filled the room wall to wall. Sam and his kid brother were the only ones knew there were two closets back to back. If Sam had a deal on he had to take everything out of the real closet so he could open the secret door in the back and get to the cotbed. He clambered over the bed, opened the firescape door, took your dime and let you in.

Problem was people got to know it and other guys would bang on the firescape and hassle you. I had a girl then Coreen Drull got scared and didn't like it and said she wouldn't go there.

What were we going do? You know that song in "Guys and Dolls" about the police station and the school and all the other places they can't have the crap game? When I heard that song I thought of the go round I had with Coreen talking over the possibilities. That was a funny song. Everybody was laughing but I laughed twice as hard as anybody else. Edna told Frank Loesser Oh my how Stiffy enjoyed that song. All I could say was Yeah great song. In those days—the kind of people I came from and Edna too—you didn't tell your wife about your experiences.

That movie was after the war and by then Coreen and I were married to different people. Edna and I ran into her and her husband waiting for a table at Ruby Foo's. Just talking around I asked Coreen if she saw that movie. Devil in me talking.

Yes she did.

Well what did she think?

She thought it was a good movie.

Well how did she like that song about the crap game?

She liked that song. The way she said it I could see she didn't get the connection. Some people don't see things. Maybe she just didn't want to let on but I don't think she was that good an actor. She might have thought I was trying see if we could start up again but it was only the devil in me.

Edna said You should have heard this man here when they did that song. I thought I was going to have to call an ambulance to get him out of there he was laughing so hard.

They got their table and we got ours and I never saw Coreen again to talk to. She won't mind me telling this because she and the fella she married are long gone.

It came to doing it standing up. The things you get used to. That's one of the great features about the human race.

I don't have much size but I got strong arms and legs and a straight back and that comes partly from doing it standing up. When a baseball announcer says on the radio He scored standing up I think How beautiful.

Coreen and I were walking down a dark street way over east, warehouse type buildings all around, just walking and talking about the problem, going nowhere, poking along. Stop now and then, work each other up, move along some more. Easy enough for girls, they just zip off and start to get ready again, leave no traces except the fat look they can get after. A guy knows if he don't hold back all that Elmer's is coming, gumming up his walking, staining his pants so people can see, smelling up his clothes for his momma sniffing around. You do it you plan to do it right.

Coreen was a girl you could trust to rinse out after, she didn't need a baby any more than I did. Where? was the problem. Where was the big event going take place? Came to a building that ended on an alley. We were going around and I got my back to the wall and the problem just naturally solved itself.

Then just naturally went on to free-standing so she can kick out, like on a swing in the park. Carried her around drumming on her box, singing The Saints Come Marching. First time I saw a real ballet I thought Hey those people have got it down. I think the saddest idea I ever heard was that ballet dancers are too busy studying their moves to think about doing the real thing. I don't believe it any more than I believed the Chinese didn't do it at all until they got married when they're thirty years old. It's coming out now it never was true. It may be news to the State Department, it's no news to me.

The difference between New York City black guys and white guys, or anyhow white guys from New Jersey and Connecticut and those places, was that out in the sticks they had cars. They learned to do it sitting down, laid back, got used to having girls crawl all over them. Spoiled them. When you're talking about a real standup guy you're talking about a black guy. Maybe a white guy with no automobile.

That's the kind of information Malcolm expects me to tell. Young guys starting out ought to know how captains of industry solve all kinds of problems. It isn't only financing the inventory keeps a man awake at night so he's unfit for the big meeting. One thing they might want to know is, say you're a rising young executive and don't have the facilities—it's just as easy to date a small round woman as a big heavy one and easier on your back. They don't tell them that at the Harvard B.

Coreen weighed in five two. Edna is five even. I improved myself. I was going call this book Little Women but they already have that book.

3

At Boot I made a buddy, fella from Chicago, Roberts Henry. His real name was Henry Roberts, but they gave us one of those fooler papers where they want your first name first instead of last like on all the other papers, and Henry missed the turn. They're going through so fast the yeoman says it's written down that way and it have to get straightened out some place else, it don't matter a damn anyhow because they pay by your serial and if you don't know your own name for the mail study up on it. Next.

You're supposed to tell the man what you can do so they can put you somewhere. Waitering, I'm going tell him.

Henry thinks that over. "You come in this here man's navy to wait tables?"

"It asks what I can do."

You say something to Henry he lets it lay there. See if it's a fire cracker going blow up, take off your thumb. See if it's a rattlesnake playing dead, waiting for you to reach out. No arguments, just let it lay.

You say something to Henry Roberts sometime he didn't even let on he heard you. You start to say it again louder and he comes in answering your first time. Makes you feel stupid. You meet characters like that in business all the time, holding back, make you come to them. Make you think they're deep. Mostly they're average dumb like most people, just their act.

Say it all over. "It asks here—"

"I'm putting down Automobile Mechanic."

Did it to me again. "You do that work?"

He thinks over will he tell me. Go ahead take your time.

"They not going give me no engine to work on till they put me in school to show how they want it done."

I had to keep telling myself Henry Roberts got his name down backwards and I got mine down frontwards the way they wanted, or I would have thought he had all the brains in the world. All the same he made me feel dumb so I listened what he was telling me even when he didn't say anything. I do his act some myself, holding back, not saying all I know. That's when I talk as good as you, only I don't say as much.

End of it was I put down I can cook.

Cook was all I could think of. Nobody ever asked me if I could do numbers in my head, but I ate three meals every day all my life and was around cooking enough to see how it was done. Where it said Experience I put down the restaurants I worked in, didn't mention some of it was busing. Frank's. Gold Plate. Cecil's. Might as well put down The White House Washington D.C., no one's chasing a boot's references.

It worked okay, got me orders to Cook School. Chief lined us up, told us to get our gear together, where to muster. Keep your nose clean. Big deal everywhere then about clean noses. Gave you the idea the only thing on Abraham Lincoln's mind when he freed the slaves was their noses. "Hey fellas let's do something like a Civil War for the Kleenex Company. Big campaign contributors."

Maybe goes back to Creation. "Now hear this, angels! I'm going make a place called the World and I'm going put people in it called People and I'm going give them noses and they damn well better keep them clean, especially Black People. Amen."

When I was a boy I thought about being a preacher. Every black kid thinks about being a preacher. Used to anyhow.

Out of Cook School they put me on busing in a mess at Norfolk. Never got a chance to fry an egg. Best I did was break a hundred and put them in a big bowl for the cook to stir. That's the first I worried maybe they checked my references.

It was a discouraging time to some fellas, just hanging around there, couldn't get any status, going send you somewhere on a miserable island in the Pacific. Different ones were figuring how to beat it. We had Gowron, he pretended he was crazy in a friendly way. He did everything they told him but he acted as if he couldn't get there to do it unless he was on his head-bike. He had to muster, he'd drive up on this head-Harley *vroom vroom* and dismount. Kick down the stand. Lock it up. They'd detail him and he'd take off for wherever it was on this special bike. *Vroom vroom.*

Put in his spare time polishing it, tightening it up, keeping it first class. Most reasonable acting person you ever saw otherwise. They tried talking him out of it but he acted as if he couldn't understand what the hell they were talking about. There it was, wasn't it? Well yeah. They gave up on him and gave him his papers. The day Gowron was discharged he drove out the gate, parked the bike outside the fence, patted it on the seat, and walked over to the stop and got a bus. Left the damn bike there. Still there as far as I know.

Henry Roberts sold stools. There would be guys in the infirmary for one reason or another liked being there. No details. Food okay. Nobody shipping you out to be Seabees on some island. The only problem was that after awhile you got well and had to get out. Henry Roberts had his way of keeping you in there. You give him a dollar and he'd bring you a package of stool from some fella who was really sick. I know Henry Roberts, he probably put some ground up nightcrawlers in there. You handed that in to the doctor and you would be good for a week or two before they even wanted to see you again. It's like now with Aids, you have guys buying clean urine to hand in for the tests. Where there's a need somebody's going fill it. That's capitalism.

4

I wasn't all that enterprising. I was there breaking eggs at Norfolk when Eleanor Roosevelt heard about it. She put it to the admirals.

"How come all those black guys aint on ships? How come they get out of boot and schools and pile up on the bases? You got trained men there. We spent this tax training these black motor macs. Electricians. Coxes. Cooks like Arsdur U. Stiff standing around breaking eggs. Gunners. Ratings piled up on the bases, sleeping, eating, turn out for details, drills, other shit, more school because the admirals won't let a black man on a ship except to wait table and they got to be kept busy. How come? Those black guys, they American, they trained. They can shoot. Wasn't them in charge at Pearl Harbor. Get cracking."

That Eleanor knew how to talk to admirals.

You put heat on an admiral he does just exactly what he has to, no more. You don't hear him say Let's jump over there to the far side of the problem, get it done. No. He goes to the Officer's Club with his buddies and they have a couple three drinks. They decide it can't be done at all, no way, white sailors won't stand for it, no sir. Everything's put on us admirals but it's the sailors. However, brother admirals, we got this Communist Eleanor in the White House. We got to do the least thing or no telling, her husband—that's a Communist too—the two of them fire you right out the navy, admiral or no.

In the navy the least thing is small craft. Mine sweepers. Picket Boats. Stuff like that working off the bases a day two three at a time watching for submarines, sweeping in front of convoys moving along the coast. No Annapolis working on that small stuff. The Personnel Officer at the Base, he looks out the window and sees an AMc minesweeper coming on the dock, the skipper was an automobile salesman in Louisville Kentucky this time last year. The Personnel Officer calls in his yeoman and tells him

"Cut some orders. Send six colored to that AMc just come on the dock. Exchange for what they got."

For Arsdur U. Stiff they set up a special deal. One only. Captain told me later Personnel himself telephoned down, said he's sorry, he's got to take his cook for the fleet, destroyer going out tonight. But hold on—we're sending you over the best cook in the navy for substitute. Statler Hotel wants him right after the war is over. Lindy's is claiming if the navy puts him on waivers. You got the best on this deal. I'm sending him right down. Now you be sure you appreciate that. Send me that cook you got now right away, okay?

I was scared I couldn't do the job but I just kept this picture in my head you do one thing, then you do the next thing and if you get stuck you look in the book and hell I was the best cook on that particular ship anyhow. I looked in the ice box. Box of steak. Can't miss with steak. Put home fries with it. Onions and potatoes is all there is to home fries, touch of tomato to make them bright. Canned peas. For dessert I hotted up a number ten of apple sauce, crumbled in cookies, dusted on cinnamon. Seemed like cake. Put it down, that was the first meal of the imminent restauranter Arsdur U. Stiff. I got better. Having a chance to work at it I don't mind saying I got pretty damn good. First time I ever had that I'm in charge feeling.

The guys would lie on their bunks and sit in the bleachers watching me, could I stand up to cook. All white guys from the south watching will this jigaboo get sick and go into the sack and die and leave them starve to death. Will he say it's too rough, nothing but cold beans and cold ham and a cuppa. Wasn't a minute all day or night you couldn't get coffee. Bosun saw to that, he tied the pot to the rail.

I'll tell you what lonely is, you be a new man, the only black man on a navy ship way out on the ocean, all the other guys southern white watching you. The edge I had over any other black guy was I was the cook, nobody black or white wants to screw up the galley. Always a question about making the cook unfriendly, will he spit in your soup. Use your imagination. I wouldn't send anything back to the kitchen if it was the best restaurant in town, if it was a hundred dollar dinner, if the chicken was bleeding to death right there on my plate. Leave it there, push it to the side, forget it, eat another roll. Get a Hershey bar later. Do anything but don't develop bad feeling with the cook you can't keep your eye on. Same on a ship. About all a sailor has to look to is the next meal. Don't make waves.

I didn't know myself how I'd do, never had a shot at anything like it before. Have to say there's times in my life I felt better but I could see others worse off. Puking. Lying down every chance. I told myself Stiffy you going make that stew. You going roast that chicken. You going stand here two more minutes and get this done. Then you going stand here two more minutes and get the next thing done. After that we'll talk some more.

We put three four days into that cruise and I never missed setting out a good meal. Fried chops. Chicken. Made biscuits. Rolling around most of the damn time till Charleston.

Captain used to swing down the ladder once twice a day, hang onto the pole, look around see how things are going. He was my age, twenty-one two, just graduated college. Worked a few months in a bank before they commissioned him. Slight-made fella, average build for a man starving to death. Had brush-clipped blond hair and these girly blue eyes. He was a gutty kid, though, the kind they use to have for quarterback at Columbia. Stand back there at safety and they'd take a shot at a truck. Be dragged ten yards hanging on.

All the time questions. If he didn't have any real questions on hand he had how-you-doing type questions. If it wasn't questions, he had a pick-up in his voice like saying Don't mind hearing if you have something to add in on this.

Seeing an officer's shoes come down the ladder guys would stand up, he waved them down, started the questions. How much fuel did we use this morning? How is your arm Devore? Be sure you take it to sick bay when we dock hm? What are you reading Jones? Who's winning all the money? Did the barometer turn around yet? Wind's down hm? How are you doing down here?

Dillworth V. Emmery Junior, Lt Junior Grade. Yeah him. Junior Grade, that has to be about the piss-poorest title any government ever gave out. Worse than Second Class Cook. You have Admirals, Ensigns, Commanders, Captains. Then you have this Junior Grade. You wouldn't know it was higher than an ensign unless you knew. You wouldn't trust anybody named that with something you'd give a grown-up man. Wonder a man would accept such a title, being an officer already.

On a ship you didn't call him that, you just said Lieutenant, let on you didn't know know he was Junior Grade. Like somebody out of prison, give the man a chance. If he was head of the ship like Emmery you always called him Captain or Skipper. Had the dignity. Emmery had a good sea stomach. He'd stand there watching me work. Asking. Cook you seem to be hanging in there okay? Will you be ready with a commissary order when we dock? Are those canned chickens on the order? Are you getting along okay? How is the weather down here?

Last day out the weather broke so there's just a slow heave on the ocean and the sun came out. I was up on the maindeck hanging alone on the sweep reel out back and the captain came by.

"How are you doing, Stiff?"

"Doing okay sir."

"We don't have weather like we had every week hm?"

"Hope not sir."

"You stayed in there very well, you're a good sailor. You're a good cook too. If you have any problems you let me know?"

"Yes sir, no problems sir."

"I see on your orders you're from New York City?"

"Yes sir."

"So am I. Not many of us from the big town around."

Didn't talk like anybody from New York City I knew. Found out later there's lots talk like that, they just didn't hang around Harlem. Didn't talk like other white guys either. They learn it in their schools so they don't need Masonic rings to know what club they're in. Gets stuck on some fellas like their skins, same as Harlem got stuck on me.

I liked Emmery all right from the start after I saw he wasn't putting me on the way he talked. He talked the same to everybody. I figured one reason I didn't have worse trouble with the crew was him saying something before I came on. "We're working for the same navy, nobody writes his own orders, hm? Give the guy a shot. Or else. Don't pile any shit on the road, okay?"

Every little bit helps even if you don't specially appreciate the attention.

I got straightened out with the crew as far as those things go before too long. After we docked I was getting ready to go for the commissary order when this seaman from Alabama, Reemes—he looked like he sooner tromp you than walk around—this Reemes came off the bleachers and offered "I'll give you a hand wheeling the chow. Lemme know when you're ready."

With Reemes on board I knew I was home free. I got into the raps and card games like everybody. The way it worked out I got to be the main man on the ship because I never got orders off, stayed on the whole war. Everybody else transferred off, new men come on, I'm still there.

We got different new captains after Emmery, some didn't know bow from stern, some could run a battleship, some fellas easy about liberty, some fellas kept you on ship for no reason even when you're in drydock. They come, they go, I'm still there. Went up to cook first class, probably the only cook first in the whole AMc navy.

Got to know everything about that ship. Where the spare parts were. Who to see on all the bases to get something done.

Ask Stiffy.

How you use the signal light answering challenges coming into port. Those ace signalmen are full of themselves, blink at you so fast it could be welding. Main thing is don't get flustered. Send back Slow Down Slow Down dittydah dittydah and keep on sending till they quit showing off and got down to a-one a-two a-three. Small craft speed. Get over the idea somebody in Little Creek Norfolk's going to shoot you out of the water because you don't tell him your call number bang when he welds at you. Up on the signal deck got to be my station coming in and going out. Nobody in the navy sent Slow Down any better than me.

Navigation was something else I could do though there wasn't any need. Mostly we were out no more than a few miles from land on a sure course, sweeping ahead of convoys hugging close to shore. Put the binoculars on shore points—towers, cliffs, stuff like that—find out where you were. The quartermasters we had you knew right off by how they handled the sexton, weren't easy with it, you wouldn't want them telling you where you were by how high the sun is. I could figure it out if it came to that. I wouldn't say it if I didn't believe it because it'd be my neck out there just like yours. Some of the captains were just as green as the quartermasters.

"Quartermaster!"

"Aye sir!."

"Where we?"

"Hoboken sir."

"Very well. Where's next buoy?"

Except Emmery, he was a sailor, sailed in Long Island Sound. Sailed those races to Bermuda and all. I was on a night watch checking out the captain's cabin like I was supposed. I saw the navigation book on his table. Flashed it. All about how to know where you are from the sun and stars. I got the basic idea right off. Next day I asked the captain if I could borrow the book. Sure. He kept checking me out on it, asking questions. He could see I had it down.

"How is it that you're cooking? Why didn't you put in for quartermaster or yeoman?"

I told him nobody ever put me in the way of that stuff.

"Lot of shit piled on the road." That was his favorite saying.

When talk got around to what different fellas were going do after the war, I'd say I'm going get a job cooking.

After I added up that even with my paycheck going home I had three thousand dollars extra from knowing when to stay and when to fold, I got a bigger idea. I said I was going open a restaurant, be my own cook. Look me up when you're in New York. Name will be in the phone book. Stiff, Arsdur U. U for Ummer. My momma's family was Ummer. In the service was the first I got the nickname Stiffy. People my great granddaddy Ummer knew in Bedford Indiana put a chain on his arm and held it in a fire till he passed out. Lost the arm. He wanted paid for some work he did. Makes me mad every time I think about it. Nothing against you personally but I don't want to talk to you any more today. Come by tomorrow.

5

Could have bet on it. When I told my idea at home they said What you know about running a restaurant?

You gotta trade now, you can cook, get a job.

Save your money in the bank for your old age.

Could have told them they were going tell me that. I might as well said big chocolate cookies. But I was a grown man now. I had this determination.

I didn't tell my idea to anybody else, only the real estate companies. After I looked at about twenty places I had a good idea what the places were like, what they were asking. Heard them say Key

Money, nodded like I knew, asked around and found out. Heard about inventory and various ways to figure it like how much it cost or how much I was going sell it for. What steamers and refridges and such in this condition would go for. How many customers came in a day, who was good to get rolls from, how much business a year from that many seats. The health inspector, what kind of guy he was, what he got you for. Licenses. All that stuff.

When I got it down so I could talk restaurant business like Mr Horn and Mr Hardart I lined up a lunch room owned by a fella wasn't making it too good. Trying to have his wife run the place while he hung onto his job with a hardware store till he saw how things would work out. Didn't have his name on the place, called it The Eatery. Gives a man the extra incentive to do things right when his name's on the window.

The main thing was having the belief I was going make it. Most things doing it one way or another don't make that much difference. The basic thing is decide and go ahead. Put that down. That's what Malcolm wants to tell. Be positive. That's how to sell books. You take Lee Coco. Customer of mine. You see how his book sells. He told me he never thought that electric razor fella would be any competition but I'm something else.

I decided I could make it in that Eatery place. I got ready to sign the papers and take the money from my bank account.

I was on the way to the real estate office to tell them I was in, already had a pen in my hand, walking down 7th Avenue when I saw Uncle Cousin Foss coming toward me.

Hadn't seen him since before the war. Uncle Cuz was a big knock-you-down size man, beautiful man, African black like us Stiffs though he wasn't a real uncle nor cousin neither. Mainly he was friends with my momma from years back before I was born, just kept on being somebody you knew. Did advertising work for the Amsterdam. Went downtown to the advertising agencies and liquor companies and all and came back with the orders. He was the most important person I knew.

Thought he might not know me in my new Groshire suit and seven dollar Champ hat. People weren't used to seeing me got up like that, and he was that much older and more important than me and I felt real good he knew me right off, didn't have to think who I was. Came toward me showing his big double chop hands.

"It's Ar sdur back from the war."

Broke the words apart in his big rumbly preacher's voice. You add that to the man's size you have a freight train coming down on you one tie at a time and you're stalled on the tracks. Fearsome.

"Uncle Cuz. You're looking as always."

"You're looking man ly. I've been wanting to run in to you. Tell me about this new bus iness you're in."

How come he could blindside me with a question like that? I hadn't told anybody but the real estate people. Seemed to know what he was talking about too. Didn't say What have you in mind to do? Went right to it I was going into business. Maybe momma got hold of him, told him if he saw me to tout me off it. I stalled him.

"What business is that, Uncle Cuz?"

"What bu siness? I wouldn't know what bu siness. All I know is Rawn Cli fford told me Purdis Stiff's boy was looking at a steam ta ble and a pie rack he ad ver tised. Wouldn't that say some thing?"

"Well yeah. Didn't know Mr Clifford knew me."

"Why wouldn't he know you? You were born here. You grew up here. Your folks are known. Are you hi ding Ar sdur?"

"Nothing like that. I was just playing my cards close. Didn't want it to get out what I was doing till I was doing it. I'm still getting ready."

"That is pru dent. That is laud a ble."

So of course it would be dumb not to tell a man like Uncle Cuz what I had in mind now that we're standing there looking at each other and I'm on the way to close the deal. I told him. He clapped his double-chops like he was going sit down and eat me and took us off the the middle of the sidewalk away from people going by.

"Ar sdur I am im pressed. Yes. I am im pressed. Where is it go ing to be?"

Not having anybody else to tell my plans put a head of steam on me and I told him all he would stand still for. Basically people listening don't find what you say as important as you think it is. If you have something important to say and you're not sure there's room in the particular ear to take it in you're as well off talking to a dog. Better off with a dog maybe. A good dog looks you in the eye like he's listening and not waiting for the opening to tell you something he don't know a damn thing about costs too much. Uncle Cuz was a listener. I appreciated it.

Gave me some ideas too. Experiences he heard about. Told me to check if the vent fan opened on something or was just stuck on the wall to give people the idea it could be hotter in there without it. Told me about a fella had a restaurant use to hit the pipe with a hammer on a cold day to give the idea heat's coming. Kept you there long enough to finish your meal, couple hits every half hour were enough. Told me his theory that the same food spread out was more im press ive than stacked high. A wide steak was better than a thick one that weighs the same. Maybe. My idea was make it wide and thick too. People don't mind paying for their money's worth.

The main thing was he knew the location and backed me up on it. Good idea to be where people knew me and could get there easy, get me off to a fast start. His eyes were shiney for me going in business on my own, not working for somebody else.

"Now Ar sdur let's talk about mo ney. Your av e rage bus iness loses mo ney in the be ginning. How are you fixed?"

"I got enough saved up."

"There is no such thing as e nough mo ney. J.P. Mor gan doesn't have enough mo ney. He bo rrows from banks. I have con fi dence in you Ar sdur. You can have five hun dred do llars any time you want."

A lot of people done—make that have done, now we're talking about Uncle Cuz—have done good things for me, nobody more than him with that offer. That was the first I heard about needing more money. It may have been sneaking around the back of my mind all along. Hadn't faced it if it was there, had it all blocked out by the idea whoever I talked to would give me the chocolate cookie treatment. Never forgot Uncle Cuz, always had him for a partner.

"It would be a shame to run out of mo ney just be fore the en ter prise became pro fi ta ble. Don't you know any body with real mo ney?''

I didn't have any names. Said the first one that came to me.

''I know Mubbles. Is he still around?''

''For get Mubbles Thomp son. If an ything is worse than not having e nough mo ney it's getting it from the wrong par ty. Don't you know any body else?''

''Well yeah, but I don't know. The captain on my ship, the last thing he told me when he was transferred off was be sure to look him up after the war if I needed anything.''

''Talk like that is a pe nny a bag. What kind of man was that?''

''Pretty straight up white guy. Just a kid about my age.''

''It doesn't sound pro mising. Where does he live? The other side of the world? Flo ri da?''

''Lives here in New York. Well I don't know where he lives, somewhere out on the Island. All I know is where he works, in a bank on 5th Avenue.''

''Say'' Uncle Cuz said. ''Ima gine that. This young man works in a Bank—'' He set that word Bank off in my face like a bomb—''on 5th Ave nue.''

Gave me a little more time. ''And here we are on 7th Ave nue talking about five hun dred do llars. Ar sdur let me tell you the mo tto of the I B M Type writer company. One word. Are you rea dy? Think.''

I did that.

Three

MONEY

1

"I MEAN IT, look me up. Be sure you ask for Junior."

Captain dropped down to the galley especially to say it when he got orders off the ship. Probably meant it too at the time. If you come from the same city you have the feeling you're in the same club back home when you're not there. People you don't say hello to waiting in line for the movie, you run into them in a hotel in St. Louis you say How about lunch? You get home it turns out the club moved. Now it's where you just left. You run into that fella in New York, all you have to talk about is St.Louis. If Emmery and me have any messages for each other, it's going be about the Navy. Nothing between us here. After I gave it a second thought, that's how it looked to me.

"The captain didn't ask me my address to come after me in case I didn't look him up."

"What do you stand to lose Ar sdur? You al ready in vested in a new gray shark skin suit. It costs you a sub way ride. When a man is a ju nior he is co nnected to a se nior. That's a good sign when ju nior is in a bank."

"I knowed that."

Uncle Cuz laid one of his double-chops on my shoulder to hold me still for the speech. "Ar sdur. If you plan to be a bus iness man it would be a good idea to speak E nglish . . ."

I told you about that speech.

2

Checked myself out. Looking pretty good there among the ghosts going by on the window. Brand new man since the navy. Seven dollar hat with the feather. Cocked it another touch. Too much, took it back to where it was. Pulled the shirt cuff out to show the half inch. Blue tab a little bit grabby on the throat, makes you want to go up like one of those periscope heads from outer space. Got used to thinking 15½ when the man asked my size. Have to think 16. Getting to be a big boy. Looking at 25.

Try me sideways like I'm tooling up to move along, no hurry. Chesty guy. Sleeves hanging right, pants breaking right. Scanned my new Boston cordovan wing tips. Looked like they had trees. Real Stiff feet in there.

Go.

Basic thing is to speak up. Talk Uncle Cuz English. Slow it down so you know how you're going say the third word on. Slows your thinking down too talking in a language not your own but you have to make a choice.

Next basic thing is the eyes. You don't want to be looking around for something to look at. You don't want to be looking too pleased just because somebody looks at you. You want to look like it's their move but they don't own all the moves, you have some say about that. You want them to know you're a contender. When I was a kid inexperienced in white country there was no natural way to put my eyes. White people think black kids have a special mad on by the way they look at you. I'm not saying they're not mad anyhow. I'm just saying it makes them madder having to think about their eyes. One way to beat that is to have bad eyes and wear sunglasses all the time, let somebody else worry about your eyes.

My system is different. I set my eyes How do you do, Tell me your troubles, I'm listening. Sounds like nothing at all. Works wonders, mostly on me. I took so much practise having the look that it turned out that's the natural way I got to be. Used to hang back and just look on. Now my eyes take me into things. People want to tell me things and that's a big talent for a bartender. Better than some of the faces you see. Faces like the Bible says going cross the street, pass on the other side.

Okay push that door.

Something going on here, yeah something. I'd been in banks before, never anything like this. Looked more like a palace.

Ceiling way up on the third floor with an avalanche of glass chandeliers ready to come down on you soon as the weather warmed up. Marble pillars you could hardly get your arms half around holding it all up. Had the idea of marble pillars going on and on, a forest of pillars going on through the mirrors on the back wall to New Jersey and west. Inside space always looks bigger than outside. I doubt if the bank stretched as far as the Hudson river if you walked it out.

Everything light colored toast from the low setting. Walls. Ceiling. Pillars. Carpet had the home-made look, sheep-color ropes with scraps sewed in, worked up by piece labor in a house without too good light. Even so looked expensive, not like the ones they use to sell you for your bathroom. Here and there they had Persian type rugs down on the wall-to-wall. Rugs-on-rugs. Hey! Whole place looked rich, like nobody cared how much things cost. How often it had to be scrubbed and painted.

I could hear momma in my head Arsdur did you wipe your feet good?

I thought I came in the wrong entrance, I couldn't even see where they kept the tellers, wasn't a cage anywhere. Had to take hold of myself not to look like I came in by mistake, going out, checking the name on the wall and having to come in again. Asking dumb questions. I found the tellers loose among the customers working at little creamy-color French type tables. The kind you expect to see mirrors and brushes and bottles on. Tellers working there. Do a little manicure business on the side.

Later I found out the Vault was what they called a personal bank, did you a favor taking your money if you had enough of it. Took care of rich widows and orphans. Didn't have any more real idea what to do with money than the man in the moon. Bonds. Governments.

Blue Chips. Buy it and put it away. Every now and then looked around to see what the smart fellas were doing and did a little of that too, like CD's, so they could put out a sheet telling customers about this new financial instrument they invented. Basically they stayed with the fixed numbers and customers who didn't care about the difference between one percent and another as long as it was triple A. Been getting away with it since before the Civil War.

Don't knock it. Not my investment style either but the chandeliers alone were worth more than an average country. I'm not talking about big league countries like the USA and England. Russia. I'm not talking either about countries with names they got in a contest, names they just made up like Esso. Like Upper Volta. Benzine. We never had those countries in school. I'm talking about your average country. Greece. Italy. Canada.

Real good-looking school teacher type girl at the desk with the Reception sign on it had her eye on me. Horn rims. Yellow hair wrapped cheese danish style around her ears. White blouse with floppy sleeves, the kind they duel in on the late lates. I put it to her who I was calling on. Her eyes checked on my hands, if I was carrying a letter or a box.

That's something, you know. Then anyhow. Black man from Harlem walks into The Vault Bank and Trust Company on 5th Avenue and says he wants to see Mr Dilworth Emmery. Junior.

"Are you here for a pickup?"

Half the time people don't hear what they say themselves, let alone hear what you say. You get a question like that a normal healthy guy makes a little move to see if he can advance himself. You can't tell. The unlikeliest woman you ever heard of could be on fire and mad her own husband can't see it. You just happen to be going by. Nothing too personal but just as good. You here for a pickup? You know about Freud, his ideas. I read a long article about this particular idea in the old Life magazine. Made an impression on me because you know from your own experience you open your mouth and something comes out you never heard of before. Been inside you all along and you've been keeping it down, not wanting to let on to yourself you're that low quality of person.

"You can tell him it's Stiffy from the Kestrel."

"Would he be expecting you?"

Hard to know how to answer that. Say a gypsy came around after lunch and read the leaves. I see water. Dark man coming into your life. I smell cooking. Hey yes I know exactly who you have in mind. In that case the captain is waiting for me to knock on the door.

"He may not be looking for me right now. Just ask if he can see Stiffy or tell me another time."

She offered me various options. If I tell her what it's about maybe somebody else can help out. She thinks he's in a meeting, she can ask his secretary. She can make an appointment.

She decided she better make some maneuvering room for herself. Got up and went under an arch and around the corner after taking a look back to be sure I wasn't carrying anything and nothing was lying loose on her desk like the insurance man says could be an attractive nuisance.

I guess I shouldn't be taking off on the girl like that. She was doing her job. Probably would have handled anybody else the same way. It could be she gave me even a better shake than a white guy. Could be she was on her best behaviour seeing I was a black guy. All the same, there's a lotta history behind the idea that whatever's on her mind, good or bad or not much of either, we're looking at each other off center.

I used to give myself this test—is that a guy who'd come around and stay with you if some neighborhood bums try to drive you out of your place, fire bombs, unfriendly incoming. Didn't get too long a list. Then I figured out Hell never mind about the white guys coming around, how many black guys would do it for you? How many white guys would do it for another white guy? How about you? I tore up the list. Got to go easier on people. Live and let live, that's about the best it's going be. Les McCann had it right Compared to What? That's the thing, Compared to What?

3

Basically I'm a shy guy and getting shyer stuck up out there in the middle of the floor, nobody paying any attention to me except from the side of his eye. I was getting to feel I wasn't too much to look at either. Never mind color. Not sharp like I looked in the window. Fire plug type guy—hold onto your dog—with dabs on my face from the chicken pox and the split lip. Standing there with my hat in my hand, wishing I'd never taken it off—give me a little shade—but you can't put a hat on your head while you're standing in the middle of a palace. I mean, once you get your hat off and you're inside, you can't put your hat on unless you're ready to make your move toward the door. People seeing you taking your hat off and putting it on all the time don't get too good an opinion of you.

Shouldn't have come. Anybody like me comes in here they know I'm asking for money. Nobody wants people asking. People want people telling, like Here I want a million dollars. You say it like that and you either have a gun in your hand or you already have a million and they know you're good for it.

I'm standing there thinking everybody's saying Look at that black guy asking for money, and wishing I had some shade from my hat, waiting for the school teacher to come back and tell me he says Who? when around the corner and through the arch comes the skipper in a high power heel-and-toe event. Wore a yellow shirt with the cuffs turned up, not looking like a banker. Reaching for a handshake. I'd been thinking about the handshake, whether he'd offer now that we're civilians.

"Stiffy! I've been looking for you. Come on in." Took me by the arm and and hauled me back to the inner sanction up a small flight of stairs to offices opening off a balcony. "I knew you weren't dead because I ran into Dick Clayton"—Clayton was the last skipper on the Kestrel—"He told me he gave you your discharge papers. I've been hoping you'd stop in. What are you doing with yourself?"

"I'll tell you, captain—"

"Do me a favor and make that Dill. We're civilians now."

"Aye aye sir. First chance I get."

I told him I was getting ready to open a restaurant.

"You'll have a winner."

Before I had a chance to pick up on that, pull this piece of paper out of my pocket with the figures—you know, I'd appreciate having your views, captain, like Uncle Cuz gave me for tactics—he climbed on with the questions, same old way. What happened to the guys? Had I seen anybody? Did I know Reemes made chief? Did I hear Caputo got married? Did I use my navigation any? What about Feinlogan, did he ever get his pay record straightened out? What was the new pulse box they put in, GE or Westinghouse? Did we ever sweep a mine? Was there a brand name on that damn good canned chicken we got?

Couldn't get back to the restaurant. Wanted to talk about canned chicken so he could tell Hope the brand.

We were in this splendid room with a brass Directors plate on the door—"We'll slip in here, nobody will bother us. I left some people in my office"—talking about canned chicken. I knew I was the poorest man ever had been in there including the cleaning man.

Size was the first thing I went by. If anything was two sizes bigger than it had to be I knew it belonged to a rich man. Except a suit of clothes, of course—that belonged to a fella had it hand-me-down. But you take a Cadillac car with a leather top and those egg windows or a house with a three car garage—that meant people didn't only have extra, they had two sizes extras, and this Director's room at the Vault bank would make your average two-size-extra millionaire touch his hair to see if it was combed.

Say you have a dining room. That room is supposed to be big enough for the table and the chairs and people to walk around. Throw in a sideboard. Throw in a glass cabinet to show off your silver. Big enough? No, if you push back your chair to be comfortable, stretch your legs after dessert, you know people won't be able to walk around you. If you tip back and go too far and fall over, you hit the wall before you go down. That place is only one size big. In the Vault directors room they seat forty around a table on slope-arm chairs, green leather with enough brass buttons for the doorman at the Plaza, and you can march by the sixes all around without jostling. Tip over, you go all the way down and still leave room for a march by the fours without anybody stepping on your face. Three sizes six sizes big.

Look up, we have more glass chandeliers. This time ambry and blue, could be jewelry. The ceiling was half a barrel—

I just now realized when I said it, the shape of the ceiling was a trade mark. Took me all these years to get the idea. I never thought about it before, just came to me. You see something like that you wonder if the guy who built it planned it that way. Could be an accident like a joke you don't know is funny till after you say it, like somebody fed you the line. Here is a builder could build the ceiling flat, peak it, could make it a dome like they have in St. Peter's in Rome. Instead he makes it like half a barrel and puts it over the Board of Directors of the Vault Bank and Trust Company. That guy either had the IBM idea or Somebody Up There was feeding him lines.

Ancestor paintings around the walls. Hoover type men knowing their picture's being painted. Stretched out English type horses.

Another thing was the panelling. I don't know how this works but you can look at panelling laid up so you can't see the edges and you still can tell how thick it is. X-ray eyes. You know if you're looking at plywood or the real thing, and this was real bird-eye maple. Not a quarter inch thick either, at least fivequarter and that's five times as much wall as a man needs to say he just panelled the game room. That's the way you do things when you don't have to think about money. It's like air. You don't think every time you breath in. You don't let on to other people how you never give it a thought. Other people want to talk about money as if it was real, you go along. You want to be polite, like you always admire people's kids no matter how lousy they are.

It wasn't enough they could seat forty around the table, at the end of the room was a sofa and a coffee table where you could have a little private meeting, and under the table was another Persian rug on top of the wall-to-wall. I never saw that where I came from.

I'd seen fat houses and offices in the movies. I sort of knew that for some people they were real places where nobody ever asked how much anything cost, didn't care, wasn't an idea that came up. This was the first time it hit me that people I could know lived like this.

Me and Dill Emmery sitting on the sofa with two rugs under our feet and a rock from the desert on the coffee table, chewing the fat about canned chicken and old times like there's nothing else in the world.

At the same time I know we're getting to the place where he looks at his watch and says Holy cow three o'clock, I got people in my office, and that's it. When I said I was going open a restaurant he heard loud and clear underneath I come in to ask him for money and he wasn't going let that happen.

So while we're talking canned chicken and what happened to the guys I have another show going in the back of my mind about money. Nothing you don't know but you know what Malcolm had on that page of sayings he has—Listen once, hear twice. I don't know exactly what that means but it was there on the page. It may not make too much sense coming out of you or me but hang it in a magazine—or better yet hang it on another party who says it in Zulu or French—and you can get mileage out of it. Here's what this hundred and ten year old Zulu wise man driving the taxi told this reporter in his native language—Listen once, hear twice. What I'm getting at is Don't always grab all the credit for yourself. Give it to somebody else and you'll get more out of it.

You must have said something made me lose my trend of thought. I was talking about canned chicken. No I was talking about money.

When's the last time anybody you knew ever offered you any money without it being asked like my Uncle Cousin Foss? Never. Uncle Cuz he's one of a kind. Fact is if there's one thing people are more peculiar about than sex it's money. You ask a man with all the money in the world, he won't give you a dime without it becoming a big serious deal. You talk about separating a man from money and it's not like arguing with him about politics or religion, it's like death. Serious. Real real serious.

When you know a man's going ask you for money, the first thing is you see if you can head him off. You talk about every last thing not to give him an opening till you can say I got to run, I'm late for this three o'clock meeting. Another way is you signal him by getting your troubles on the table first, things he can't have any idea at all you're suffering, like your cousin passed on unexpectedly and you're responsible for his widow and nine kids. Every thing in the family dumps on you. The object is to worry the other fella you have a better case for asking him than he has for asking you.

If a man brings up an idea that might lead to him asking for money, you can't say anything like Yeah that's a good idea. If it's such a good idea, why wouldn't you spring for it? Instead you say something to set up that you had a bad experience with an idea like that made you swear on the Bible never to do it again no matter how good it sounds. Or it could be a good idea but it might get wet if you left it out in the rain and you just don't have the experience of wet ideas. You don't dare ask what he plans to do if it rains because that says right off if he's got an embrulla you're on board.

There's the idea rich people have that money is bad for anybody but them. The fact you don't have money proves you don't have the experience of it, and if you don't have the experience how do you know what to do with it if I give you some? It's bad for your character, people handing you money. You should get the experience the same way he did, getting a check from his daddy. I heard a guy once at the bar saying how much harder it was for him because his daddy made him president of the company, instead of letting him come in anonymous and work up. Fat chance. He comes in anonymous he's still punching the clock.

Luck's the real thing, and what's lucky about asking a man for money and getting it? No sir, go find your own luck, mine's bad for you. My money is like a bad liver they give you in the hospital, it won't match your blood. Here is this good looking liver you think is going save your life and it can kill you. Yeah.

A bank's like a hospital, only instead of livers it's money. The particular money a bank has might not be the right kind for you. It might upset your system. Now we don't want that to happen, do we? I heard of a banker once told a fella A year from now you're going thank me for not lending you this money you're asking for. Can you see that? Nobody ever thanked anybody for not lending him money. Damn few people thank you even for lending it, mostly they cross the street when they see you coming.

You go to enough testimonial dinners like I do and you hear once a year at least about the banker some dumb guy asked for a loan. They tell this story so you know how great the honored guest's reputation is, it's a privilege to know him. Not a chance, the banker told this fella, but I'll tell you what I'll do. I'll walk across the street with you and people will see you know me and you can ask them.

Yeah. That banker was positioning himself in case anything went wrong and people came to him about it he could say Not me, I didn't lend him a dime. We were just crossing the street and I was telling him he should save up instead of borrow. It's you fellas that sprung. You should have better judgment. You can't lend money to every bum grabbing your arm to cross the street or you'll be broke too. I thought the man was blind.

One thing nobody but my Uncle Cuz is going give you is money. Might give you a little time. Advice—that's something everybody likes to give. Not money. Sacred. You just don't do that with money.

I was doing all this free thinking for Emmery, knowing he was in the banking business and therefore a worse case even than your average non-lender, when sure enough he flashed his wrist watch. Here it comes. Three o'clock. Got those people in his office. If he'd taken me in his office it would have been that much harder to get rid of me.

"Okay now, that's all out of the way. Tell tell me about the restaurant."

Positioned like I was at the time I didn't know Dill Emmery too good and I didn't expect too much of any white guy anyhow. I was there mainly because Uncle Cuz pushed me. It wouldn't ruin my day if we just shook hands and he said Nice to see you and I went back up to the real estate company and make the deposit on The Eatery. I know better now. Dill, he opens up. He is sure you get to say what you came for. I try to be like that. If I get slack at it, say a man I don't care for too much comes to me with some proposition, I think how Dill would talk to him and I do the same. I don't always spring for it but I let a man talk.

I told him a place, you know, for coffee and eggs in the morning. I'll do my three egg omelettes, and a man brings the family for Sunday dinner now and then and I can do my special things. Duck and sausage gumbo. Catfish with Mexican sauce. Chocolate banana cake. This is going be the favorite place of my customers.

"You're going to work from six o'clock in the morning to midnight seven days a week?"

"Won't be that bad. Six to nine. I don't mind work."

"I know you don't. Did you have somebody check out the lease? How long are you tied up? What if you want to go out next year and open somewhere else? Is there room to expand? Have you got renewal options? How do you know the last guy did as much as he said? Did you see his IRS? Any building plans up there that could tie up the street? Did you ask the real estate agent? What did he say? Don't you have your own lawyer? You mean you're using the real estate company's lawyer? Can you get a liquor license? What happens if there's a fire? What happens if you get sick? Who'll keep it going? Where is it?"

I told him about this place I had lined up on on 134th. I didn't say anything about money. Let that come up.

He looked at me a few seconds, had that look of holding back something he had in mind to say. Got up and went to the window, big window patched with small squares of glass and lead. Looked out from balcony-high onto a corner of the church and on down 5th past the stores and St. Pat's. Hiked a foot up on the heater box that ran along under the window and hooked a thumb into his belt. Held a pencil in his other fist, pushed his thumb into it like he was testing where it would break. Thinking. His shirt had a loop on the back of the neck for hanging. First I'd seen that feature. Good idea.

4

"Why don't you start where the money is?" He pointed down the Avenue. "Out there. It's just as easy to sell an egg for a dollar as a nickel. It takes the same gas to cook it. Hn?"

I could see that. I said "The real estate is expensive too."

Three years since I last saw him. You can't get too good an idea about an officer in uniform. Has all this power put on him by the suit of clothes, like a witch doctor comes on with this big fur mask, waving a spear. Who knows what's under. Best thing I could say for Dill now in the Directors room was okay forget the chandeliers and the rugs-on-rugs, the guy looks like he knows how to do this work whatever it is. Asking questions like before, but more snap, like the answers were owed him.

"The most expensive real estate is the cheapest. It delivers the traffic. Isn't that right?"

Not my traffic. No one around here's coming for my special black-eye peas with pepper gravy. Shouldn't have to tell him the whole time from when I came up out of the subway on 55th I didn't see a black face, not coming out any of those hotels, the Gotham, the Berkshire. Not out any of those stores, Saks, the bookstore, St. Pat's. None in the bank.

"Maybe for some people. I got my own trade in mind, doing business where people know me, see me around."

"Shovel that shit off the road. If you set up somewhere around here and run the kind of place I know you can you will do business. No question." Big difference between that and what Uncle Cuz said about being on my own turf.

"I don't have hardly enough money to open in Harlem and you're talking 5th Avenue."

Cut me off as soon as I said Money. Back to square one.

"Why a restaurant? Why not a bar? The money is in bars. Around here more people drink than eat."

He came off the window and sat on the edge of the big table all-fired up about the bar, looking to carry me with him. Easiest thing in the world for him to think about a bar instead of a restaurant. You could see by looking at him here's a man who doesn't care all that much about eating. Left more on his plate than he ate on the ship and he didn't weigh any more now than when I fed him last.

"Anyhow forget money hn?" he kept on. If you want to do a bar in the fifties we'll find you some money—"

Let's not forget money so fast after it first came up. I don't know anything about bars in the fifties. Take it again from the top. Let's find some of that forgetting money you're talking about for what I got lined up waiting for me to sign and lay down the deposit on

134th.

He went right on, not paying attention to what I just said in my head. "I'll put you in touch with a real estate man who knows his way around here. We will have to bring in somebody to see to the license. Fred Lebrand will set up your books."

"Whoa there captain, whoa."

"Come on, Stiffy, make that Dill."

"Whoa both of you. You got to understand I'm a little guy with this plan to open a restaurant in my neighborhood. I can't swing this downtown bar stuff with high priced talent looking for licenses and doing books and all that. I do appreciate what you're saying but I'm not connected there."

"All right, start over again hn? I'm saying that when you walk out the front door of the bank, all around you is the best place in the world to do business no matter what the business is. If you want to make it in a restaurant make it a restaurant. I'm saying think about making it in a bar. They tell me a bar is simpler to manage and makes more profit per square foot. Can't you see yourself running a great saloon?"

"Never gave it a thought. I got this restaurant deal."

"I can't believe there is a man who wouldn't want to run a first class saloon. You really never gave it a thought?"

"To be truthful I never did. Restaurants are my bit. You can't cook a highball."

"I wanted to run a saloon as long as I can remember. I would have if the war hadn't come. It's too late for me now."

Now we're getting really nowheres. He's telling me his dreams. Really wished he could do a bar. How could you figure that. Didn't want to be a policeman or an aviator. Wanted to do a bar. He's disappointed I don't get it.

Gives you another way to tell a man you can't lend him any money. He isn't planning to do your dreams, he has his own? Okay let him print his own money. You got this made-up thing like one of those UN countries. Benzine. You see the name in the papers. Yeah. Bars on 5th Avenue, that's a Benzine idea. You're having a serious discussion in the UN with people like Russia and France and this fella comes in How about me? Who are you? I'm the ambassador from Benzine. What's he got to do with anything. Dill kept pushing this Benzine bar idea on me.

"If you would consider it I know we could get some people together to back you. I'm thinking of people who wouldn't just put money in but could contribute to a successful operation. If Fred Lebrand would handle your accounting I could ask Dick Greenberg to do the legal work—Robbins would want to think about coming in. There are investors out there who will see a way to get a handle on this. Mike—Carter—"

Out roll the names of these parties he's going ask in on this thing going on in his head no place else. Lebrand Greenburg Robbins Straight Burden Forbes Breger Barnes. Names didn't mean a thing to me. Names didn't even have to be real. He could be putting on a magic show for his own entertainment, talking about money and investors he knew I wouldn't catch him up. Stiffy, he got here just in time to lay this blue sky on.

All I heard was I wasn't getting any of that bank money, and those names and ideas he mentioned had nothing to do with me. You learn what your family talks about at home, what kids in your neighborhood do. Then you do something inside those ideas the rest of your life. Emmery was from another neighborhood. An okay fella but from another neighborhood.

"I'm looking to be in business for myself, be my own boss. You're talking nine ten bosses. I appreciate it but I don't want you doing that for me. I got to get cracking on my restaurant. I'm taking your time. I have to be going. Nice catching up with you."

"Oh man" he said. "I'm not getting across. I'm a banker. The hardest thing is to find a man to bet your money on. That's the first thing I learned about banking after Be sure there's enough collateral. Now hear this, Stiffy. If you have a restaurant in Harlem I want to be in. If you have it on 55th I want to be in. Restaurant or bar, I want in. I think I know a few people who can do you some good, but that's up to you. Just make room for me. Will you do that?"

Well, you know, on top of what Uncle Cuz said about having confidence in me, that made me feel pretty good. People having confidence in me. I couldn't see where that came from but there it was.

"Think about it. How about coming in Friday for lunch and talking some more? Maybe I'll get some people in hn?"

5

On the way out we stopped by his office, which wasn't too much, considering the class of the whole shebang, those pillars and the chandeliers and the rugs on rugs. Peeked in. Tight quarters. Three four people gabbing in there over spread-out paper.

Brass on the door said Dillworth V. Emmery, Jr. Assistant Vice President. Took me awhile to learn that Assistant Vice President is the first title you get in a bank. After that comes Porter, Mail Clerk, Reception and Trust Officer. The lowest bank job that gets paid in American money is Executive VP. They gave Emmery Junior that job to let the vice presidents know they weren't too bad off.

Out front a secretary was positioned to cover two offices. Behind her was a picture different from the ancestors in the Directors Room. One of those pictures that isn't about anything, just color dabs like kids do in school and you say That's nice and you know one thing he aint going be is any artist, no way. I've studied it out but couldn't tell you why people pay big—I mean big—prices for pictures like that. Some of it's my fault too. Dill got me writing checks to that museum he's in over on 53rd. What are you going do when a good friend asks you?

Never go there myself except when he says it's some big occasion, put on your tux and be there. Edna says she likes some of it, sees music in it. Sees Charlie Parker and Diz, that type music, in paintings over there the size of a house-wall done by a fella who admits he just drips paint from the can on a drop cloth. That's her idea. She may be right. She can sit in with those stream players when she wants, scattering notes like gravel under a hot car's wheels. I never saw much music in that type playing and I don't get the pictures either.

Dill's secretary Casey was a cheerful woman, bright as could be you could tell by looking at her, same way you can tell how thick wood is from the top. All business.

He asked her how he was for lunch Friday.

She looked in a calendar book and showed him something and he said Move it and she showed him another day and he said See if they can do that.

"Keep Friday open for Mr Stiff. You're going to get to know him. One o'clock on the button. Right here. Hm?"

6

I went by the school teacher not looking at her except by the white of one eye. You could tell she wanted a chance to show she wasn't a half bad person. Show me next time.

By the door was this elbow-high table with deposit slips and pamphlets and I saw this one entitled Quarterly Report. Thought it would be a good idea to read up on that. Give me something to do on the subway.

Never saw one before. First thing I noticed was they left off the pennies. Somebody got to keep those, probably the fella who did the counting. When it came to the dollars I had a Jimmy Durante feeling. You know his song *Did You Ever Have The Feeling You Wanted To Stay And then had the feeling you wanted to go? Wanted to stay? Wanted to go?* Numbers didn't seem big enough. Hell they had to be right, it was a bank. Interest income $9,180. Even I knew that wasn't much even if it was only a quarter of the year. How come?

Same with Salaries and Wages. $3,220 to pay the whole shooting match. Only a thousand a month for Miss Danish 1946, Casey, those tellers, that brass up there on the balcony. A thousand a month you couldn't recruit a section of boots. Something wrong. Couldn't figure it, knew I was missing something. Went at the numbers again.

Noticed the little line at the top Millions Omitted.

Meaning make that three month payroll $3,220,000. That was more like it. *Wanted to stay.* After that I got into the groove of reading words first, numbers second.

Read the little piece about the satisfactory quarter considering the unsettled conditions and the government sticking its fingers in the markets and so on, and finally it couldn't be done without the contribution of our dedicated employees, signed.

D. Vault Emmery, chairman, president, chief executive officer.

His picture there. Looked just like Dill was going look filled out a little in a few years if he learned to eat. Same sucked in cheeks. Same jaw coming at you. Same hair going lift straight up soon as you stop watching it in the mirror.

Man held three jobs, bound to give up one or two before long. You talk about a connection, that would be Uncle Cuz's idea of a connection.

7

On his fiftieth we gave Dill Emmery this big party in the upstairs room. All those people who knew him from the banks and the commissions and what in all came. The fella who used to be mayor was there, tall wavyhaired fella looked like a movie actor. People hoisting toasts and tributes. I knew what Edna had worked up and pretty soon they got her to the piano.

"I wrote a song for you, Dill" she said and began progressing.

People thought she might do one of his favorite songs like Tiger Rag, but she did this special song.

People think Edna only writes the tunes but you look on the labels for Powah, Eubie's Back, Pig In A Poke—a lotta her songs, you'll see Words and Music by Edna Bundige. She never spent much time at it, just dummied in words for the tune usually and they turned out good enough. Didn't use the words anyhow on her records, just a phrase here and there, her style. Hammond never paid attention to the words less there was going be a different singer doing an Edna song and singing all the words. He listened to the tune is all, thinking who to get on the date with her. By the time it got to the print sheet it was an established fact. Done. Words and music by Edna Bundige.

"The title of this song is Lotta Shit Piled On The Road."

Everybody who knew that was Dill's trade mark broke up. Edna kept vamping while word was passed around for people who didn't know Dill that good and couldn't believe what they heard. That was it, Lotta Shit Piled On The Road. Edna did it gospel, hushed everybody down, had to hear every word. Belted it. Now and then some guy would go haw haw haw and set people off but they swallowed it back because Edna was going straight down the gospel blues road. Hear, I'll sing it for you. I'm no Armstrong but it won't kill you to listen for a minute.

Lotta shit piled on the road
Lotta stuff to sweep away
You clean it up, another load
Gets piled on the road.

Lotta ways to turn your back
Lotta ways to look away
Lotta things are done to keep you from
The shit piled on the road.

Fast as you shovel more's on the way
Take more than your lifetime
To get it out the way.

What's that on the road?
Aint pie a la mode
Can't forget—Not forgetting yet
That's it—a lotta shit
Piled high high high high
Piled on the road.

"Bless you Dill Emmery" she finished "a guy with a shovel". Could be a lotta people there went out and did some shovelling, at least that one week.

People say What's so great about Dill Emmery? He has all that money. He gives a stack of it away, he has more left than he started with, no way to stop money piling up once it gets into compound interest. He has that name, he can say anything he wants to anybody and they still want Dill and Hope at their parties. Yeah. But he doesn't buy out. He makes house calls. He goes bail for tough cases. He does windows. He gives blood. He don't just walk across the street with you. He'd be a good stop on the Underground Railroad. If that Anne Frank kid needed an attic over here, Emmery's the place to go.

The reason you never heard the song is it wasn't put out for for the public, we only made enough disks for the friends. Collector's item. Don't have a copy myself, I gave up the last one to Mrs Astor for somebody she was working up to donate money to the 42nd Street library.

Four

PARTNERS

1

YOU TAKE A rich man, he doesn't care one Iowa or any of those dustbowl states or all of them put together what anything costs. He wants something, it's his. The main thing isn't that he decides to buy it, there's no decide to it. Decide means you spread the papers on the table and talk to your wife. Your basic rich man can go from I want to I got.

Don't get the idea a rich man is just a hog eating his way through the store. That's not it. I know rich men you can see where their shirt collar's worn. Not cheap types either. Just not interested. Once you get it into your head you can have what you want, you see you got plenty after all without adding on all the time. Except money. You got to add on money. Seems like you owe it to the money to add on. Other things, you can see when you got enough. That's how we got away from bigamy. The way it works, the fella with the worn collar, it's probably on a hundred dollar shirt. So what? Probably outwears four other shirts and looks better even with the threads showing. Feels better. Feels like a hundred dollar shirt just from paying that for it. By the time we get finished with inflation it's a $200 shirt and I didn't even pay half. That's how those things work.

By my way of life all the partners Dill brought in were rich men. They were all around the same age as me, plus five maybe, all had college, nobody had to give any of his pay home. Most had jobs in the family business starting with Dill and Mal and Wally.

Fred Lebrand's daddy was an accountant before Fred. Wally's daddy did real estate. Barnes was a broker neighbor of Malcolm's in New Jersey. His wife Gwen was into good causes like me, had her life ambition filled being a backer to a black guy in a bar Dill said was okay. Robbins did apartment buildings and was into low rent housing for the mayor. Greenberg was a partner in a big law firm. I never knew then exactly where Mike and Carter had their money from, but they talked the same peculiar way Dill did and I knew they weren't running books.

Doesn't make any difference who was and who wasn't on his daddy's payroll or had checks coming from his granddaddy's estate, the basic point is most of them were used to money. Knew how to talk about it. How different people used it. They had the road map. Gave them a head start getting somewhere.

One of the things about having money is that you want to show you know what it costs even though you don't care all that much when you're looking at a hundred dollar shirt with a stripe that appeals to you. So I had these peculiar actions going on. One minute I'd have your friend Mal telling me I needed a nice $5,000 ship model on the wall behind the bar. That's when he was too used to money to think about it. A minute later he was telling me nobody reads book matches, save the money, every dime counts.

Me, I wasn't used to spending on anything, ship's models or matches. Every dime, I couldn't believe I was spending it. Uncle Cuz and I were going in a Harlem restaurant with four five thousand dollars and here I was in a bar operation on Madison took $70,000 dollars to set up. Starting out today that would be a half million seven eight hundred. I was running it. Responsible to partners and trying not to be scared to death.

Lucky the place Wally found for us was a tavern before. It had this beautiful oak bar I never would buy myself, didn't have my head up that high yet. Nothing like the party ahead of you going bust, leaving everything to you at bargain prices so you'll take the lease off his hands. That's the usual thing in bars and restaurants. No reason for you to buy new. Bars. Tables. Ice Machines. The fella before you, his job is to buy new and break the piece in. Get the kinks out. Put a nice hand-polish finish on it. Then he has the duty to go bust. That's the capitalist system, the first man is supposed to take his depreciation and the loss and bust out. He smartens up and next time he buys used. All the players understand used is the way to go. Why do you think we have all these mergers instead of from the ground up? Used corporations. Cheaper that way. Malcolm understands those things.

If the builder didn't know Dill and Wally were in it, with all the real estate they controlled, I hate to think how long it would take to get open. People will do things for you if you are known to have money just the same as if you paid extra for it. If that fella who was mugged and left beside the road had been known to be a rich man, people would come out the buildings all around to help him. Wouldn't have to wait for a Samaritan. Wouldn't be looking for any reward. Just showing respect because he was rich. People care more for your money than they do for you. I don't run my business that way. You come in here you're the same as the president of the United States. The one we got now, maybe you get the table first.

2

One partner in particular was on my case all the time and of course he'd be the one I was edgey with. Easy to see why that was and no reflection on him. Freddy Lebrand was a man everybody knew would keep his eye on the money. Some fellas have trouble talking about money, looking at their fingernails, apologizing for bringing it up. Fellas on the dock go right to it Hey there old pal I'm looking for two grand you're late with interest or I'm taking out your knee caps. Freddy wasn't the type to break your knees but short of that he had no trouble getting on you about money. That's his business. As long as Lebrand was in a deal everybody left the money part to him.

He's the one, when I put Edna on the payroll, came around before she had a a real chance to break in, after a couple weeks.

"You're in over your head. Let her go."

I wasn't going do that.

"You've got partners to think about."

"Thinking about them all the time."

"You're going to run out of cash next month and your ass will be in a sling."

Talked like that standing there rear-backed with his chin down, bobbing and jabbing and looking around like a sore-head marine pigeon having breakfast. All that jazz on account of eighty bucks a week and two more tables taken away.

"I'll take the responsibility."

He could asked what I meant by that and I'd have to say I didn't know, just came to me to say it. All the money I owned was in that business. I already gave it all the time I had.

"We'll talk again next week. Take my advice and tell her it isn't working. People get fired off jobs all the time. Get your ass out of the sling."

Hoot de toot toot.

I never took that advice and look how it turned out. He wasn't slow to admit that either in his own way. "Good figures" he'd say "I like those figures. Next week you can beat them."

Real bright fella. I can read figures, Freddy inhaled them. He took in numbers like those deep-breathers take in smoke, bury it inside themselves, give it back out when they're halfway through the next sentence. When he liked something he added opening his eyes wide to the pecking and the bobbing and deep breathing. He'd pull back the corners of his mouth—had the shape of a smile but it wasn't any more of a smile than a dog ready to come at you. Reminded me of Satan dropping in on the Lord after going up and down and to and fro in the land and the Lord telling him he could have Job for a project. Real challenge. Job. Yeah. Wouldn't bother Satan how it came out one way or another, you win some you lose some. The main thing was to dig on the man. I don't think it made that much difference to Fred if figures were good or bad as long as he had something to get at you with.

Same time we were getting the store ready I spent time with Freddy setting up the books. We didn't get along too good from the first.

"You people haven't had much experience with figures" he said.

This was his best side, showing me he understood us people. "All you will have to do is put the register tapes and the cash in the deposit bag. We'll do the rest. We'll watch your expenses and tell you where to go."

Tell you where to go too. He never asked me what I could do and what I couldn't.

First monthly I looked at I told him I wanted more breakouts, wanted to separate the bar from the tables and see the wholesale discounts separated out. Doesn't take you long to get into that lingo once you catch on how things are done. I picked it up at the Bar School.

"You don't need that" he told me.

"Maybe not but let's see. I'm dumb. I need to see more."

Let him know I was no pushover but he didn't learn too fast. Apart from him just being the way he was he was teed off by the way Dill agreed to split up the stock. That goes back to when I told Uncle Cuz about this big snowball Dill had rolling down hill toward the bar.

Uncle Cuz got hold of his friend Counsellor Marcus Bragdon and they worked up this deal where no matter how much the investors put in I had the last say. I had to get them their percents on the loan and the A stock but as long as I did that I could do what I wanted. All I needed was one other partner with me. I had Uncle Cuz. I had Dill too.

Fact is I had everybody and we never had any big trouble but Fred Lebrand just didn't like the idea of me putting in that little bit of money and having the last say. Money was the one thing with him. If he'd been the one writing up the Last Supper in the Bible, you might not even know who was the guest of honor, only who picked up the tab. He was in the saloon deal because he went in what Dill was in if he couldn't talk him out of it.

3

I went to bar school nights over on 6th. I never knew anything but beer and a shot and a bottle of 89¢ wine. Man, you have no idea what people put in their stomachs. Alexanders. Pink Ladies. I'm talking grown men floating cream on top of coffee liqoor in the middle of the afternoon. Zombies. Five different kinds of rum, one of them Myers 140 proof, maybe 160, I didn't count.

First Zombie I ever did I turned the bar over to Sid and went around to sit with a customer who ordered it. He said it was so damn good I told Sid Make me one. I was getting ready to go out for dinner in the slow time. Tasted it. Nice. Smooth as a Coke. Sat there sipping and rapping till I finished and it was time to take off. So long for now I said. I stepped off the stool and kept right on going down like into a coal chute. You think you insulted a Japanese wrestler.

I learned a lot from one of the instructors who liked to ramble on, wanted to tell people how much he knew without saying it was on account of having belly-upped himself in his own place in the Village. He told ways loyal employes steal from you if you're the owner. Malcolm will like this.

"Here's how they get into you. Say you write the orders in books with numbered pages. Say you get sloppy and don't look at the number on every page when you add up the day's sales. You don't see the one missing where the waiter wrote the order, took the money, stuck it in his pocket and tore out the page and threw it in the can. Say you get a waiter who makes it his business that you can't read his writing. It says anything he says it says. He's a good waiter, which isn't that easy to find, so you give up and stop reading the items, just tally the dollars. He sets up his own business on you, selling dollar items and changing them to 50¢ between the customer and the register. He keeps half, gives you half. Lemme show you."

He showed. Anybody planning on being a loyal employ for somebody else wasn't supposed to watch. Told about cigarette machines and liquor salesmen. I thought you just went into a store and bought a case for a few cents off the bottle price but that's nothing. I learned how to cut deals for free goods. Clocks. Glassware. Twofers. Inside information on different styles of heavy bottoms on glass so you can spray Canadian windex in there and a customer thinks he's set for two hours till he finds out in ten minutes he's empty. We have glasses now where a $4 drink evaporates if you turn off the air condition ten minutes. I don't use those.

About towels for the rest rooms. That's a science. Some bars don't make a dime from liquor, make it all from blowing cheap hot air on you instead of having a man hand you a good cotton towel.

Learned all these things the other fellas did I didn't want to do. My barware's the same you use in your own home. People appreciate that. They must or they wouldn't steal it. Would you believe people put old fashions in their pockets? Ladies are the worst, born cliptomaniacs, some of them take everything on the table but the check. Ask me sometime how some folks show their appreciation. Average people though, they appreciate if you ask them a fair price and then don't shave the odds. If it has to be another quarter, ask for it but don't give them the windex. Orrin Riley came in here one night screaming mad. Stayed over at the Sherry. When he checked out they handed him a laundry bill for bed sheets. How about that? Told the story up and down the bar. Great piece of free advertising.

4

Got through Fred Lebrand, the building, the bar school, all of it without losing an arm, and unlocked the door April 25, 1946 eleven a.m. Exactly the time we said, only two months later. Poured rain. Everybody went by had collars pulled up, hats pulled down, eyes squinted on the ground for puddles and wet dogshit, saluting to protect from embrullas. People hopping from doorway to doorway and trying to squeeze under the cornishes. Wearing newspapers on their heads. Wearing fogged-up eyeglasses they'd be about blind and I'm trying to get open. Couldn't care less they had a new bar on the block, the door wasn't set in enough to give cover.

Madison was two way then, neither way moving and the bumpers closed up so anybody on legs was shut off if he wanted to cross the street, had to go around. One blood caught in the rain in his shirt wants to cross over. He boosts himself up on the hood of a car and jumps over onto the next one and the next and onto the other side like Uncle Tom's little girl. By then the driver of a taxi he tromped on had himself out the window hollering. So the blood came back to exchange hollers with the taxi. The two of them are out there under Niagra Falls—the taxi, he's only half out, he can't open his door any more against a fender next door. The blood is standing on the hood soaked through to his muscles, and they're screaming at each other till the blood tore off the taxi's wiper and beat it back to the sidewalk. The taxi couldn't do a thing, only hang out the window far enough to get soaked some more and holler blue balls.

Meanwhile he's banging his door against the fender next door and that guy's blowing his horn and hollering for him to pull over and show his driver's for the insurance. Pull over. How about that. Pull over. Like it's Staten Island. They exchanged fingers instead.

Sunday in church I forgave the taxi what he called the black guy. I forgave the black guy for tromping on the hood and breaking away the wiper. Fingers, hell they're nothing, like you walk on a rug and lay the static on the light switch, gets it out of you. You do that for yourself not for the switch. I opened on a hard day but I was better off inside than they were out there. I remember being in church and having exactly those thoughts. It was a hell of a day to open a bar and be your own boss. At four o'clock we had $8 to show for four hours work by Sid, me and the waiter Carlos who doubled as dishwasher. It cleared some and the partners start drifting in.

By closing we had $92 and change minus it turned out the cost of a new cashmere dress for a lady who touched her sleeve onto some paint in the lavatory. The painter ducked in there and touched-up the doorframe day before opening. Green paint on a purple dress, not a bad combination but she didn't appreciate it. She came from the Ladies walking very very slowly, holding her arm out and looking scared. I knew I was in for something. She didn't say a word, just came up to me as I was coming to her and held her arm out like it was her baby killed by a car bomb, showing me this nice purple and green color combination. Something for Dill to put up in his gallery. Her husband coming from the bar was going strangle somebody, going take somebody to court he doesn't yet have any idea why, all he knows is the dead baby.

It had to be cashmere, couldn't be rayon or bamburger, something cheap. A dress that backs into a painted doorframe or has a Pink Lady dropped on it by a waiter—every one of them was bought last week, last month at the latest, and the ones that aren't cashmere are 100% pure silk.

Bad luck can be as good as any other kind. Bernie and Kitty Molinaro got to be two of the best customers I ever had. It cost me more than the opening day's receipts and I found out what a deductible on the insurance is, but I took my medicine, didn't try to cut any corners and when it wouldn't clean out I sent a check for what they said. Sent it with a bottle of what they'd been drinking for good measure.

That's another thing I believe—if you're going do something for a customer, do it, don't see if you can do it for half. They came in with a party of six to say they appreciated how I handled it. I couldn't guess how much business came in here from that painted dress in forty years. One anniversary party in the upstairs room ran $4,000 right there.

That's the main thing I told them at Harvard Business—you can run a shop where you win some and you lose some and you're satisfied if the law of averages works out on the bottom line. Or you can go the extra mile to settle a complaint and never let a customer get away from you if you can help. I don't know anything about that first kind except when I'm a customer of one of them I don't like it so why should I do it to you? If you want to be proud of the tax you pay, that's the way to run your business.

4

Didn't take long for us to catch on pretty good. The bar would get heavy from late afternoon when the offices start letting out and stay pretty much that way till the last fellas living in town or the close suburbs had to lam for home. We had the crowd from the broker's and the bank crowd and all those offices. When it got going good the place hummed like a subway. Not loose and coming apart like a New York subway. London subway, say. Big animal eating a four pound chicken, bones and all. Humming to himself That's what I call a chicken. I could turn my back on it and listen and tell you how much we were doing. We paid our bills. That was mostly a man's crowd. We didn't do that well after they left us for dinner. When they were out with their wives or dates we weren't that much the place to come to because we didn't have entertainment till Edna came.

The first thing I thought was put in some food specialties we could get known for, like steak sandwiches and famous desserts. I could hear people saying Let's go to Stiffy's and have a steak and a drink. Piece of pie. Stretch the cocktail hour on out into the evening for us. Give me a chance to do something famous with my lemon pecan pie.

The only problem was we had no kitchen and no place to put it. That was before we could get the room next door.

That's when my mind turned to thinking about that square-grand piano sitting back there not paying the rent.

Far as my day regulars were concerned they couldn't care less if we had a piano. That was one of the risks, that I was just hiring noise to annoy the business we had developed. The fact is my regulars didn't care one way or the other. I could have hired on Paderewski. Harry Truman. Turned on a record, it wouldn't make that much difference to them. I could kept on with nobody. Nobody told me I had to have it. Basically music was something I always wanted around me and then I figured it would bring in late business. I wasn't pressing it, just turning it over the way you do. Mentioned it to Charlie Duvall.

Then this talented young lady from Pittsburgh walked in with Duvall's card.

Not counting the first three four months it took to get known Edna took right off. They had pieces about her in The Times and The New Yorker and Cue magazine. We had Society. We had them coming in after the shows. We had them making a night of it, taking in a couple of sets and going home to bed early. We got that class of people whose names were in the columns, and then those people who heard those other people were here and wanted to hang out with them, and Winchell and Lyons and Kilgallen who wrote them up coming to see who's here, who's got something to tell them.

Another thing was jazz cats carrying trumpets and saxes in here after hours. Lewis set up his vibes. We had Grub Wallace here one night with two taxis of percussion—bells, tomtoms, every kind of clanger ever invented, high hats, temple blocks—Let's go Eddie, let's be heard Eddie. Everybody who didn't know Edna real good personally called her Eddie. Closing time and after, the cats from all the clubs around came in to play behind Edna. Desmond and Sonny Rollins. Diz. Sam Jones. Thad Jones. Don't get me started. That's not for Malcolm. I'm saving that for Nat and Feathers.

Those name people and jamoramers, they got to be good friends of mine—and it was Edna brought them. She loved playing here, the appreciation she had. She wouldn't take any outside dates. Practically had to shove her out the door to do that Jazz at the Philharmonic gig for Esme Hammond, then she wouldn't go on the tour. That was an NBC thing, she would have been Esme Sarnoff then.

That's some record, Bundige and Peterson at the Philharmonic. When that record came out Hammond came in and sat at that table right there and Edna sat with him after she came off her set. John said that was the best Peterson ever played, had the most heart in it, pushed to it by Edna. Edna and Tatum would be the only two could push Peterson that way. We lost a good one when John passed on. Same type guy as Dill Emmery. Same hair too, like they just got up off the electric chair. Those Mohawk haircuts the kids wear, they got the idea from Dill and John.

The only places she would go wasn't for playing dates, it was to sit in like they sat in here. We closed early those days, one o'clock. She'd go sit in at the Uptown or the Downtown or the Gate or Birdland or wherever. Mostly it was Minton's. I'd sometimes drop off there with her. Real jazz people there. That's all she would do outside the house except a benefit. She'd do benefits and she'd do records. After that it was all Stiffy's. Same as now.

Take a piece in Lyons column saying how it was sinful she wasn't put on one of those trips to France and Russia, those places, to show off America. If he'd asked he would found out the State Department sent an ambassador to ask her how come she turned them down. Harrigan. Used to be governor.

Thank you, maybe next time she told him.

"You can't do that" I told her. "You got that coming to you. You're the best. Wilson says here Edna Bundige is a National Treasure."

"Sounds like a horse."

"Makes no difference what it sounds like. You got a chance like that you got to take it."

Edna's face never changes much, except when she's playing, making those little pops with her eyes, working her jaw like salt water taffy's gummed on her teeth. Basically she goes with that visiting Indian look. Nothing to get stirred up about here.

"Too cold in Russia."

"Get a fur coat. I'll get you one. I don't want you staying back on account of the bar. I'll get somebody in. Bushkin. That Tristano kid you like."

"You let me run the piano."

She reached out and touched me on the arm. Little thing. Means something from a gal who's not touching and kissing all the time. Not the kind you get used to right away and use up.

Things going too good. Soon as Fred leaned on the bar that day I knew we had trouble.

5

"Come on back to your office."

That Lebrand had this brassy way of talking to you. Could have said I love you and you'd feel like throwing a spitoon at him. Not like the other partners, but he had his job. Come on back to your office, and walked off without even looking to see if I'm following. I felt like letting him go and look around for me when he got there and I'd still be here but I didn't want to put myself in his class. Enough to fight about in this world without taking up every last thing.

We went into the cubbyhole I had behind the hatcheck. He pushed the door closed. I hardly knew the room had a door. If I was in there I liked to keep an eye on the outside and let people know they could get to me. I had an old desk and a layback chair you could catch a nap on and another wood chair. Desk like a museum for things you don't have any use for right now but if you put them in a drawer they're gone forever. What are you going do with a special gnarled screw? It came off something. You're going miss it the day you let it get away from you. Same with October Downbeat with the rundown on foreign records. I don't know what year. October.

One thing you worry about is having too much cash around. You need back-up cash for the register and you need cash for weekends when the banks don't open. We kept that in a wall safe behind a picture of New York harbor. First place any cracker would look for a safe is behind a picture in the office, but where the hell are you going put it? Days receipts Sid or I put into a bank bag with the register tapes, never counted it, just took off a regular amount to put back in the register to make change with. The register tape went into the bag.

Every day 11 a.m. Fred's man came in, compared the cash to the register and carried it to the bank to deposit. Every day that is except Saturday and Sunday when we had the biggest cash from the days before. Those days accountants don't work. Fred's man was the only one ever closed the door.

Got the picture? Doesn't make any difference. The problem I'm talking about had nothing to do with it. Just telling you how a small bar handles things, before we got a bookkeeper and put him behind a scissors door. Overhead. Every time your business needs a new person or another room takes you forever to pay your new overhead. As soon as you expand you make less than before till you catch up with your new rent and your new payroll. Your average business expands too far, comes a little recession no fault of theirs and the second hand furniture goes on the market for the next fella.

Lebrand went right to it, no beating the bushes. None of this Sorry to bring this up. None of this We seem to have a problem. Right to the kneecaps.

"What went on with the last night's money?"

We had symbols printed on the tape every hour so we could see how much business we were doing. I never paid too much attention to the hours. I went mostly by the whole day. Nothing wrong I knew about.

He reached a roll of folded register tapes from his pocket. Marked up with x's and checks, initials, memos like tapes get when you're tracking. I knew he had something on me, couldn't think what. You can know you didn't do a thing but being asked like that makes you care more what he's thinking than what you know. Common experience. Basically it's on account of we all know we did something we never got called on, so when we get called there's all the guilt boiling around inside you.

Best experience I ever had of that was the two of us driving home from the Poconos. We were old married folks by then. Edna took a date in Pittsburgh helping out Previn with his Symphony and we had a visit with her family and we decided we never take a vacation, let's get a Hertz and drive home through the mountains. See what mountains are. We went all through Pennsylvania looking at mountains. Had about enough and we're driving home through New Jersey. I catch onto a police car hiding in the trees down the road and I'm down to 45 in no time flat, I can read, and he comes out and pulls me over for doing 50 in a 25 mile zone. I agreed to 28. How is anybody going convict you for a lousy three miles? Wouldn't do it to anybody but a black man.

Took me to see the judge in this gas station town. Judge there in the front room fixed up for an office in a little white house like a spider waiting for the cases. Sweet looking old man for a judge. Knew he was running a racket. Knew everybody else knew it.

How did I plead he asked me. I started to tell him all about how I didn't think I was over 25—maybe a mile or two—and I was a careful driver, never before been arrested for speeding.

That was the truth. Made this long trip through Pennsylvania on our way home from vacation, driving careful. Had nothing to be in a hurry about, wife wasn't going have a baby. He's nodding his head agreeing with me all the way. Sympathetic old bastard.

When I'm finished he's still on the nod. Home free I figure.

"How do you plead?" he asks me all over again.

I looked over at Edna to see if she'd back me on the 28 if I asked her to witness. No use. No use at all. She'd say the whole 45. That's Edna. I see sooner or later I'm going have to say Guilty to the lousy three miles.

"Well I heard what the police said, your honor. I just don't know how that can be but he said he read it off the radar."

"Tell me—" looked me up on the ticket "Mr Stiff, how many years have you been driving?"

"Thirty years your honor."

"Never once been stopped for speeding?"

"No sir, your honor." And that was the truth. He had to be able to see in my face it was the truth. Home free. Warning maybe.

"Mr Stiff, let me put it this way. You know that in thirty years of driving you've been over the limit many times and never been caught. If you weren't over the limit today put it down to justice catching up this once for all those times it missed you. Count your blessings. Pay the clerk $35 and costs."

I still see that judge smiling at me like I'm home free and then saying pay the clerk. That's my idea of a judge. Got at the truth of the matter.

"What am I looking for?" I asked Lebrand with this guilt.

"Who had a hand on last night's money?"

"What's your problem? Is the cash short?"

"How did you guess?" Said it like How would I know if I wasn't in on it. Looking at me to see the guilt.

"Tapes showing money that wasn't in the register?"

"It didn't get to the tape. The cash tracks the tape OK. Somebody got his hot hands on the money and never wrote it up." He liked to shove the knife in a little extra after you thought he already had it in all the way. "You should know by now you can't hire these clowns and put a black tie on them and turn them loose without paying any attention to what they're doing."

"Is that a fact? How about that. The things this man knows."

"You may think it's funny."

"I'm not thinking at all till I know what the subject is. Are you going let me in on it or am I going back to work?"

Out comes another paper, this one a chart. The whole time looking in my face to see if it's painful enough or should he throw in a couple more jabs like How about Sid? he's in charge of the register. If he said Sid's name to me I would have climbed down his throat. How about the guy from his own office that came in every day and closed the door?

Didn't take me but a minute to get what the chart showed. Two weeks, hour by hour, everything going pretty much on the same line except nine midnight last night flatted out, real quiet. Double busy after midnight.

"If you have somebody who works ten midnight and not either side you don't even have to check any further. That's your man."

"Where would I get anybody to come in just long enough to steal and then go home?"

"Figure it out for yourself."

"I'm doing that."

"Who's got the hot hand?"

"Edna."

"Save the jokes."

"No joke. That's how it is."

The man didn't want to believe that but I let it lay. His face started staggering around looking for a place to hold on. By then everybody knew what Edna did for the place, pushed up the night sales, got our name in the columns. Fred Lebrand he'd rather see me gone than Edna. Shoved the knife in him a little extra like he did on me.

"You asked me a question, you got the answer" I told him. "Stop by some night, hang around instead of for a quicky on your way to Grand Central Station. See what's going on."

That all went back to the night Tatum played at Moonrow's in Pittsburgh. Edna got past some of Tatum's fancy work but she never got over that night, knew that was the express she had to catch. Tatum played one song for four hours. Got up once to go to the can. Cats from the neighborhood heard about what's going on and came in with horns, saxes, clarinets, harmonicas, strings. Whole band gradually moved in around him. He'd bob his head and sit back signing somebody Take a chorus. Basically it was Tatum four hours on Things You Are. That must be a hundred ways he did it. Wished I'd heard it myself.

Last night on Fred's tape Edna was on her second set leading off with Georgia Brown. Basically her set was five six tunes. She did the usual three four choruses on Georgia. Shook out another chorus stuck in her fingers. Led on to another. Pretty soon it's eating peanuts. Half hour through the set she's played nothing but Georgia Brown, she remembers Tatum and decides to go all the way.

Catching on that Edna has a no-hitter going coming out of the inning, everybody starts paying close attention. Leaning over to the next table, people they never saw before, asking were they onto it. Going all the way on Georgia. Hey! You hear that, Georgia in a rip waltz? She still in it? How many ways has she got?

Have to say I wasn't paying too much attention. There were three of us handling the bar and covering the register. Had my ears open less than my eyes. I had two waiters out there I had to keep an eye on. If I don't want waiters hanging over customers for refills as soon as the ice hits bottom, it doesn't mean I want them studying the moon on my time either. You ever notice that soon as you tell somebody he's doing something you don't basically like—say feeding a cat at the back door and you don't want it to be yours—first thing he says is Do you want me to kill him? No don't want to feed him and don't want to kill him, you want to do the Mr In Between. Shut the door. Call the Humane. Do something else but don't feed him and don't kill him. Use your imagination. Some waiters, if you tell them not to hang over the customers, that's the last appearance that waiter's going make for that customer till the man starts waving his arm to hynotize him off moon duty so he can get his check and go home.

Yeah, the chart reminded me I noticed the bar slow down. Things come and go and you get a chance to get your head up. Had this gypsy gal in front of me. Mole beside her nose. Lavender grease on her eyes. Lavender tortilla on her shoulders. Selling this john she came with a bill about starting up a jewelry store. You don't hear too much what's said the other side of a bar unless people are talking up to be heard. This fortune teller was talking up because even I could see the fella didn't come to get this particular message about an airline pilot she knew flying back from Greece with a ton of jewels in his pockets. Nothing like it anywhere. You wouldn't believe how cheap. Popping this fella good about these big Greek chocolate cookies. He wasn't listening too hard, they weren't his cookies.

"She's still on Georgia Brown" he said.

We had a long skinny room before we broke through and took in the next building, hard room to work in with tables strung off to the back. The piano was off the end of the bar, quarter-turned to the back. The usual way Edna worked she had her jaw up and a touch to the side bringing her side-view back to us at the bar. When the fella mentioned she was still in Georgia and I looked over she was in a right hand solo, slow, full of air. Backphrases. Catching up. Working the tune and taking the chords apart. Stuttering. Saying something when you didn't expect. Going down a flight of stairs, taking the last step and there's no step there but she catches you. Shooting bullets at the keys. Including the pinkie keys. Edna could kill a hog with her pinkie, still can. Left hand taking five in her lap, surprised the other hand did all that by itself with nothing holding it up.

Always some people talking in a bar, paying no attention to the music. Musicians don't like that but they're working a bar not a concert. Peterson's the only one won't stand for it. You sneeze when Oscar's playing and he closes the piano. I don't blame him but Edna always said it didn't bother her. She wasn't listening to them either. Up to the musician to grab as many as he can from those folks who came to drink and those folks who came to listen. When I looked around at forty tables and a full bar hardly anybody in the house wasn't hearing Edna. Argument going on at one table trying not to let on to everybody else. Big eyebrow action. Everybody else on Edna up there fighting that damn bull, depending on her pinkie to wave him past, can she get away with it and Hey she waved him by.

She put her left hand on some chords, signal coming off that chorus. She had in mind to sing and did it right into the ovation, dipping her chin I hear you, as usual. You could go all night without seeing Edna smile at the house, just that dip of the chin Thank you for being in it with me. Sometimes she smiled at the moon. Different moon than the waiters looked at.

She never came off that set. After ten went right on through eleven and it was near midnight when she decided to roll it off. Georgia all the way.

Believe me, I was flapping my hands with everybody else. What Fred read on the tape was people forgot to order till she dipped her chin and let her hands fall loose.

I went over to walk her past everybody who'd want to bang her ear on the way to the Ladies. She was sweating hard and only one of those little doilies ladies carry to dry off with. I took her elbow to keep her moving. It had a little earthquake signal from Tokyo going on in it.

I told her "Great set kid. Don't come out for the next one till you feel like it."

Edna did the same thing to us that next night after Fred brought in the tapes and I stood there watching the whole show. Twenty minutes of Just You, Just Me—and then Just Nothing at the bar in the middle of prime time, from when they caught on she was staying on the one number till she signed off. Buried herself in the song, jogged her head a half inch—Hear you—for the applause after specially great choruses and went on taking the song apart and fitting it back new ways. Old ways too like old Double Your Money Bach would have done it. Some piano.

What was I going do, tell her lay off, she was shutting down the bar that paid her salary? Not me, not a piano like that.

At least she kept inside the hour and the bar got partly caught up. I let it go while I thought it over till one night she went three hours again wrapping a couple Ellingtons together—Sophisticated and Sentimental Mood and I heard a little Solitude in there too. The register had a restful night till she quit. Couldn't blame her for stretching out in the office on my layback chair.

Fred was on the phone as soon as he saw the tape after that second three hour set, and late in the afternoon I had Dill leaning over the bar.

"Fred bucked it over to me. He says you and I can talk. Don't you think you can get a handle on it some way without hurting Edna's feelings?"

It wasn't Edna's feelings held me back as much as it was this great spirit in the house, something happening that wasn't happening anywhere else in the world. They knew out there she didn't do that for money, it wasn't any performance, it was preaching. Wasn't anything you shut down for the drinks. I didn't say that to Dill.

"Gimme a little time to work it out. We'll take care of it."

"Keep it on the front burner? A week?"

"Sounds okay."

5

I also didn't mention to Dill what happened last night when she came off the Ellington set and went into the office to settle out before going to the Ladies to wash up. Beat. Wet. Stretched out in my layback chair with her eyes closed. Not in the shape a lady likes to be looked at you might say and I was looking at her for the first time in the five years we worked together, had a chance for the first time to study her out. Always knew she was a nice person. First time I saw she was a woman. Took me five years. How about that?

What I mean is before that she wasn't the kind of woman I thought of as a woman. In the beginning she wasn't a woman anyhow, she was a seventeen year old kid. When she came in with Duvall's card I looked her over the same as you would naturally look over any female. A little on the heavy side, tell by the way she walked it was muscle, not fat. Working figure. Took me a couple years to notice her legs one day and think those are good legs for that kind of figure, solid ankle, balloon calf like Zweisel's #3 goblet. Even so add it all up, hair shoved back, nothing in her face saying she had what I call personal interests, and I didn't have her in view as a woman. I had an idea she might be the type that cared for the girl she had rooms with. Might be good friends with this girl Eunice Cole. Eunice had the strict look that type gal sometimes has. You make up these things about people if you have an active mind and I'm not going around saying my mind is deactivated am I?

After Edna brought Momma Bundige to New York for a week to see how things were here I had this extra reason not to be the one to give her experiences. Momma Bundige told me

"Now you watch out for her, you see? I know that's not your job to do but I'll pray for you. That's what I do, that's what I'm known for. You watch out for Edna and I'll call you to the Lord's attention."

I wasn't too sure I wanted that attention but she put the ball in my court.

Edna did have some boy friends and it passed through my head she might be going both ways. You make up these things. Until Damron Arbo showed up none of those fellas amounted to much with her. It isn't that easy for a musician to go steady except with another musician. The hours don't work out. You're dragging home to get some sleep and a shirt salesman is halfway to breakfast. When your head is deep into your own work like Edna's you're not looking around that anxious to bring somebody into your life. He has to qualify himself. Still you have feelings, you know, no matter how busy you are.

She was at Minton's one night I wasn't along. I had her in mind and watched out for her but I had other obligations. I was going with a girl I'll call Lynette X. She's a respectable married woman now and I'm not going put sand in her gas tank. People doing books think they have the license to talk about people. They talk about their own momma and daddy like they're strangers. I'm not up to that. After the navy I put in time with several girls before Lynette. I might have started up again with Coreen but she married. I can mention Coreen's name, she's gone. She didn't wrong me by by not waiting. What would she be waiting for? I didn't have any ideas to do anything except what we were doing. I didn't have the objective to avoid being married to Coreen. I didn't have any objectives at all except being in the restaurant business.

When I got together with Lynette she was in the show line at the Palace. The bar was working out okay and I had my own flat away from the family. She didn't exactly move in, she kept her own place but we spent a lot of time together. I told her from the top

"Look we got it good together but anytime you find some guy you think can do better for you I won't shoot him. I'm not that prideful kind. My idea is people should live their own lives."

"That's fine with me" Lynette said.

Everything was fine with Lynette. Nothing excited her except getting her hair mussed. That was what mainly concerned her at that particular time of her life, how she looked. She had the idea she was in the world basically to look good. She knew she looked good coming into a place on your arm. You know about atoms how they move around without touching each other. That was Lynette. You had this feeling she went around saying Yes and saying No without thinking too hard about what it was you asked her as long as she looked okay answering. You could take off her clothes and she had her eye all the time on how you laid them down. She had to pick up her panties and fold them in two and put them on a chair before you got back in business. Couldn't just kick them off. First thing she did after we finished was put on a lipstick. Like laying somebody you had a contract with, she does this and you do that and nobody comes up short. Yeah well, I came up short but you expect that. She was that kind of woman and I was that kind of man and I wouldn't say it was a bad arrangement at that time for us two people. Went on two three years, couldn't be too bad. We cheated out on each other some. I knew it. She knew it so you couldn't say it was real cheating.

In that time Edna was growing up, growing legs, learning how to handle fellas and she met Damron Arbo at Minton's. I didn't know anything about it. No reason I should, she was on her own, didn't tell me every least thing.

Old Marcel Pennywhistle sold me a table for the Haitian Ball and after the close we all went over to the Manhattan where it was going on. I heard about this great party the Haitians put on every year and I had Lynette with me and Edna and Sid and Eunice. Dill and Hope came and Pat and Gwen Barnes. Folks I knew would appreciate being there, something different.

Those Haitians know how to have a party. They had dance acts and jungle drums and Marcel did his whistle and different bands moved in behind each other keeping things going. We talked and dranked and watched the acts. Had a problem getting a drink. Marcel warned me you had to bring your own bottle to the Manhattan and I was sure not bringing any over from the bar and be picked-up for running an off-premises. I clean forgot to stop at a liquor store.

There I am with a table of guests, the famous bar owner Stiffy Stiff and you can't get a drink with him. They knew about problems like that and had a runner go out and get us some booze. We had a lotta friends there stopping at our table.

Pretty soon I notice this fella come off the stand after a band change-over and walk toward us and he kept coming and it turned out he's coming to our table and he is one beautiful man. I mean beautiful.

You get a beautiful woman she is just more of the same. I shouldn't say Just. I mean she has more of the good things you know about, nothing strange about it, but a beautiful man is unnatural. He's gone around the circle and started to come out something different from a man. A usual good-looking man can have his hair and his eyebrows too close together, he can have big ears. Say Lister Andrews. Clark Gable. Details like that let you know he is real. You get a beautiful man, though, he is a model sent over from the agency to set up us ordinary guys. He can have chain-breaking muscles and talk like a bassoon but he's gone around the circle and come out unnatural for a natural man. Don't ask me to explain. I'm pointing it out. Arbo was made from five dollar a quart French ice cream. He had haughty eyes and black snails for hair and his momma was queen of the tigers. Unreal.

"I'd like you to meet Damron Arbo" Edna said and introduced him around. He bowed to everybody without mentioning any names. He was the one being met. He put out his hand for Edna to come on the dance floor with him. Hey. Friends. When did that happen.

They had a mambo going and he held her off with one hand while he did that easy step and glide they do. If you get a good beat you can go around the world with that, you don't have to be a dancer but they could dance. They did some things standing in place, rolling their knees. Went through them like you snapped out a carpet. They leaned away from each other talking and stepping and Edna didn't apologize for anything, no sir. She moved with him like it was jazz, a sixteenth behind the beat and catching up and laying on breaks with her feet and shoulders and rolling those knees. Have to tell you the caboose stayed with the train. Looked fine.

Okay that was the clue for all of us to get out there and do. You can be sure Lynette knew how to dance. We were close dancers and she would come right into me. We danced together a lot and knew how the breaks would go. You could say the same for Dill and Hope, except that the best I can say for Dill's dancing is if you think of him as a sailor sending flag signals you get the picture. He yawed away with that arm and his feet had no connection to the time but I never saw a man enjoy dancing more. For him it had to be a reward for hard work like a bottle of beer after you dig a deep hole. I don't know what it was for Hope. For her it was the way they danced, it's the way her man danced so that was it. You shoot one ten it's still golf. Some people like being out there walking in the sun, don't care all that much about the fine points of the game.

Pat and Gwen were pretty good dancers. Moved with the beat. He topped her around, pushing her can to keep her spinning. Nice going there I told her going past. This is living she said.

Sid and Eunice didn't do bad either. Some stout fellas carry weight like it doesn't weigh anything. Nice going there I said.

Kept getting snapshots of Edna and the Haitian through the crowd. Response steps. Challenges. Spins. I never saw her dance before. Never thought of her dancing. Liked the way Arbo danced too. Different. Straight up and on center no matter how he moved. Didn't lean the way we do. Had dignity.

"I'm going Haitian style" I told Lynette. "Hang on."

"That's fine with me. Any way you lead."

I held her off with one hand and we glide-stepped. She liked that. You can be sure Lynette knew she looked good making those moves with her good figure with that space around her so she could be seen. "I got the best looking girl here, Lynette" I said.

Every last word of that wasn't gospel true because those Haitians have some women that come right out of the ads.

"I don't see where you could do better" Lynette said.

After the party I was going drop Edna off in the cab I took with Lynette but she went with Damron.

6

"If you plan on spending any time with that man, keep your eyes open" I told Edna. She gave me that flat Edna look. Made the whistle sign with her lips.

"What do you mean by that?"

"He's a little too good to be true. A man that beautiful, you know."

She kept zeroed on me.

"People want to please him" I said. "People want to do what he does. He could be snorting. He could be into needlework. He could be a boozer. You don't need that."

We did alcohol. We did reefers like everybody. Never did any harm. Eased you out. Some people can't do it that easy way, they got to excess everything.

"I get you, daddy" she said.

"Keep your eyes open."

"What's bothering you?"

I told her my theory about beautiful men going around the circle and coming out unnatural. What I mean was there was some woman in them.

"How would I find that out?" she asked me, and I see she's kidding. As though she wouldn't know better than me.

"That's all right" I said. "You may not know about fellas who go both ways."

"How did you find that out?" she said as though I was telling her something secret about myself. Hell I never had the least inclination that way.

"I was trying be helpful. I promised your momma I'd look out for you."

"You're doing good."

I didn't know if she meant it or she didn't. The fact is any momma would say Arbo looked like a pretty good boy. Wouldn't harm my case with the Lord to leave him in Edna's life. He had a steady job in the house band at CBS. He picked her up after hours and they made the other clubs. Edna was taking the comp course at Julliard then.

He picked her up there and they had afternoon time. What other steady is she going find with free time in the afternoon except another musician? She showed him art over at Dill's museum. They took in a movie now and then. Seemed to be going along fine. But I never liked the man. Didn't think there was anything to him except being beautiful.

Then things start moving fast. I was at the Chicken Shack and Charlie Duvall came over and asked how I was doing. I told him how. He asked if I might be looking for any piano talent.

One of those cards he throws out hoping it's going land somewhere good.

He said "There's a Haitian cat going around looking for big green to open a club. You know about that?"

It hit me in the stomach. I knew what was coming but I wouldn't let on.

"I wouldn't be surprised if there was ten of them."

"This fella says he has Edna Bundige lined up."

"You know how people talk, Charlie. Last I heard she was going make a tour with Cab." Nobody was going find out looking at me I was surprised on anything in this world.

I didn't know how to handle it. Long before that I learned Never go on what somebody says somebody said. Hold off till you can hear with your own ears from the party direct. You can bet that most times it never was said. Least it wasn't said like you heard it first. You have to tell yourself Hold off. The hard part was deciding whether to wait it out or take it up with Edna.

I practised saying different things to her. I wouldn't mind all that much if you did better for yourself. Don't I always encourage you to take the concerts and the tours? Going into a new club with somebody who doesn't know anything and doesn't have anything but your name to sell is Nowheres. It being worked up in secret from me, that's what hit me in the stomach.

But hold off, hold off.

I began looking at her close. She had something on her mind all right. She was never a big talker but she had even less to say than before. Always looked like she was thinking hard. That was when she began playing the long sets and we got up to that night she was stretched out in the chair in my office. Sweated. Hair brushed back the easiest way to do it, mouth sagged open. Held a sweat towel in her hand. Beautiful hand for the work it did. Every joint packed tight with piano music.

Her arm was settling down, wasn't all there yet, still tuned to Tokyo. I liked her body lying back like that. No doubt this was a woman now. Figure falls into place a different way when you can say a female is a woman. A woman a little heavy in the belly looks good lying back. Liked that face, that was a lasting face, didn't have to be done over four times a day. I had a whole new idea about my life. If her eyes had been open I would have kissed her.

It wasn't more than a minute before they opened and saw this dentist Arsdur U. Stiff with the split lip and the gibble on his eye hanging over her. Some sight when she could be looking at Damron Arbo.

"What time is it?" she said trying to tune in that little gold wrist watch she had. "How much time have I got?"

She brought the towel up and swiped it across her face. Left it on her chest covering the gully.

"Edna listen" I said. "I want you and me to be together. You're the greatest woman in the world. Come on home with me tonight." That was the best I could do, not giving any thought to it before.

"You keep secrets good" she said.

When you kiss a woman like that and she opens up and comes back to you, man you don't forget. Different experience. You're connected all the way to Tokyo. You've got yourself more than something made of all these parts. You're into that woman's good times and into her troubles. What happens to her is the same as it happening to you. I'm not pushing these ideas on you. You're a young fella and I'm telling you there's something beyond what you thought if you find the right woman.

No problem later on bringing up Damron Arbo.

"Somebody to go to the movies with. Go dancing. You expect me to sit around here like a sister?"

"I heard he was going open a club."

"Oh he told me that. He doesn't know any more how to do that than fly. He told me he would star me. Can you feature that? I got it all now, I'm the star at Stiffy's. You wouldn't let a man like that bring you butter from the store."

I didn't bring up anything about Damron Arbo's looks and mine. She could see. She decided. She had her own idea of beautiful like I have mine. You want good chords you got to put in flats.

Five

THANK YOU, MISS REPLOGLER

1

NOW WE GET to how we solved the business problem. That's what Malcolm is interested in telling. He knows how we did it, he was in on it. I don't say he thought it was a great idea at the time. The truth is he thought like everybody else it was a terrible idea but he says tell it like it is.

I got to it a little roundabout.

In the morning before I left I made sure Edna understood this wasn't any one night stand, we were going get married if that was all right with her. I made us an omelet—That's high class cooking with no notice she said—and we sat talking marriage. Brand new word to me. I said come in early and we'd go around the block and have a bite for dinner and I'd give her my first present.

That was the day Dill's hanging over the bar yakking at me to take care of Freddy's problem about the bar going dead. I didn't let on what I had in mind to do. Edna and I went around to Panella's Back Room. Little place where he did five six menu items on the grill. Filled him in while his bar was light. Making early footing I said I always thought that was something I'd like to do in my place, except with some of my specialties not the grill food. Plenty of places with grills. If the omelet didn't get to her, this did.

"You sound like a real cook."

"I cook some when I get a chance, mostly Sundays. I learned in the navy. I was a navy cook."

"I never guessed that."

"There's a lot about me you don't guess."

"Give me the time. You mean real whole meal cooking?"

First time we ever talked like that. Usually what we had to say was about different jazz styles, different customers, what was going on in town. Outside things. I knew more about her than she knew about me, which was natural. She had to tell about herself when she asked for the job and that led to discussions later on.

I told her about my specialties like knowing what to do with lemons. I told her about putting lemons with strawberries making preserves, and lemon juice with some chunks in chicken, and my lemon barbecue sauce. I told her about my shrimpotato salad. My chicken done with fresh bacon fat. You had that here. Really interested her.

I asked her what kinda cook she was.

"Not too much. Momma couldn't take me from the piano enough. You like to do it, why don't you put cooking into your place? You got more tables than here. I bet you can do a big dinner business."

"No room for a kitchen. Have to take your piano away to get a kitchen. I don't know whether I like piano or cooking more but we got the piano. Maybe some day. Speaking of that I've got my first present for you. You think it's going be a ring but the ring comes second. Tomorrow we'll go over to 5th Avenue and you pick out your own ring. The first present is going be a backup bass like you always wanted."

Surprise, that's the thing. Blew her over. She didn't think I paid serious attention when she mentioned she liked a backup bass.

"You mean that?"

"Anybody you want. I was thinking to ask Philly Lucas to come in with his electric bass for a good sound. That something that could grab you?"

Trying to steer her off the thump thumping string fiddle.

Didn't work too good, she knew what she wanted. "If you're going to do that, see if Vance Addison can make it."

"You wouldn't want the electric?"

"I like the bass fiddle fine."

"If you change your mind and want the electric let me know."

Okay, a string bass. Anything she wants. That's step one.

Next morning I went over to the bank to tell Dill about Edna and me and impress my idea about the dead bar on him. Spread the credit, don't hog it, there's plenty to go round if something works okay. If it doesn't, it's going be blamed on you anyhow. Partners going say Well I wasn't sold but that's the way he wanted to do it and I didn't want to cut him down. After I told Dill about Edna and me and he told me he's giving the wedding dinner we went into the other subject.

"I got the answer to the dead bar when Edna's on."

"Good news."

"Jiu Jitsu."

Well I didn't lead into that right. Should have explained it better first. If you want to put over an idea you don't just say it like that Bang. You have to give them a chance to get used to it. You don't bring something close up to a man's eyes when he's looking far away and expect him to see it right. The man jerks away, he thinks you're going hit him in the nose. Do the same thing nice and slow he won't even blink. Same with a new idea. Don't put it so a man backs off.

I had this idea about Jiu Jitsu as long as I can remember, as far back as being a little kid when I first heard about it. Let the other fella do just what he wants to do and kill himself. Neat idea, the same as the saying Give a man enough rope and he'll hang himself. Same as Go with the flow. If you can't lick em join em. It's a basic idea. Goes away, comes back, goes away, comes back. Like Parkinson's idea. You got some little thing to do and all day to do it I guarantee under Parkinson it takes you all day. Like a rabbit giving a turtle a ten minute head start and having all day to catch up, he takes all day. Maybe never does catch him. That's Parkinson. Basic idea. Same with Jiu Jitsu. Basic.

We had this Miss Replogler for a gym teacher in sixth grade. First female I ever had a thing for. I would say that was because she wore bloomers. I never saw anything like that before. What I remember most was the wand lessons, lining up ten fifteen in a row eight ten rows deep going through the wand drill. You don't even know what a wand is. Thick like a police club. You don't even know what a police club us. Yeah a place they hang out, that would be your idea.

Cops used to carry a round stick about two fingers thick and two feet long to poke you in the ribs or hit you on the arm with. Had a leather throng tied through a hole near one end. They used to put the throng around their wrist so if they tossed the club it would go only so far before it jerked back into their hand. They'd walk along the street—yeah that's what cops did, they walked. They had a word for it called Walking The Beat. Good song title. Walked along throwing the club and catching it, throwing it and catching it like cheerleaders if their batons had a string on it. When you thought of a cop you thought of him throwing that club and catching it.

The wands they gave us in gym class were the same thing only maybe a foot longer and no throng. The wood was yellow, the cops' clubs were black. The wand drill was holding it with two hands spread over your head and doing spread jumps in place. Or swinging big circles with it, things like that. You always had to hold it by both ends so you wouldn't get the idea to use it like a baseball bat and beat somebody's brains out. They wouldn't trust a gym class with anything like that now because people start with the idea of how much damage can they do to you.

"No wands today" Replogler said this time. "Today we'll do Indian wrestling."

We all knew Indian wrestling, did it on the street all the time. You pair off and get a good grip with our back feet and line up your front feet sideways against each other and take a good hand grip and on Go you try to haul the other kid off balance. If he touches the floor with his free hand or lifts his foot away from where it's supposed to be against yours he loses. I know you know that but there's fine points. Everybody knows checkers but still there's a world champion. There's something for everybody to be best at.

Replogler walked around the gym changing pairs so we'd be evenly matched and showing us fine points like getting more power and balance with your knees bent. Instead of trying to outstrongarm him all the time do the same thing you do in football. A guy wants to charge at you and he has more guns, just step aside, let him go into the hole where you just were and when he goes by give him a little elbow to help him keep going. It isn't up to you to provide a solid place for somebody bigger than you to hammer on. They have all this power revved up to knock you down and if there's nothing there when they knock they're going keep on going till they hit the next thing. Fresh air maybe. Ground zero maybe. Let the man have his own way and fall on his face.

"That's Jiu Jitsu" Replogler said. Standing right next to me in her black bloomers. Smelled like an iron radiator. That was the most sexy experience I ever had till high school. Couldn't forget anything that happened right then. "This is a Japanese way of wrestling. Find out what your opponent wants to do and help him do it. In that way you add his strength to yours."

Neat idea. Don't fight city hall. Jiu Jitsu. Basic idea.

Along about then Dill was trying to take a look at his watch without giving any offense."Hm hn? Hm hn?"

"That's how we can handle the problem" I said.

"Do you want to hire a Japanese wrestling act?"

"No just use the idea. If they don't want to order drinks while Edna's in her big set, we'll close the bar."

"That is one of the all-time great ideas."

"You'll see it'll work."

"What will work?"

I explained it again.

"Just for the nine ten set. See how it goes."

"That's scratching your left ear with your right hand. Put on a cover charge or a minimum. Get it done."

I didn't want to go that route, took too much of the me-and-you out the place. I don't like it if you have to think upfront the first thing is Stiffy wants something extra. Sold you a stripped model and now it's How about FM? What about wheel covers? Cigarette lighter. Tires. Cover charge.

"Do it my way. Jiu Jitsu."

"If you say so. Not enough shit on the road, you pile on more. Have you sprung this on Fred yet?"

I got to Fred in due time. Didn't make any difference. We were going do it my way no matter.

2

We were ready Wednesday night. I would have held it for Saturday but Lebrand actually said please, please if you're going do it don't give away the biggest night of the week. I showed him he could get somewhere with please. One night was as good as another anyhow.

Most of the partners came in with their wives or girls. Uncle Cuz showed with Eunice. Insiders made up a big piece of the house, that was the only part that didn't please me, that it wouldn't be usual and somebody could say it wasn't a fair test.

We had a standing room house from late afternoon. No dinner letdown. We had guys who used to come after work and be off for Scarsdale on the five-thirty six o'clock calling home. Emergency with a big client. We had regulars call in they were taking early dinner and wanted to be sure of tables after.

We did the best we could. The partners gave up their tables and looked for leaning room. Pat and Gwen came over from New Jersey and Pat appointed himself assistant maitre d'. His first job was to jolly the girls to close up to one table. They hated being an AT&T going away party but they pitched in. Malcolm picked up on that and put in a call to the Plaza to send over six rose bud corsages. He can be a fun guy. Did you ever think if Malcolm put on a bulb nose he'd look exactly like a circus clown with those big eyes and the wrinkles bouncing on his forehead?

Eight-thirty we had a little informal conference of the partners going behind the piano. Uncle Cuz said we were already ahead of the game with the early crowd. Going give it all back as soon as she gets to the piano Fred said.

"Anybody think what's going to happen if the Fire Marshall comes in here?" Mal asked. He pinned Dill. "We better close the door before we're in trouble." Two highest price doormen in the history of the world. It's a Guinness.

Twenty to nine. We went into the Jiu Jitsu. I gave Sid the high sign and he went down the bar with the bartenders passing the word.

Same with the table waiters. No service while Edna is in her next set, friends. She's going do Blue Skies and Nothing But Blue Skies All Night Long and it's going be a long dry hour if you don't get drinks on the table ahead.

Man I was on a high looking out on all that action, the house keyed up and buzzing. People glad to catch my eye and make faces meaning Congratulations. Some night. Me, I was thinking, me, I did it. I know how to do things. Gimme the shot and I can do a World's Fair. I can run the country. Gimme a shot at the U.N. Get me that room next door so we can expand. Like Uncle Cuz says Ex pand. We had the night people and we had a gang of the day people too. Place polluted with friends wanting to be with Edna and me on a big night.

Over on the door Malcolm had a problem and looked back toward me to send him inspiration how to handle it. Talking to a little black guy pointing over to me. Malcolm posted his neck around for a comfortable way to aim his eyes. Trying to say No Maybe and Sorry at the same time and hoping I'll send him something through the air. You could see the little black guy's teeth shine all the way across the room. With teeth like that a man that high had to be Ray Alldrid. Ray telling him Ask Stiffy, Stiffy will tell him Okay. Yeah Stiffy will but where in hell am I going hang him.

"This gentleman says he's a friend of Edna" Malcolm said. "I've explained we couldn't even get Edna's mother in."

Ray chattered his head Yes at me, telling me with his eyes without saying it I'm an ofay-suck it if I don't get him in. Ray was a man if the devil turned him back at hell's door he'd know it was on account of color and demand in. Best trumpet player in the world too for my money.

I told him I'm glad he stopped in and pulled him with me.

"Just going by and saw the mob. What are you giving away?"

Push on through. "Edna and Vance have some special music on. Word got out."

"That's what the frisk told me." Had his trumpet case clutched across his chest. "You must be getting rich."

"Doing okay. Every night doesn't look like this. Scrootch in here. They'll be on in a few minutes. I got to be moving."

Except for Uncle Cuz and Eunice, Ray was the only black in the house. I never asked for it that way, I wasn't running any Cotton Club. That's how it worked out, though. Not many brief case types among black people then, and brief case types were what came into a Madison Av bar, except the black cats who came to play and that was after hours.

Ray would see that first thing. That was known. He had a bellyfull of the race thing as who didn't but Ray was known to be a man who wouldn't have any of that without letting you know how he stood on it. I planted him, looking around as best he could from his low location, speaking with his eyes Who needs all these ofays.

I didn't have time to take that up with him but it only takes a second for the whole history of the world to pass through you once something gets it going. Slave ships. People being hit with bull whips. People not being able to use a toilet, get a bed in a hotel, get a meal on the road. Being hung and burned and white people standing around laughing or going about their business not paying attention. White people just like the people in the room, people like you not getting involved, not your business, not you putting great granddaddy Ummer's arm in the fire. All you do is know about it.

Damn I was mad. Explaining myself to Ray Alldrid a man I didn't know that good and I got a big night to run here. What the hell does Ray Alldrid know how I feel, how I do things, all he sees is all this white here and me sucking. Piss on your shoes, Ray Alldrid, I got work to do.

I'm not saying that's off the record. Put it down. Black people are coming in, you got to deal with us, you got to know what's on our mind.

3

I had it all worked out in my head, the waiters laying down their orders in the slot, picking up, coming back with more orders. The average time to fill an order. How many checks would be paying out and how many carrying past the set. I stood at the slot to keep things moving. Had it all in my head ahead.

Blew it almost. You just can't figure everything ahead you haven't done before. Couldn't figure how much you're slowed down when every seat is taken and folks are standing around. Couldn't figure all those filled orders backed up waiting for a tray. Couldn't figure the goddam tape jamming in the register. One table on Grasshoppers—eight desserts like that slow you down, lose a couple minutes off the average mixing time in my head. Table 14 wants twelve Zombies?

I looked over to see which was table 14. Gwen Barnes giving me the big grin. So blond you think she had white eyes. I'm her good cause that paid off. Pat must have told the Zombie story and the girls decided to have some fun. I guarantee it's the first time any of them played Russian Roulette. I told Sid to cut down to two shots of eighty proof, make one of them Myers for the brown taste and lay on the shrubbery. I gave Gwen the okay sign and showed her a one for a warning. They were all either going pass out just from thinking they had the full treatment or they'd go around the rest of their lives saying they put away two and hardly knew it. I didn't want any of those people insulting any Japanese wrestlers in my house.

We held Edna and Vance back to a quarter after till the bar cleared and I signalled Sid to throw the spot for them to come on out. I didn't like not starting on time but the bar was jumping, had to clear it.

Big hand. Edna dug into the seat and waited for quiet. Vance behind. Scarecrow with a Joe Stalin mustache. Tuxedo with the wing collar. Never saw him work without it. Wish I could get that elegant type look Vance gets without half trying but I don't have the body lines.

Edna never worked real dressed up with long skirts and sequins and feathers in her hair, all that show business gabardine, but she did a little more for tonight. Wore a neat black dress with dog fur around the skirt and a gold belt. Looked perfect, just the way she should look for her.

She tilted the voice mike. "I'd like to welcome the great jazz musician Vance Addison who will be playing along with me tonight." He took his applause.

"Irving Berlin's Blue Skies" she said and dropped the mike away.

Began to pump up the vamp. Laid down two silver dollars. Just like the first day I met her. Going be my wife. Wasted all that time. She timed it just short of an hour like we talked over so she wouldn't kill herself and she'd have something left for the next set if she wanted to go at it the same way. Hey, now I could give her the kind of orders you take from somebody you know is thinking about what's best for you. Take it easy. Don't beat your brains out. Stay inside the hour.

Everybody knew from the time they'd been on and the way she was playing into a run-off that the set was ending. They sure knew they'd had their money's worth. One of those fellas who wants to let you know he knows when the piece is over was on his feet to get the ovation going. A couple others started up, not wanting to be late. Edna took the closing chords into the bass octave, slowed it down. She was dipping her chin toward Vance saying thank you to him when from nowhere came those two silver dollars riding in on a trumpet.

Nobody was ready for it, a trumpet coming out the middle of the house, least of all Edna and Vance but they hardly blipped. Only needed the two notes and some scribble tying them together to tell them it was a real trumpet, not some neighborhood kid.

They kept the close going, turned it into a comp while they looked to see who it was playing that long soft line that sounded almost like it came out of a tenor sax. Edna already knew from the style it was Ray when Vance found him buried amongst the folks around the bar, only this smokestack on a ship sticking up, sending out music. I read Vance's lips when he said the name. She waved Come on up and picked up the comp while Ray played his way up to the stand.

There went the next hour and another with it. One of the greatest sets ever. All Blue Skies. Shame we didn't have any recording but Feathers and Ballot and Hentoff wrote it up as one helluva session. Edna Bundige at the piano, Vance Addison on bass and Ray Alldrid trumpet. Look it up. You can imagine the scene when they finally wound it down. Won the World Series in the seventh game with two out in the ninth.

Tell you what I was thinking when they finished the last chorus, killed it on a growl in the low octave while Ray scribbled his name on the ceiling. Edna dropped her arms. She put her hands out to Vance and Ray and dipped her chin to the house, every one up applauding and hollering and shaking their heads at each other Wasn't that tremendous? Wasn't that something to tell your kids you were there for?

That wasn't my thought.

I was thinking this isn't my place any more. It's Edna's place. People would be saying, probably saying it already and I never had my head aimed to pick it up, Too bad she's got herself hooked up with that bartender where she works. Won't let her out of his sight. Holding her back. His meal ticket.

That's me, standing there flapping my hands like everybody else. Saloon-keeper pimp making a living off her, selling her for the drinks to these white people. Looking at myself with Ray Alldrid's eyes. Selling her like Damron Arbo tried. No warning, hit me just like that.

Biggest night we ever had till then. Thank you, Miss Replogler. Proved they'd order up the drinks ahead, although we lost something in the extra hour.

Six

KENTS

1

WHILE I'VE BEEN telling you about that night Edna opened with Vance it's been on my mind that I said the gypsy in the bar was wearing a tortilla. Of course I know better than that. My mouth was on automatic, expecting the right word to come up in turn like always, and instead we have Mexican food on the menu.

Gets that way more and more when you're my age. I know all the words I ever knew, only I can't find them everytime and sometimes there's a shoe salesman in my head keeps on bringing sizes and styles from the back, everything but the right one. You know if you could get back there yourself you'd have it right in no time and be on your way. You say Damn I'm going back there and get it. It's there. Had it yesterday. You do that and you just intimidate it back farther. You may never hear from it again.

If you tease at it right it could come to you anytime.

To tell the truth the reason I'm vamping over it now is I I haven't got it yet. I know it as well as I know my name is Arsdur U. Stiff, only I can't put my finger on it, can't tug it out. It's an illa word. Mexicilla. Montezilla. If you nag at a little knot like that it just draws in on itself, it takes Fu Manchu's fingernails to get a piece of it. Got to wait these things out. Don't tell me. Make me work. Brains need as much exercise as any other aspect.

The question is do I know what I'm talking about.

Say I'm in school taking a test where you fill in the answer. What's that word they use for a shawl? Don't know. Been to Mexico three times and he can't tell you what they call a shawl. Says he knows it but can't pull it out. Give him a zero. This is Mr Dumb.

Say in the next class they give you a choice test. In Mexico they call a shawl a Caboose? A Tortilla? A Montezuma? A This-is-the-word-I'm-looking-for? On a test like that you can show me all the words in the dictionary and you can't fool me. I'll pick the right one, no doubt about it. All of a sudden this is a real smart fella sitting here. Same fella.

I can tell you what they look like, how they wear them hanging from their elbows more than their shoulders, better than the kid who knows the right word. He just knows the word. Big deal. I've been to Mexico, I've seen them. And still I'm the dummy and he's the smart one because he's got the word. We have people in control of the words like we have people in control of the money, and that doesn't say either party has any more brains than a trained dog.

I know you young fellas ask around How come he thinks he's so smart and he forgets everything? That's easy. I got the important things down on choice tests in my head. Looking right at the answers. It isn't the same as remembering a fella's name with nothing to go on.

Still vamping. Thought I'd have it by now. Let it go. Don't tell me.

2

Well I went ahead and got married without saying a thing to Edna about how low I felt about losing my place and her excelling me. I promised and I did it.

Wally Breger, one of the partners, had a piece of the Western on 57th and he got us an apartment. Three blocks, five minutes from from here. We didn't have to track back to Harlem every night.

Black people going into a hotel like the Western you're a gunfighter in a new saloon. Looking everybody over without being seen to do it. Being looked over the same way. Finding a wall to put your back on and a good view to the door. It isn't that any one's coming on you with a fast draw but we have Parkinson's Law. I mentioned the name to you before. They have two Parkinsons, one has the Disease, the other has the Law. I'm talking about the Parkinson with the Law.

He says you only have one head and no matter what you put in fills it to the top bone, no more no less. Most people have more head room than they know what to do with so they fill in with tv and whatever trouble happens to be lying around. Say you have sore feet. You think about sore feet all your spare time, same as if your problem was having no feet at all.

When nothing else is going on in my head what I fill in with is Are people treating me different?

Say you set a fire in the hall in front of my door. That's treating me different. Say you look at me like you want me to go away. That's different too. Between the man with the gasoline bomb and the man who's looking for me to get lost, I'll send a drink over to that last man's table. After we take care of the fire party we shut off the free drinks. In the bar I figure everybody comes in decides for himself he's going do business with me. They got a pass with me. I didn't know about the Western View Hotel. Barney Rudolph, the manager there, always treated us first rate. Couldn't do too much for us. Only other black party in the hotel was Marsden Hennifew the concert singer. Treated him the same way, Hennifew said.

So there it is, the main problem in the Western was being treated too nice. That's different too. Parkinson says if those fellas with the big smile and the glad hand are all the trouble you have left, you just naturally concentrate on getting that kind of person out of your life too. They won't be around when you need them. If somebody comes fire-bombing you, those friendly type white people are all going be out of town. Stick with your own.

Yeah well. That may be. But when the bums come around to burn you out, not too many black buddies going show up to help you out either. This human race is no big thing. Just people here and there you can rely on. You hear all kinds of things from me.

Sometimes I think I don't give a damn how lousy people are, if they're all black I can work it out. That's my Ummer mood. Other times I think I don't give a damn if a person's black, if he's lousy what good is he? Don't ask my true feeling. If I knew I'd tell you. Depends on the day you ask me. Right now I'm going easy on people black white red yellow or striped not looking for trouble with me. Don't tell me tomorrow what I said today.

Edna and I never moved from the Western. Went upstairs a couple floors to get more room. Got a new bathroom. First was all crackled, gave you the idea you were inside a mended wash pitcher. Never felt the need to show I was prosperous. It's all Astrodome compared to what we were used to anyhow.

You can bother your life too much laying on things just because you can afford them. Say you get a cat. Nobody needs a cat but you get one, you can afford it. Then you say Get a cat-scan, no use running around the neighborhood for the least little service when you can have it done on your own premises. Then you need people to run it and places for those people to sleep and eat and first thing you know you're into putting up a new building and dealing with the unions and you didn't need the damn cat to begin with. As long as Edna could have a piano and I could walk to the bar, that was the main thing.

More and more on the way to the place I'd stop off at Greg Wyman's to look at the morning tape. Easy for me to do. Wyman was a customer of mine. Some of his players too. Anything with numbers draws on me if it comes to my attention, and here's this stock broker in the next block.

I let Sid open up. The business was making good money. We could afford the help. That thing about Stiffy's being Edna's place and not mine ate on me. Ate me up. I never discussed it with Edna, wasn't anything she was responsible for. Just bringing it up would be like asking her to stay home and raise babies or go work some place else.

Some men take to drink or women. I took up with the stock market in a small way. Just getting used to what was in the books and what the numbers going by on the screen were all about. What it was like to put an order in. Win a little. Lose a little. I didn't like the losing part but I took it. I wasn't a genius yet.

Wyman started up about the same time I did, in that room upstairs in the next block. I didn't know anything about brokers, I didn't know he was there. All I knew was people at the bar talking what GM did and they coulda had IBM and how about that Zenith and what's your idea for the Dow and looking at their watches saying they wanted to get back for the close.

This fella knew those people. Didn't come in too often. When he did it was late afternoon asking for House of Lords on the rocks. I didn't know that particular brand. I don't know where people get the idea they have to have this or that brand. I got over that the first time I saw a Standard of New Jersey tanker putting gas into the ground at the Gas-X station. Never mind the brand, any of that Scotch tastes like something you have to take to get well.

Maybe that's it. Like the muscle fellas say Push through the pain, it don't help till it hurts. I gave that to Bill Bernbach for an ad slogan for Cutty. Give Cutty a try—push through the pain, you'll get used to it. Some people even think they learn to like it. Bill never used the idea. Even a smart apple like Bernbach gets his head down, doesn't see the possibilities.

I had another idea I gave Bernbach when we had all this publicity about making cigarettes out of scrap tobacco. Sweepins. There's a brand name for you, Bernbach. Sweepins. Go find a cigarette you can hang the name on. He never used it. Would be an overnight hit. It's got that Don't give a damn macho idea in it.

You're thinking Who'd buy a cigarette named Sweepins? Well who'd buy a cigarette named Chesterfields? Who'd buy a cigarette named Camels? What's the first thing you think about a camel after his hump? Right. That's worse than Sweepins. When I was a kid if you were a standup guy you smoked Camels. Don't see them now except for people trying kill themselves. Camel could use a new idea like Sweepins.

While we're at it, who'd ever put down serious money for an automobile they called a Toyota? Unbelievable. Toyota. How does it sound I drive a Toyota. Nobody would say that. Yeah. Everywhere. They got all these guys making big money doing research coming up with names like Esso and ABC corporation and every parking space has a Toyota. If you run a real business it doesn't make any difference, you can sweep the name off the floor, call it Toyota. Call it Chevrolet. You could never get anybody to name anything a Chevrolet today.

Yo-Yo Ma. You think anybody's going pay forty fifty bucks to hear a cello player let alone one named Yo-Yo Ma? Well you better believe they do, it's the man's name and he's world class. That's the best thing, put your own name on what you do. Seeing your own name on the sign makes you shape up. Stiffy's. See that? Stiffy's. I'm on the line.

My wholesale guy said this House of Lords was a cockamamie brand Distillers didn't sell in New York. Sold it in Ohio. Places like that. He said he'd give it a try and one day sure enough he came in with a case.

"You really got it" Wyman said.

"I had to take a case. You better keep on coming in here and drink it up."

"You betcha. You're the first bar ever did that for me."

Agreeable fella, middle thirties, easy to talk to. Carried himself like he knew how to throw a ball and tell a joke. Could sell you a thing or two. He had mixed-color hair like wet wood Stacombed down. Stacomb was a product we had that grouped your hair together like licorice sticks, the flat kind with the ribs and sugar beads. I haven't seen those licorice strips lately either. With the sugar beads in the ribs they looked like bars of music. We used to have them in black and brown and sometimes you could get them red. Wyman had hair like that only blondish. I asked if he did something around here.

He had a card in his wallet. Gregory Wyman and Company. "Greg Wyman. I'm a stock broker. My office is in the next block over Gristede's." Asked me if I owned any securities.

I wasn't into that. Building up a new business used all the money I could get my hands on.

"You run a good bar" he said. "You'll do all right. When you're ready look me up."

"I'll do that. May not be tomorrow."

"Anytime. Fill that again. I figure I just made a customer."

Never forget the first time I was in his office. I was early for the bar, around nine nine thirty. With that much time on my hands I thought it would be a chance to see what Wyman was all about. I figured he'd be open when the banks opened. I didn't know the market didn't open till ten o'clock those days.

I walked over past Gristede's and found the small door with his sign on it. Almost missed it. Gregory Wyman and Company spelled out. Stocks and Bonds. Nobody knew anything about commodities, options, shelters, all that stuff in those days, it was just bread and butter stocks and bonds. It didn't say Member New York Stock Exchange. He didn't make that till later. Had a deal with a member firm to trade for him.

The stairs were closed in like a chute and went straight up, the usual stairway for an old building. He put the elevator in after he bought the building and showboated it. Wasn't any show boat then. You came off the landing into a hall with a bare wood floor, old floor with ridges like cat scratching wore in it, and a couple light bulbs tuned to the economy setting. A hall where if you knock on one of those doors nothing happens. When you're ready to walk away somebody cracks it four inches and says Yes? Places that say Baltic Trading Company. Companies you draw a report on it tells you the principals weren't available.

The floor was like it wasn't open, maybe a holiday I didn't know about. The first year I had the bar traffic was so light one day I got scared to death the way you get when you're new in business and you think everybody decided to go some place else, they don't like you any more, you had it. What's going on?

"It's a Jewish holiday" Jim Perse told me. "Yum Kipper. The name day for the saint of herrings. He died tragically of a bone stuck in his throat so they close the store and don't eat or drink anything. It's Lent on a grand scale, only it's over in a day. Not a bad deal. I offered to trade a Jewish friend of mine my name for his on Yum Kipper if I could have his for Lent. He wouldn't take me up on it. I told him he was from a stiff-necked people. He said No just a touch of arthritis bothered him only when it rained."

You asked Perse a question and he was good for a half hour of that jive. Didn't make a bit of difference if it was true or not he laid it out for you exactly the same way. Some things you really wanted to know the facts on you would say Is that true Jimmy? he would say How would I know? or What's the difference?

Will it make your feet hurt? That was his question. If it didn't make your feet hurt it didn't make any difference.

You couldn't tell to look at him he had money from somewheres. Tooth out on the left side when he stretched his mouth. He could forget to shave. He had to have it in the bank though because he lived at the Barclay and he'd spend ten at the bar day after day without blinking when a shot was a dollar dollar and a half. He'd drop a five dollar tip now and then. Never saw him drunk. He just thought twice where to put his foot down when he eased off to to go home.

He curled up on the stool with no weight between his ass and his elbows, curled like a shrimp, drinking and seeing how long he could grow the cigarette ash in his skinny fingers before it fell off. Had spike hands like saints in those old pictures. If you got into a conversation with him be prepared to listen. Any subject, like Elaine May and Mike Nichols. Evolution. Training police horses. He was going on and on to this guy about cockroaches. How they liked to lay their eggs in beer caps. How Dolley Madison introduced them to the White House. I bet you don't know how to spell Dolley. Look it up, then you won't forget. How they mated by standing up and pumping their arms like cheer leaders. I listened in. I learned all about cockroaches.

"Is that true Jimmy about them mating once for life like pandas?"

"Would it make your feet hurt if it wasn't?"

Basically he just sat there growing the ash on a Camel cigarette. One of the last users. Hardly ever smoked the things, just let them burn. One day Sid heard him groaning "Oh God Oh Mother of God."

"What's the matter, what can I do for you?" Sid started up a bromo. Perse held up the hand he wasn't using for Sid to shut up and kept his eye on the cigarette. "Oh Mother of God."

''What is it Jimmy? Tell me what I can do.''

''It's the ash'' Jimmy said keeping his lips still. ''I swore to go off the hard stuff if I ever grew an ash that held all the way down to my finger. Look at the damn thing.''

''Shake it off'' Sid said.

''I'm no pervert. You're talking to the wrong man.''

The ash hung there bent and lacy and burned back almost to his fingers. Still going. Smoking. Sid stepped back carefully not to disturb anything so he wouldn't be blamed. When Perse couldn't see, Sid let out a quick shot of breath and the ash broke off.

''That was close'' Jimmy said. ''I've learned my lesson. I'm switching to one of those long brands.''

He never had any more trouble I knew of. That was a real contribution Sid made, saving a good customer like that.

Matilda. Mantillo. That's it. Mantillo. I know you knew it but you didn't know it any better than I did, it just wouldn't come up for me. Wrong kind of exam for a man my age to be taking.

3

When I got to the top of the stairs it looked to me like Greg Wyman was having himself a Yum Kipper. Wasn't sign of a thing going on except a machine clunking behind the pair of doors across the hall. Gregory Wyman and Company lettered on that pebbly glass they use for hallways. I could see the bolt wasn't thrown between the doors. I moved a door open and sent my head in to draw fire.

Signs of life but not too much. Laid out like a courtroom with rows of chairs. One of those white spitoon globes on. Smelled Chinese, could be a restaurant in the back. Bulletin boards all around with papers tacked up. The clunk machine was across the room, I guessed what they called a stock ticker, only it wasn't turning out the narrow tape they threw at parades but a mile-long sheet of typewriter paper pouring out a page a minute, piling on the floor.

I went in to see what it was all about and just naturally took the sheet in my hand like it was a transaction between it and me. Mr

Dow Jones knew I was coming in that door and had all these messages for me about ship movements in the Mediterranean, what the rain was doing to the corn in Illinois, small truck inventories, may be a copper strike in Bolivia, the interest rate in Germany. I could see all that stuff coming at me, telling me what was going on, asking if there was something in it for me. Spilled off the table onto the floor, lapped around my ankles. Must be people around could see a string sticking out somewhere you could pull on, I thought, get you out what you want. Smart people.

Behind that news ticker was the one I knew about that had parade tape tap-dancing out. Working up steps at rehearsal. Warming up. Testing it said. Market wasn't open yet. Anybody out there bidding on 260,000 FMC? You all know we got this new company listed today? Let's all give Swimsuit Corp of the USA a big hand. Let's hear it for SSC closed yesterday 14 on the American. Testing.

I gathered some of that tape in my hands. Pinched it to hold it still so I could read and it kept coming, climbed over my hand, up my arm like a pet snake.

Made me think of a picture we used to have on the cover of the telephone book of a naked old man under attack by a family of snakes. Some said he was Chief Lackawanna, the one they named the railroad for. Those were railroad tracks he was tangled up in. He didn't look like an Indian. Never saw a beard like that on an Indian, like shaving lather whipped up from a pig bristle brush. I don't know what that would have to do with telephones, probably something to impress you how tough it was getting a call through all those wires. Make you appreciate them.

Others said he was a story from the ancient Greeks. He was supposed to be a famous well-hung Greek hero trying to sort himself out for a date with one of their Love Goddesses. I don't know what that had to do with telephones either. Could be to get you to sympathize with what they had to do to get the bills right. There was a time they gave up on the bills, started putting every call on a separate piece of paper and stuffing it in an envelope. Here, you sort it out, you made the calls. Give you ten days to get it done and pay up. Some people got a hundred little slips of paper. Took them all the time from the invention of Alexander Graham's bell to get that simple idea how to screw up the whole system and find a judge to say Hey you got it. They did that till they caught on people were talking about this big dignified company as if it was a joke. One thing you can't take is people talking about you as if you're a joke. They went back to the bills.

It was before all the improvements that they put out the phone books with the old man wrestling the snakes. Couple of his kids hanging around in the picture not doing anything useful, watching the old man carry on. You can see the old man has some real distress. He has a right to expect help from the boys.

"Hey Cedric, some of this must be you, can't all be me."

"That's you, dad, you just go on over there to the Love Goddess and she'll straighten everything out."

Would be a good ad for these call girl services they have now. I never saw so much paper as came out of those tickers. Never saw anything so careless of using up material, showing they were too rich to care.

Grabbed me. Yeah.

I put my hands on the machines. Good dogs.

I knew there was something there for me. I could feel it working inside me. It had a taste. Anytime I smell Chinese I go back to that first day at Greg Wyman's when I met those two print machines. If you're looking for the exact time I got interested in the stock market you can say it was then. It was a long time after that I found out about my KGB being the Dow.

4

At the far end of the room from those printers a janitor was pushing up a broom storm and humming Lazy River with sound effects—*baroombeboom*—the way you do when you know no one's listening. Wore one of those shiny coats made from the silver paper they used to wrap gum with. Maybe they still do, I don't ever think to chew gum any more. You bit on that paper it made your teeth buzz. Kept his hat on to protect from the dust. He finished sweeping and stuffed the broom in a closet, moving along brisk, humming away. Took off the hat and stuck it on one of those bentwood customers. Took off the shiny coat and exchanged for a gray blazer he was sliding into when I realized the janitor was—Whoa! that's Greg Wyman himself.

While that was sinking in on me he ducked into an office marked out by chin-high partitions and switched up the light. Maybe the man won't appreciate me knowing he sweeps up. Maybe I can let myself out easy and come back another time. Maybe I can just sit here a couple minutes and then act like I just came in, not waste the trip. Heard him on the phone.

"Good morning." He said it in a highly dignified voice, not the one I heard in the bar. Wouldn't know it was Wyman if I didn't know. "Would you please ask Mrs Humdinger if she is able to speak with Thomas Hayes, research director of Wyman and Company? She is expecting a call from me."

Thomas Hayes. Whoa again! Who's on first?

Then I heard *Whack* like something hit the wall and the same again. I couldn't figure what that was. Fly swatter maybe.

"Good morning, Mrs Humdinger . . . Fine thank you and I trust you are the same . . . Good. I said we would be ready with some recommendations for you today and I am calling to let you know they will be delivered by messenger later this morning. *Whack* Well right at this moment we're recommending *Whack* General Motors and *Whack* International Lust. Mr Wyman will stop in to see you at ten o'clock Saturday morning to discuss those with you. *Whack* And Associated Freebies. We will be issuing a special report on AF. Nice to talk to you. *Whack Whack.*

First reaction I had to Greg's act was Man there's something hurts your feet. Being able to put on an act like that, that's a man you don't want to get a head start on you. After I got older I thought I didn't know if it mattered that much. What's the difference if there's only one of him instead of two?

Everybody has his act. Some people have the act of acting huffy about your act. I got more into Jimmy Perse's mood, except when it gets as high as president of the United States I like to know the real man in charge of the store. We get somebody like Tommy Hayes in charge you have an unreal man in a real bad situation and we could be in trouble, man, deep trouble.

I made a little fuss with my feet. Spoke up into the empty room loud enough to be heard over the partition.

"Hello? Anybody home? Is Mr Gregory Wyman here?"

Wyman came out to see who was calling. Wearing in his handkerchief pocket the feathers of one of those darts from a saloon game.

5

A few years later—may have been quite a few because Greg's hair was all faded then and his neck folded from dieting and putting on, dieting and putting on—we found out we both had tickets to a Sugar Leonard fight and decided to have dinner together, take a night off from the wives.

We were good friends and had business together. It was his idea we ought to put in a ticker, we had so many of his players drinking with us. That turned out to be a good feature. People weren't in such a hurry to get back to the board when we had the tape right there. Not bad for him either. Players would see something and go to the phone and it meant broker business. Having it was another thing that made us different from other bars. Image. You know, Image. Got to have that Image.

We walked across town to Gallagher's, had a drink and tried out subjects, loosening up waiting for the oysters. Got into stories of how it was when we first went into business. I told him how I didn't know a thing. Told him about Bar School. He told me when he went in for himself he was short of money and had to do everything himself. Couldn't afford to hire people. Did his own books. Wrote his own letters. Had an air staff like those air bands people do now, putting on a record and pretending they're playing. Telling each other You're too loud, they can't hear me. You're too slow, pick it up, pick it up. Nice riff, pal. It's all going on in their heads. Only with Greg he was playing all the instruments himself. Couldn't even afford anybody to clean his toilets or sweep up.

I didn't let on just then I knew all about that. You don't have to say right away what you know. Sometimes if you wait it turns out you're just as well off not to say it. I don't like to experience that specially if other people do that to me. Makes you think they're lying in wait for you a little bit.

Sometimes I test a man out by telling him a story twice, see if he stands up and says You told me that one. I trust a man more if he doesn't have any act with me. Either that or he ought to be good at it so I don't know. Not many people are that good covering up. I couldn't name you one. Yeah that's true, it could be because he's so good at it.

I let him keep telling me about that air staff and how he got into it in college doing a ventriloquist act at parties and all that and then I told him I knew about Tommy Hayes and picking stocks by throwing darts at the Journal stock page. Didn't faze him at all.

"I was the first" he said, and that's true. Picking with darts is an established thing now but Greg was the first. Today you've got the Dart Mutual Fund, it made the first ten last year. You've got the dart kit and the dart stock game. Greg never made a dime on any of them but he did all right sticking to what he did best. Got a good price for his business and the Market Letter. Nobody needs a billion dollars, believe me.

"I kept Hayes on only for a month or two. He was a terrible stock picker. He had a stiff shoulder. Collar rotation problem. I told people we had to let him go and he was working for Orvis Brothers. He put them out of business. Before Hayes I had a Chinese research man, Lee Wu. He was the best research man I ever had. Did you ever run into him?"

Must have been before I was in the market. He went into Chinese gear.

"That was when errebody thought Chonese smot fellas. Exotic anyhow, something you would remember. Ah so, Wyman and Company put on Chonese research director. I was sensational. I made the Journal. The Times wanted to interview me. I said Wu was press-shy. I left Wu traces around. I'd put a Chinese skull cap on the rack and a clay pipe on the desk. I'd burn incense before the opening—just wave the stick around in the air once or twice to put an idea in your nose that the great Wu had been there. It got to be too much. I had to get Wu's father taken care of in Hong Kong.''

Chinese Mafia, hey?

''No, he had a terrible accident, a construction scaffold fell on him, and Wu he had to go back and take care of the family business. He wasn't missed very long. Wall Street always has a new wonder man ready to take over. I still bring Wu back now and then when I pick up a phone and I'm not sure who's on. Hayes would have been all right if I hadn't thrown my shoulder out playing tennis and distorted the distribution.''

Something else Greg Wyman never made a dime on was that song from The Wall Street Crowd. You saw that? Yeah helluva show. That character who opened the show with the One Man Business song, he was a take-off on Greg Wyman.

Sitting there waiting for Greg to get off the phone to Mrs Humdinger, I thought This is a Broadway show. Man comes on singing, pushing a broom. Broom-dancing. Ticker gives him the beat. Ticker challenges the man. Man challenges back. Man changes his clothes. Puts on an act. Spotlight picks him up at the telephone putting on more act. I told Edna.

''That cat Greg Wyman, he's a one man business. He puts on a one man show.''

''He's who you see. He's who to know'' she came back. Her head got rhymes without working at it. Never thought of herself as a word writer, just wrote words that happened to come into her head to fill out the ideas coming off her hands. That's how we get songs like Inkadinkadoo, people forget they only vamped the words and somebody printed it up. Lotta the president's speeches are done that way. Inkadinkadoo speeches.

Nothing more about that till around nineteen late fifties. Abel Barasch was horsing around at the piano like he did any time the seat was open. We were closed, chairs on the tables, cleaning crew pushing vacuums. It had to be three four a.m. Edna and I and Abel, and Lauri Court sitting off to the side like she wanted you to be sure you saw she's holding back on the suffering. I wanted to get out of there and get some sleep but when Abel was working on a new show he liked to talk about it, especially if he was stuck. He needed people to brainstorm to. He never talked to Lauri about show business, her job was to stand lifeguard for him. I never saw anybody really talk to Lauri. Best you could do was the weather. I think of Lauri Court she's up on one of those towers at Jones' Beach in a white suit with a Red Cross on her chest and a white rubber cap with a chin strap keeping an eye on Abel. Didn't know what to do with him after she saved him except get back up there and save him again.

Funny how different people get together. You can't always see from the outside why that works. What's in it for her. She didn't seem to like his kind of life at all, not the people, not the hours. On top of that he was a slob and she always just washed her hands. He couldn't talk to her about what's on his mind day and night, the next show. She wasn't even one of those who say Great Great no matter what the man does so you can't believe them anyhow. There they were though, twenty years I knew about.

How would you like that, people on the outside not knowing anything about it asking how come he didn't ditch her? How come she didn't pack her bag? People were saying that about Edna and me. I knew it.

Abel was thumping out numbers two-four bang-bang, croaking lyrics, breaking off, No got a better idea. Do it another way. Break off again. Abel had good song ideas but he couldn't sing worth a dime and he couldn't play the piano as good as me, but he was a great believer in himself and he could put a song over. That's the thing, the belief. You give me a man who thinks he's Einstein, if he can stay out of the nut house he'll get a lot farther on in this world thinking he's Einstein than thinking he's himself.

We had a pretty good idea of the show from what Abel said about the numbers, and it kept coming up that he wasn't happy with the opening. Meantime it's four five in the morning and the rest of us want to go home and get some sleep. The only way that could happen would be if we got him away from the piano.

Wasn't easy. The man was built like a seal.

"Here" Edna said throwing a block to shift him aside on the bench. "We'll give you an opener free. Stiffy give him your thing about the one man show."

It was out of my head. Blank.

"You know, sitting in that office before the place opened and the boss sweeping up."

"That idea, yeah. Just an idea I had. There's this office before the market opens. Fella's running a one man business. Does everything himself. Sweeps. Answers the phone. And so on. Changes his clothes right there."

Edna chorded up a background while I talked. Found what she wanted and started singing. People will listen to Armstrong because he is known to be a singer. I'm not known but use your imagination, that's what it's for. I can sing as good as Abel ever could.

I'm a one man business
A one man show
I'm who to see
I'm who to know

She came up with one more line—*Tommy Dorsey had a brother*
Abel fired back *Karamazov had another*

So there's Barasch half-drunk with one piece of butt on the seat with Edna and she's noodling a song. Abel put an upbeat curtain-raising tempo on the floor and worked his arms like a fat bird taking off.

"Good, that's it. You got it." Edna closed it down.

Abel stayed put. He stopped trying to fly but his head still had the beat.

"I think I like it."

"Good. Go home."

"I'll call you tomorrow."

"Call me about anything but that. You've got it all. We don't have any more. It's yours. It's late. Let's go."

Lauri was up on the signal to help him into his coat. He got in one sleeve and dragged the rest behind. Camel hair dragging on the floor and Lauri trying to get hold of enough to throw it over his shoulder. Halfway to the door he began hollering

Chester McLaughlin boom that's me
And Company boom boom that's me
And Inc boom boom whaddaya think? Boom boom
Chester McLaughlin and Company Inc

I'm a one man business
A one man show
I'm who you see
I'm who to know

and so on out to Madison Ave bellowing *I'm alone I make the coffee put the cat out change the light bulbs dump the baskets dust the pictures give the orders take the orders mind the store boom boom boom boom* dragging the coat and Lauri complaining for a Taxi Taxi. He had the whole song down then and there, except for the usual changes. At the first night party Preston said the curtain was going up and Abel had him by the lapel with a new line for the patter that set the song up.

First Abel saw the number in performance was Philadelphia before they brought the show in. He sent Edna a check for a thousand dollars and a pair of tickets for New York. "Thanks sweetheart for getting us off to a hot start. Love and kisses. Abel."

That's it, that's what I'm talking about. That's how it worked. No notice was taken that basically it was my idea. Not that I wanted the credit. Show business wasn't my business, I had no wishes in that direction, I had plenty in front of me. It was the idea that Abel didn't give me a thought. I could be furniture, somebody hanging around after hours while he kicked it around with the main person. He wasn't in my space at four o'clock in the morning on account of me. I was left out. I was the guy who ran the bar and had a lock on Edna. Damn pimp.

"He should have sent it to you" Edna said.

"It goes on the same tax, honey."

I wasn't going let on to her. We had no problems between her and me. Still there's more to the world than you and only one other person. It gets to you if people out there don't have regard for your basic manhood.

I told all that to Greg the night we went to the fight together. I started out to tell him only how he happened to get written into that show under the name Chester McLaughlin and wound up telling it all including me being left out. You get to talking, you know. That was the night we got to be extra friends.

6

Couple of months after we were married I had my first hair-raising experience in the stock market.

I'd been reading about cigarettes killing you. Thinking about it. How there were new brands with filters to neaten up the smoke before it got into you. The name that made an impression on me was Kents. Camel was the big name then like always. We had Lucky Strikes and Chesterfields you never see any more. We had Pall Mall, you never see them. Gobbled up by filter brands. We had Marlboro and Phillip Morris, they're still up there. Mostly it's filters now. They were just getting started. Stories in the papers and big ads for these Kents. I was fresh out that morning and thought I'll try a pack.

I used to have a machine over by the door a fella they called Saxy Tony Saxi put in. Saxy came in every couple days and took out the change and filled the rows. That was before the cigarettes went with the hatcheck.

I went over to the machine to buy these Kents and we didn't have the brand. I never paid any attention to what was in the machine. That was up to Saxy and my Camels were always in there. But these Kents had to be something my customers wanted, and they wouldn't want to know anything about it being Saxy's route. With the customers it's all Stiffy's. You can't tell people a man has a concession in your place of business and you don't have a thing to do with it. While I was studying out the machine, Saxy wheeled in his handtruck with new stock.

"Just the man I'm looking for. See that we get some of those Kents on this fill-up."

"You and everybody else" he said. "I can't get them."

"Meaning what?"

"Meaning I can't get them." He was filling the rows with the usual brands, no place for these Kents. "They can't keep up with the demand."

"Say that one more time. Slow."

"You heard me. They can't keep up with the demand."

How about that.

Zap!

"Take it for a half hour" I told Sid and hotfooted it over to Wyman's. I was going up the steps before I realized I didn't even know what company made them.

Get the idea out your head I was a wild flier, one of those Bet A Million Gates guys. I took it a dollar at a time. To me buying 100 shares of a $5 stock and seeing it go down to 4½ was humongous. I was working on getting that up to 200 shares of a $10 stock and not blinking too hard if it went down a dollar. Got into the idea of putting stops under winners so you didn't give it all back and getting out of the losers without losing too much sleep. Get out, get your money, put it on the next horse.

I made plenty mistakes thinking those fellas who wrote those articles in the newspapers and Malcolm's magazine knew that much more than me. Got talked into dogs by stories that made you crawl up on your daddy's lap and ask for more. You know, fairy stories.

I was bowing down too much to others, not doing my own thing. That's a hard habit to shake, the idea those fellas must know more than me because they put it in the paper. People only know what they know and half of them don't even know that. The only people know a thing in this country are college professors and garage mechanics. That type person. That's a fact. A few of them know a few things. The rest you hear about make a living telling you things they picked up, no sweat if there's nothing to it. They don't get paid for being right, just for having something down in time to make the paper.

I'd go into Wyman's and look around. Who was there. Run the printouts through my hands. See what was on the bulletin board. How the market opened. What my stocks were doing. Kept walking out to the end of the diving board thinking I'd drop in some real money for this or that stock. Lacked the confidence.

I was getting to feel it was my place like an operating room feels to those people wearing masks and shower hats. Holding up their arms like they're on a string worked by somebody up top. Knowing the special language. Knowing all those people around, what the place is suppose to smell like, where everything is. When things supposed to happen. How things are done there. Like being inside a machine, being part of the works. I appreciate that.

Tickers going, pumping out paper. Broad tape movering by on the wall over Greg's office, strip of shiny screen jerking the symbols and numbers along like somebody's on the end hauling it in, taking another grip and hauling some more, trades coming in one end going out the other. The American tape ran underneath like a kid trying catch up. You don't see too many broad tapes any more. Now they use mainly the Bojangales clicking off that wall-size game of dominos. Everybody watching the game. Playing in that game with real money. We had papers around talking our language. PE's. XD's. Shorts. Longs. Futures. Averages. Curves. Priced flat. Round lot. Head and shoulders. Saddles. We had mergers and takeovers coming in then and McGarvey was one of the big players.

Hardly a day you could pick up the paper without reading Allen McGarvey and associates were said to be taking over this or that company. Telling you what McGarvey's Market Letter was telling the select, confidential, insider 100 List of subscribers what to do. That's all, 100. $25,000 a year to subscribe, no extra charge for air mail. And none of this If you're not satisfied let us know and we'll return your money in a plain brown wrapper.

McGarvey was right there at Wyman's, one of us players. Him coming in was like the big surgeon coming into the operating room. Scalpel! He never talked to anybody but Wyman and Carole—Good morning Mrs Lane—and some to me—What's good today, Stiffy? He knew me from the bar.

Against the wall halfway back Wyman had his library on a book table. Loose leafs racked up for stocks on the New York and stocks on the American. Books for Over The Counter stocks. Bonds. Every last little detail about every last company you can think of. Not a bit of it means a damn thing, not a word in any of those books and in all the papers tacked to the wall ever made a nickel for anybody in that room he couldn't make throwing darts.

Best use I ever heard of for the book table was Carole Lane's.

Carole had a big job with the Swimsuit Corporation of the USA you could say she inherited. She'd been a model there and married one of the owners. He died young and left her his action so she could write her own hours, put morning time in at Wyman's and I'd see her late in the afternoon or at night when she brought in visiting buyers to hear the jazz. One of my favorite customers. Edna's too. You could see Jimmy Perse shape up a little when Carole came in. Being in her business she had style and she had a sense of humor, she kidded right along with Jimmy. She was a person you just naturally liked.

Carole would get in Wyman's early two three mornings a week and work the book table, looking up stocks. Wore sunglasses all the time, part of her style. This particular day Frank Doelger sees her eyes are closed behind the glasses. Flipping pages she wasn't looking at. What's going on. He passed his hand between her and the book. Nothing. Notice something off about the color on his hand and looked up under the light trough. She had an ultraviolet screwed in there. Taking a sunbath.

"It's the only time I have to get outside" she explained.

She had a year round tan and always looked wonderful.

Wyman's was more like a club than any business you know of. We had all these people friendly from seeing each other, watching the broad tape together and telling each other what they have, what they're thinking about having and what they coulda had. IBM. Xerox. Everybody coulda had those. From that you go on to discuss how much Metamucil it takes to get the job done and whose kids can't make a living. Some of those friends of yours in there bleed to death if the numbers turn against them but you wouldn't know it. Wyman knew. He knew what they started with.

Except for McGarvey we were all small traders. No big trader hangs around a neighborhood shop watching tapes. Might be some fair-sized bankrolls holding down chairs in Wyman's room but that's only by the standard of the club members. Typical high roller in there probably had some real estate, apartment houses in Queens say, but if you saw high thousand lots running by on the broad tape it wouldn't be theirs. Wasn't anybody in our club shelling out 25,000 bucks for McGarvey's Letter. Nobody in there important enough to be one of the select, confidential 100 insiders or even get on the Standby to subscribe when somebody died.

That's one thing knocked out everybody about McGarvey, that a big man like that would show up at Wyman's three four times a week to look at the tape. He lived at the Gotham and took a morning walk to circulate his blood and Wyman had the nearest tape. Nobody talked to Allen McGarvey about their children or how things were in there after a heavy meal.

I had another idea why McGarvey came in. Seems fantastic, big man like that, but I'll stand on it. He came in to look at Carole Lane's legs. Yeah.

He'd have his eyes up on the tape and she'd walk past and he'd shift. Take out a handkerchief. Say a word to one of those two henchmen who hung around with him. Reach for his pocket calendar. Something to swing his eyes across Carole's can while looking like he had something else on his mind. I told that to Sid. He kept his eyes open a few times when Carole and Al McGarvey happened to be in the bar the same time.

"You're right. Why doesn't he ask her for a date?"

"Because he can see she has her eye on somebody else."

"What kind of a reason is that?"

"I don't know. I see what I see and I'm putting a reason to it. Big man, can't afford to think a woman would turn him down. Can't face that. I could be wrong."

"How would you know anything like that?"

"I didn't say I knew it. I made it up. That doesn't say it isn't a fact."

Took him awhile to digest.

"Who is her eye on?"

I mentioned Frank Doelger, one of our regulars.

"You kid me. She's old enough to be Frank's mother."

"One thing doesn't follow right there after the other. She may be old enough but there isn't anybody would say she's your average mother. Keep your eyes open."

In a week or so he came over and granted maybe I'm right.

That's going on in addition to booze and watching the tape.

I've been thinking about that mantillo. That isn't a mantillo at all, it's a rebozo.

7

I was in that club except I never told people what stocks I had. In the back of my mind I didn't want to deal with something that might look good today and get me credit but could sure look dumb tomorrow. Like I don't like to eat soup if I'm wearing a white suit. Doesn't make any difference if it's my favorite ham hock pea soup. People see a little stain that one time and the rest of your life they hear your name and they think That slob.

Some people didn't mind the risk. We had people in the club just as proud to tell you what they lost as what they cleaned up on.

We had this Dexter Gleason. He invented losers. He wanted you to know he could afford it. Moaning and groaning all the time. If you didn't see Gleason was in a Kollmer-Marcus Hickey-Freeman you would say he was in sackcloth and ashes as of old and so poor he had to rent his clothes.

"Can you believe I bought Chrysler at 90? Pitiful. It never sold that high again. Cost me an arm." He'd tell you that and shake his head like he didn't know what he was going do about himself. Same way people shake their heads over their kids hitting a ball through a window. Terrible terrible thing. Hoping you notice it's a real strong American boy that hits one like that. Gleason dropped his statement one day and Molly Caso looked it over before handing it to him. He didn't know for sure she did that but her going to the Ladies and then finding it as soon as she got back gave him that idea. Flustered him for Molly to know he had winners.

"It was there on the seat like that?"

"It must have dropped out of your pocket." Kept her eyes on the tape, wouldn't give him the time of day.

"I didn't take anything out of my pocket. Strange thing to happen." Pawing over himself to see what else was missing. "I can't understand it." Then he thought of the bright side. "I have an account with Bache. I don't do well at all over there."

Another way to look at it is that he dropped the paper on purpose. One way or another he let you know he was a good credit risk.

First thing I saw when I walked in to get some of that Kent, holding back not to look too anxious, was this other club member Darice Harrison stealing a page from the OTC book. Nonchalant like she had nothing to do with that particular hand. Third hand dropped in from the sky, tore a page loose from the ring and tilted it out. Like they say, the famous Invisible Hand. She didn't even notice it happen. Imagine that, she didn't even notice. If they had an event like that in Italy they'd have her up for saint. That's the same class person that tears out the doctor and the rug dealer page from the phone book in the hotel. No one else has any right to need a doctor or some carpet, they're the only ones with those needs. Got them everywhere spread over two stripes in the the parking lots, throwing used Kleenex on the street, sending their dogs over to your part of the sidewalk to make their deposits. Yaking the Walkman into your ear. How we supposed to run a world with characters like that taking advantage all the time? You go into the loose leaf looking up a company and you can be sure that is the page some son with Invisible Hands lifted. Member of the same club you're in, too.

I passed down the other side of the street on that one. Not up to me to get involved. People get amazed if you speak up on something where you're not personally hurting. They know they're not talking up for you, no sir, so what's it to you getting involved on that? What's it to you buddy? Are you the plain clothes on the beat here or something?

What I'm doing talking about it this way now I don't know. The point is I didn't do anything. Some point.

We had a few minutes before the opening and I hung off the line of traffic thinking How am I going go about this? Wait for my stock to show a price to tell me what I had to pay for it? I didn't know what the symbol was and I didn't want to sound too foolish asking around a question like Who makes those Kents? Didn't want to show my hand.

While I was standing aside there with my problem McGarvey walked in fast with his two usual henchmen on the flanks and stopped like he was on ice skates. Sprayed shavings on a couple regulars standing there. Looked at them like they're people who have shavings on them. Dumb people. Looked over their heads to the far end making believe he was flashing the pre-opening garbage on the broad tape but basically looking for Carole. She had her back to us so he could give her a good long look. Soon as she showed signs of turning around he wheeled his honchos on over to the tickers to take in the news.

They went through the tapes like my momma used to go over trouser seams looking for lice till one of them pointed his finger and croaked a lorangitis whisper.

"Harbor Oil."

That would be Bunschli. He was the one with the hairpiece. I had trouble keeping those two fellas straight. Bunschli was the hairpiece. Supposed to be black hair. More like a reject divot of Astroturf, green when the light hit it right. Gilders' specialty was the odd vest. Red plaid with lapels that particular day.

McGarvey gave Bunschli a teacher look and held a finger up at him. Bunschli went mum and they all looked around to see who was into their business.

Wasn't me. I was inside my permanent shadow not paying attention to them in any way shape or form. Didn't know they were there to my knowledge any more than Darice Harrison knew about the Invisible Hand.

While I hung in their doing my silence Frank Doelger breezed in and he kept on going toward the front. I knew he didn't hear Bunschli and from talk at the bar I knew Harbor Oil was a stock he played sometime. He'd tell people what he was in, he had the confidence, not like me.

He kept travelling toward Greg's office, me after him to get away from there. The bell rang on the ticker saying the market was open and floor trades began movering across the broad tape.

At the partition break you'd call the door to Greg's office—wasn't any door then just an opening to walk through—I lagged back to let Doelger have his time with Greg. He wouldn't be long. Regulars know not to tie up the broker while the market is open. Young fella, good customer of mine. Even a better one of Greg's. He had a trading stake from what a young bachelor can put away and an inheritance, and quit his job with Lord & Taylor to play the market. Must be a good man because Carole Lane kept after him to go to work for Swimsuit as a high exec. Sales vice president. Big job. Frank wasn't buying, he was hooked on Wall Street.

From clues I always figured him for a canny guy. He'd watch the tape and write notes to himself. Screwed his face up thinking about those notes. That's all I had to go on but I had the impression. Couldn't help but figure he knew something now and then. I heard his order.

"Sell 2,000 Harbor Oil at the market."

Sell? That shook me up. When I heard a stock mentioned I never thought about selling. I figured McGarvey was a buyer. Was I supposed to shove in and say I just heard Allen McGarvey's fella mention that stock? Maybe they weren't buyers. Maybe they were sellers. How would I know? Doelger seemed plenty smart enough to know what he was doing without help from Arsdur U.Stiff.

"You want to sell 2,000 HO at the market?"

I couldn't see Greg's face but I could hear what it looked like in his voice. Wouldn't show any opinion. Neutral. A question like that wasn't moving things forward, though. I could hear Doelger's face too. The one that explained something to you you should know.

"Indeed I do want to sell. See if you can get me a fast execution from those polo players you have downtown."

"Is this the 2,000 you bought last week?"

"The same. And a fast execution. If you please."

"Do you happen to know your account number, Frank?"

"What is this with account numbers? It's my account."

"I just thought you might know it. It's on the wheel."

I could hear the Wheeldex creak.

"I thought you liked that stock" Greg said.

"I don't like it today. I gave up two points in a week and I don't want to give them any more. Put it to them."

"It's your stock. You bought it. You can sell it."

"I can't sell it if you don't call in the order."

"Do you want to put on a limit?"

"Market price will do. Get it off."

"Here we go." The phone came off the cradle. "Wyman. Sell 2,000 HO at the market." He listened a couple seconds to what the floor was telling him and reported to Frank.

"Closed 17. Hasn't opened yet. They're saying 17 to an eighth. Oils are steady at the opening. The floor is saying McGarvey's Letter likes HO."

"Screw McGarvey. Move it."

Greg went back into the phone. "Sell it. Customer wants a fast execution." He would be running his thumb across his throat the way he always did when he said that. The phone went down.

"You're ordered."

"Get me that 17 and I'll be happy. I'll be in the room."

Seeing me on his way out he said "Pick a good one, Stiffy."

"That's the only kind I know."

Nothing more for me to say to him. He's a big boy.

Now I had this problem that I didn't know what company made Kent cigarettes and I didn't know if the stock cost a dollar or fifty dollars and I didn't want Greg to know I was all that ignorant. I flipped it to him.

"How about $10,000 worth of Kent cigarettes?"

"How about" he said. "Opened 7,000 shares 20½ up a half on the day. Trading is active." Had it in his head. Didn't say the name of the company like I thought he would.

"Price in there is okay. Make it a market order."

"Do you want to tell me if you're buying or selling?"

Yeah well. He was entitled to know that. "Buying."

He picked up the little square blue pad he wrote Buy orders on and wrote LL for the name of the stock. That didn't tell me a thing. I figured the 20½ into $10,000 and told him to make it an even 500 shares. He wrote that down and dialed his trader.

"Wyman. Buy 500 Lulu at the market . . . Right." He hung up and told me I was ordered. Lulu. Hell, that was just two L's.

Didn't know any more than before except I was in for ten grand. Didn't know on what.

Then this just came on me, didn't think a bit about it. I had this feeling crawling on me that I would miss out on something if I wasn't in that Harbor Oil with McGarvey and Doelger both having it in play. I didn't own it and I wasn't a short player in those days so there was no way for me to get in on the sell side with Frank, so I thought what the hell I'll buy it. I was sure McGarvey was on the buy side from the way they looked and the way Greg tried to slow down Frank from selling.

"Tell you what—get me a 100 of that HO too."

If I was an owner, it was just as likely I would have bowed down to Frank and sold. I'm telling you how hard it is to break bad habits.

One thing about Greg Wyman, the office was wide open but you never heard from him anything about another customer's business. That was something you had to pick up. Up to you to keep your voice down about your own affairs if you felt that way. He didn't give me the least blip when I gave him the order. Went right to his blue order pad.

"Do you want to give me a limit?"

Hadn't thought about it. Hadn't thought about any of it.

"Well I don't know."

"Closed 17 and hasn't opened today. It may be up. There is a rumor that it's mentioned in McGarvey's letter."

"He's in the back. You could ask him."

"It's an idea" he said. No one was going ask. You didn't do that. You had the Letter or you didn't.

"How about putting me in at what do you think?"

"That's a good number. How about a limit at a half?"

"That's it."

I was glad to get past that transaction, didn't even know why I was in it and if somebody had said Let's start over I would have said Okay forget the whole thing. That's what comes from having money in the bank and listening to other people. That's how I first got into Harbor Oil.

Kents. LL. That was my personal stock. I got it in my own way. Got it in my own head.

I was on a righteous high for those Kents like those fellas who start up new religions. L for Luther. Those fellas. That ten grand was a real money for me but nothing that would change my life too much if I lost it, except maybe kill a night's sleep thinking what a jackass I was. I wasn't gambling to have the extra money. I was gambling to show I was right. Don't ask me Show who? I never analyzed it. I guess you would have to say it was to show people who said I made a living off Edna that I didn't need that.

How did I know that stock was going up? You're asking me to explain. Explain moves from my head into yours. I had reasons but you always have reasons. Saxy being out of Kents was a reason but reasons are a dime a dozen. Isn't a stock on the board without a reason, that's why they're there. That's why Greg Wyman had a buyer and a seller for every damn one of them up there. The thing is have you got a reason that appeals to the particular way you're made. Have you got a reason that lights the KGB fuse. Zap.

I was lighted up inside with those Kents. If it was night you could see me glowing like a candled egg.

Malcolm'll want to know my investment strategy. That's it.

When I shine inside I got a stock.

8

In those days you gave a broker an order and it didn't make any difference what the amount was, if he knew you he never flinched. He didn't give you the stock till you paid for it, but he went on the line to buy it and he didn't expect your money for another three four days. I thought that was one of the great things about America, ranked it up there with the Supreme Court, that people would take your word, no witnesses, not signing anything.

Do you know what can happen to a stock in those three four days before you get your money up? The price could double. Just live that long for it to happen but it's possible. Never mind, you get it at the promised price. It could hit bottom and keep going. The Financial VP could clean out the safe and disappear to South America and you haven't even paid for the stock. Tough. You ordered it, send in the check. All on a handshake. That's in business, mind you, the money business at that, the most cutthroat kind. You can't match that for trust short of marrying somebody.

I never got used to that much trust. Always had my money in hand, except this time the Kent subject came up so fast I hadn't got to the bank. Harbor Oil even faster. I started telling Greg I had to pull the money out of savings and into checking and he'd have something in the account in the morning and all that jazz but he wasn't paying attention. Had his ears tuned over the partition to a seat war developing between a couple customers.

"Somebody in Mueller's seat" he said. This was at least the size of World War II and he had to get into it. Mueller's voice coming through loud clear and stern.

"It's my regular seat. I always sit there. Would you mind?"

"I didn't know there were reserved seats" this other gal says. "I didn't know it was the opera."

Sarcasm was all Mueller needed. This was her home. She came up the stairs behind Greg the day he opened and only went to her rent-control to tell her husband what happened in the market that day. She knew stock symbols and earnings like kids know big league batting averages. A steady nickel trader like Mueller figured to make a couple hundred bucks a week. Of course you couldn't expect her to do that unless she had her regular seat, fourth row on the aisle. How could you pick stocks from the fifth row?

"Listen Miss Simp I was a customer here before you learned to read." Mueller was ready to swing her pocketbook when Wyman jumped off the block to get out there and make peace. Right behind to see the fun, I just got outside the office when Carole Lane was in front of me with her head tipped up to the tape.

"Look at that Lorillard" she said.

Sitting over to the side, Dexter Gleason had his eye on it too. "Look at Lorillard go."

I turned around and saw a string of trades up there . . . LL 9500s $21^5/_8$ . . . LL 2400s $21^5/_8$ . . . LL 500s 22 . . . LL 23000s 22 . . .

That's how I found out I owned 500 shares of the Lorillard Tobacco Company.

I felt real good about it.

I let Greg handle the seat war. I watched the tape.

9

Another stock they were trading that day was HO.

The oils turned weak but Harbor Oil didn't know about that. Opened at Frank's selling price and all up from there.

17 $17^1/_4$ $^1/_4$ $^1/_4$ $^1/_2$ $^1/_2$. I'd be in and he'd be out at the same price. Frank came over and leaned against the wall with Carole and me. He knew he was out on an early tick. With the price going up, he didn't look too happy selling out at 17 like he said he'd be.

"I don't understand your system" Carole said. "It's your favorite stock and as soon as it starts up you sell."

"I didn't like the way it was acting."

"This isn't an act. Look at the volume. This is real. Are you sure you wouldn't rather be in the rag business?"

That wasn't a question he was supposed to answer right there. That was Carole Lane digging him a little. In a motherly way you might say but you could be wrong.

"Harbor is in McGarvey's Letter" Gleason advised everybody.

He was at the end of the camp chair row behind Mueller. He didn't know McGarvey was in the back of the room and he didn't say it loud enough to carry but loud enough to annoy Frank.

"Have you seen it yourself?"

"My brother talked to somebody—"

Frank cut back on him "Just say you didn't see it, never mind the rest of the garbage. It's just a goddam rumor. McGarvey. McGarvey.'' Irritated. You know, irritated.

I'm poking Frank and mumbling at them to cool it, McGarvey's back there. They finally caught on and shut up. I don't think McGarvey heard the fracas anyhow. It was a long carry to the back of the room, and he and his vest and his hairpiece weren't paying any attention to us. Their heads were aimed up at the broad tape. A few seconds more and McGarvey had enough.

''Let's go gentlemen'' he said. ''Time is money.''

And out.

Fella named Saniford, not one of my regulars like Frank and Carole but I saw him now and then at Wyman's, came up to Greg who just finished re-arranging the seats. All excited.

''That was Allen McGarvey.''

Yeah it was.

''Did you hear what he said?''

What did he say?

''He said Time is money.''

That's news?

That Saniford he was frantic. ''Time is money. McGarvey said Time is money. I want 50 Time Inc. I want a fast execution.''

That's all a real fact. In an hour it was all over the market. Reporters looking for McGarvey all over town. By noon Time Inc was up five dollars and in the last edition they they said it was in McGarvey's Market Letter that money was to be made in Time. Only it wasn't the magazine, it was the clock company. The San Francisco market gave away Time inc and the next day General Time went to a new high in New York.

That story was never in the paper but you could look it up in a report a professor at CCNY gave to the Economical Association. Some outfit like that. He had the whole McGarvey story down, things even I didn't know. Professor George E. Neumann, good customer of mine. He's the one that got me interested in colleges. You'd be amazed the things a man like Neumann knows. He told me about that Texas oil man who flew his own army around invading foreign countries he was unfriendly with. Big man. Professor Cornwell said this Texas general offered McGarvey 50,000 bucks in the lobby of the Plaza to get up to the first ten Standbys—not even a subscription, just high on the reserves. Putting on a show for the benefit of the leather boots with him. McGarvey gave back the High Noon, slunked him all the way back to Phoenix. One of those Oklahoma type places.

You could play off McGarvey another way too. Take the time Walter Cronkite had Wriston that big banker on TV for an in over your depth interview and asked him if he was a subscriber.

"Heck no I'm not that important. I'm only a Standby" Wriston said. "I don't even have a high number." Showed he was a modest man. Took out the gold reserve card with W.B. Wriston Standby Subscription Reservation Number 58 signed Allen J. McGarvey. The chairman of the great New York City Bank wanted the American television audience to appreciate that he was in with McGarvey but at the same time he wasn't too in. Like being born in a log cabin in case he wanted to go into politics later on. Look good in his biography. He was a plain man of the people only on the Standby. Bottom line probably was he prayed like everybody else for the fellas higher up on the list to get a heart attack. Don't bet Abraham Lincoln if he had a shot at it wouldn't trade the log cabin for a ranch-all-on-one-floor with all the conveniences and let politics take care of itself later on.

I had the idea at one time to make a market in the Standby cards like they do in taxi medallions. The taxi medallions go for a hundred grand today. Used to go for ten twenty grand and what are they, only a license to beat your brains out making a living one day at a time. Get on McGarvey's list, people figured to read the stock page a day ahead, almost as good as being wired to the Dow.

I gave the idea of making a market in Standbys to Gordon the lawyer from Greenberg's office. I thought he'd have the connections. You know how lawyers are, he was slow, before he got around to doing anything it was too late, the demand for the cards had passed. Timing is the whole ball game. That and having something like that Lorillard Tobacco Company to time with.

Put it down. Lorillard was first. Then Harbor Oil, and I never looked in a book. Never even threw a dart. Something inside me glowed and I went.

No I don't know how Wyman made peace in the seat war. I never thought about it again till just now. You live long enough things come back to you.

Seven

LA BANDIDA

1

WOULDN'T IT SEEM only right to use the product your own company made? I tried for a pack in the news shop at the Berkshire. Made me feel good when Selma told me she couldn't get any. I had this picture of every smoker in the world scheming to get a pack of Kent cigarettes and it taking years for Lorillard to catch up at a penny extra per pack for scarcity times 90,000,000,000 packs. Big numbers for us stockholders. Across the street at Grusom's they had some under the counter for special trade. It disappointed me some you could buy a pack that easy.

Jim Perse was going into the bar ahead of me and by the time I checked over things Sid had a Cutty down for him and he was hunched on the stool growing an ash. I went over for a chat, broke the pack open and lighted up.

Inhaled, knowing it was healthy.

Looked it over. Rolled the body. Rolled the filter. Let out the smoke taking some back through my nose. Gave it the full treatment. My baby.

"You ever smoke these, Jimmy?" Showing him the pack.

He thought about should he admit it.

"I have."

He didn't give me any opinion and as I was conducting a market survey I didn't want to influence him one way or another.

"How did you like it?"

Jimmy saw I wanted his best shot. A man doesn't get a chance to be in a Gallup every day. Some people go their whole lives nobody asking their thoughts on a blessed thing.

"That was the very best cigarette made out of camera film I ever expect to smoke."

Fair enough. Me too. Made me think I might have the right general idea but the wrong company. To be on the safe side I called Greg and bought a jag of KE for Kodak too. I didn't have any zap for it, just wanted to cover the bases.

We had that stock ticker Greg Wyman sent over chomping tape into a big wire basket we kept alongside it. I checked on Lorillard and it was already up a dollar. That improved my health immediately and I kept checking all day and by the close I had four points and Kents weren't tasting all that bad. Two thousand dollars was a fair day's pay, the most I'd ever made. That's even with Uncle Sam in for halfers and he hadn't put up a dime.

Lemme tell you about the Harbor Oil. Get back to noon.

By noon I had three points on that stock. For a seventeen dollar stock that wasn't bad even if I only had a round lot.

Frank came in here around that time, too sore at himself to stay at Wyman's any more.

"Can you imagine. I always liked that stock. Always held a few shares and looked to make a killing some day. I watched it for a month. It sat there on 19, down from the low thirties, and didn't budge. That stock has bottomed, I said, and I bought it. It began to give up quarters right away and kept sliding. Last night I made up my mind I'd been a little premature. Lighten up, I told myself, get back in when it bottoms again. Look at it again for awhile. Wait till it's ready. This morning first thing I was a seller and it started straight up. Son of a bitch."

"Us common folk only deal in stocks that go up when we buy and down when we sell."

"That's the way. So here I am out of a stock I have all this faith in and it's going up."

"It could be worse. You could be in and it could keep going down."

He experimented to see if he could turn the glass without taking the ice around with it. You have to go real slow. You have to concentrate. You can't think about anything else. He finished that experiment and went over to read the ticker. When he got an HO tick he said

"Son of a bitch. Twenty bucks. Up three on the day. Son of a bitch."

He came back to finish his drink and think about it. Rangy six foot-some fella. Tennis player. Racquet games. Basketball. Maybe a rower if he went to one of those rowing schools. A guy you think of when they say He's an account executive or He's in executive training. Black hair. Ears flat. Eyes pierce into you then pass on like a lighthouse. Don't stand still like Edna's. Come round again. Go on by again researching something out there. His mind seemed like one step away from right here. Usual with him.

"Do you play that market?" he asked Jimmy.

Jimmy looked into the smoke coming up from the ash seeing if there was some mysterious information in there, a message coming through from an ancestor. Dancing girl materializing. Sent his tongue in the empty space in his teeth to see if something might be there.

"I wouldn't know one stock from another. I had a grandfather who was so good at stocks he didn't even need a company to be there and he could make money on the stock. His attitude was that there was no need—no real need—for a company. He dealt only with people who had grandchildren. Buy it and put it away, he told them. Take care of your grandchildren like I'm taking care of mine. He travelled the country preaching that gospel and selling certificates in mining companies with glorious names. One I remember was Thunder Valley. Another was The Mighty Widow. Take care of your grandchildren with a share in the future of The Mighty Widow. Buy it and put it away. Never think about it."

Jimmy held up his hand to give the blessing. You could see all these grandmothers and grandfathers lining up to do for their grandchildren what Jimmy's grandfather was doing for his. "He left a good estate for those days, considering that he was destitute when he got out of jail and had only four years of good works left."

"Did he die young?"

Jimmy looked into the smoke for the answer. "I have no idea. I don't ask people their age."

"Well did he just print up the certificates?"

"He wasn't a printer. He was a salesman. He was 51 years old when he died."

"That's young if you're going to die."

"It's young now. It wasn't young in those days. And there will be days to come when it won't be young again."

"Why do you say that?"

"You don't think things are getting any better do you?"

The bar began to pick-up and we had a new man with Sid so I got away from those two. I don't know why I ever listened to that Jimmy Perse. I never made a dime on Kodak. It just sat there tying up money I could have added onto my Lorillard. Any money he had he must have inherited.

I saw the new man knew his business and I went out amongst the tables talking to customers. Took a look at my stocks on the tape and saw they were doing good. All except Kodak. Took two weeks for me to make up my mind to get rid of it. Bowing down to Jimmy Perse's ideas.

Pretty soon Frank got down off the stool and went to the tape. I read his mouth Son of a bitch. He went into the phone booth. A minute later he came out looking refreshed. Felt good like he'd been in one of those French pisserias they have on the boulevards. First time I saw one I thought they were part of the Maginot line. I knew what he did all right, he went back into Harbor Oil. Couldn't stand being out.

2

We got into the low part of the day. Frank and Jimmy were gone and I was thinking about going out for a bite and Bunschli and Gilders came in looking for McGarvey. Had he been in? No we hadn't seen him. Were we sure? Sure we were sure. They acted like it was our responsibility to see him if he was there or not, then decided they had as good a chance of heading him off here as anywhere so they took a table. I would have gone out like I planned, except Bunschli said something that made me lag back with my ear open while the new man stood there waiting to write up the drinks.

"You'd think, being this close to him, being his best friends and most loyal associates he'd print up a measly extra two copies."

"I can't agree with you. It's the principle. You either print a hundred or you don't. If you go whoring after circulation your standards suffer." That Gilders was a real company man.

"You could say the same about a hundred and two. Would he be a whore for a hundred and two and not for a hundred? Don't we deserve something?"

"Exercise a little patience."

My waiter's standing there and they're not ordering. I know what's going on. The waiter's supposed to know what they want. I go along with that. If a man has a regular drink he wants you to know it and set it up without him saying. Puts him in the club.

There are fellas in New York still drinking drinks they learned to drink before they knew better, like red Manhattans, afraid to change because the bartender might forget. They may hate those drinks, won't order but one and sit with it, but what can you do? If you bring friends in because the bartender knows you and knows your drink you die right there if he looks at you like it was your first time. Like your wife saying Who are you? at two o'clock in the morning. If you have to tell him what you drink you might as well go through that routine some place else. A fella comes in five times and says Chivas, water on the side, so from six on he doesn't have to tell you. He doesn't want to know from new waiters. Good afternoon there, Mr Bunschli, the usual? and go right to the Chivas and that customer will come all the way from the west side to do business with you. That's one of the secrets of my success. One of them.

"These gentlemen will have Chivas, water on the side" I told my waiter.

They loosened right up.

"I saw you trading this morning" Mr Hairpiece said. "It wasn't a bad day to be in."

"It's always a good day for you fellas. The rest of us have to scratch."

"I think you do all right."

"Yes I think you do all right" Mr Vest said.

"I don't do too good Monday Wednesday and Friday. I do all right Tuesdays and Thursdays. If I could trade Saturdays I'd be even." Time to get away. Stand there with customers too long and it's uncomfortable for them looking up while you're looking down and just filling time. They weren't going say any more about McGarvey's Letter while I was hanging over.

I told them "Don't be in any hurry to go. Cooler in here than out there" and left them getting back into their conversation. Lagged back, kept my ear in. Last thing I heard was Vest asking Hairpiece where he was on the Standby.

"Six. Where are you?"

"I happen to be three."

Surprised me these big shots didn't even have subscriptions. Just a couple high class gofers on the Standby like everybody else. At that they may have been lying to make an impression. Neither one of them took the card out of his wallet to prove it like Wriston did when Cronkite asked him.

You heard about Lloyd's insurance company in London, how they ring a bell when a ship sinks, lets the insurance agents know to get ready to dig down and pay off? The news ticker has a bell goes off to let you know when there's important news coming through. Could be something the Federal Reserve is doing to finagle the interest rates. China and Russia going to war. Things that would make you change the basic idea of how you invest your money. A couple days after we've been talking about the bell rang on the ticker at Wyman's. The usual thing is a customer walks over and reads the news out loud so everybody has it the same time. Gilders got there first.

"Wendell Willkie is dead at 66."

Mueller had her eyes on him when he turned around and showed two fingers to Bunschli. She gave me an elbow.

"Did you see that? It's one thing to be against a person's politics but that was gross."

I tried to cover for him without saying what I knew. "I don't think he meant that. It could be something else."

"Like what? Like he's holding a cigar?"

"It could be a price signal like they use on the American. It could be two something."

"Please."

3

McGarvey showed at my place that afternoon with a couple reporters hanging on. He slid in with the two henchmen and I sent over a Chivas on the rocks. The reporters pulled up chairs and kept after him and he kept shaking his head. Wouldn't talk. What did he have to say about Lorillard? Nothing. Well how about Time Inc.? Nothing. Did he know what they were saying about his position in Harbor Oil? He wasn't responsible for what people said. I was going over to change the subject and get them off him when McGarvey settled it himself.

"Have a heart, boys. I came in here to have a drink with friends. You know I never comment on rumors. I don't know any more about Harbor Oil than its name."

Bang! There went my two phone booths, those guys to their papers. The morning Trib said their reporter had caught up with McGarvey at a well known east side watering place and he accorded a rare wide-ranging interview in which he denied an interest in Harbor Oil.

The market didn't have to wait for the morning paper. Word went right through the air from my place to Wyman's, homed on that tape Frank Doelger was feeding through his fingers when the Big News bell rang. He was the first to know why trading stopped in HO while the floor trader tried to find buy orders to match sell orders piling in from all over the USA and Zurich.

He had to read it out loud so everybody had an even start.

ALLEN McGARVEY DENIES
Then he had to give Greg his order
SELL HO

"There is no market yet. Take it easy, Frank."

"Take it easy about what? Where's the famous specialist who's always there to make a market? Where is he when I need him? I want out."

I went all the way up and down in HO and before I made up my mind to get out I was back to even. Well fella, there are worse places than even. Frank lost the up and he got back in just in time to buy the down. Wrong way twice on a one-way street. If I'd sold right away when he came out my phone booth with that pisseria look on his kisser, I would have held my gain. That's when I got the idea Frank Doelger might be a little lacking.

The bottom line on that day was I got into Lorillard and foundered the fortune of Arsdur U. Stiff. You could say it was just good business sense. What do you have to know about a big company that can't keep up with the demand? Do you have to know what the ratios are? Do you have to know who the president is? Wouldn't you get that zap without having to go into any reports?

4

Things began picking up around four when the crowd from Wyman began to drift in. Carole came in with Gleason and a couple other regulars and went right to the corner angle of the bar, their usual den. Sid set their drinks up.

When I tell you Carole Lane was a health nut and wouldn't touch anything alcoholic, you know she had a lot going for her to be one of my favorite customers. She used to order things like a Collins very very easy—too much—on the gin—or gin on the side. Took me awhile to catch on she only took a sip of the Collins and never poured the shot into the mix. I called her.

"You caught me" she said. "What are we going to do about that? I want to be welcome but I can't handle that stuff."

I told her not to worry about it, she could have club soda.

She was a good-looking woman and that's the only sure-fire celebrity there is that makes everybody's head go up. Having celebrities in the house is good for your image, never mind what they drink. At Stiffy's we had different night and afternoon type celebrities. We had the show business and political types the night people looked for. Afternoons we had the business crowd, a celebrity to them was the president of J. Walter or Bache or McCall's. People who wrote checks. People who signed contracts.

Then we had all purpose celebrities like Al McGarvey and Henry Kissinger and good-looking women. Carole Lane coming through my room straight-backed as a marine, wearing sunglasses, carrying that bouquet of orange hair—those pale California oranges, not those orange oranges from Florida—with a little bit of a hat tacked on it, that's a celebrity.

Added on to Carole being a celebrity, Edna and I liked her for being a certain kinda person.

I'm thinking of a day when I first got to know her. We were crowded in here that day they had a power shutdown on the Long Island. Commuters stacked up in bars all over making up their minds what they were going do about it. Hang in town at a hotel. Rent a car. Whatever. You could hardly push through here. Somebody backed into my waiter and he dropped a tray of drinks on a table behind where Carole was sitting. Hell of a mess slopped all over a fella at that table and everybody coming at him with napkins. He busted out with the words waiting there in his mouth.

''Watch what you're doing, nigger.''

Now I'll tell you, when somebody says something like that people around don't say a thing back. It wasn't anything they said. Nothing they're responsible for. Might be that some of them wish it hadn't been said, but if anything's going happen back to that big mouth, Hey that's up to you, you're the black one. If some black guy is getting hassled by the powers it isn't the Knights of Columbus that butt in. It isn't the Jewish Anti-Discrimination or the Little League. It's the NAACP. The NAACP, the NAACP always nagging after people in the newspapers. Well who else? You?

Carole came right around on her seat, didn't have to think about it.

''Take that talk and your wet pants out of here'' she said.

All of a sudden the fella sees there's two sides to it and this good-looking red head is making him look not too good. He cools right down. Starts smiling at my waiter. Telling him he's sorry he lost his head. Didn't mention he couldn't understand how nigger happened to be in his mouth. Stuck in by the famous Invisible Hand.

Take a situation like that night I was on the bias at a dinner where they honor you by getting your friends to take a table for the benefit of something. Brotherhood Week. One of those things. Sitting next to me was the white preacher who blessed the meal. Making conversation he told me he was born in South Africa, son of a missionary. He had this experience with one of his flock who came back from a vacation over there. Not too many people been to South Africa.

The preacher had this fella and his wife over for dinner to talk about their experiences. This fella with two weeks in Africa under his belt was all steamed up about the media having it wrong about how things were for black people there. Things were getting good. They had good jobs. Good houses. They weren't heated up about schools and votes and living two standing-up hours away from work the way politicians and liberals over here were carrying on. None of our business. Leave em alone. Let em work it out.

''That man knew from my sermons that I didn't agree with him'' the preacher told me over the roast beef. ''But what could I do? He was a guest in my house. I said nothing to suggest that I agreed with him in any way shape or form. You can't do anything about the ignorance of some people.''

Yeah I said.

Under Parkinson's Law I got to take the preacher over that other fella but not by too long odds.

I'm not saying I'm anything special either. Take me at no better than even odds with that preacher because you notice all I said was Yeah when he told me about it. I didn't say How come you don't tell him what you tell me? Is him being your guest more important than him thinking you're in it with him? You make him happy when you're with him, and you're trying make me happy while you're with me. All I said was Yeah. I'm putting it out the way it went. Carole would let that friend of the preacher's know. He wouldn't say anything like that to her again.

Something else, though. Say that fella with the drinks on him was a hardnose and came right back at her like they do What's it to you sister? Then where are you? I'll tell you where you are, she's out of it and Greg Wyman or Gleason have to come off their seats and say to this joker Cool it, that's a lady. So one of them gets his head broke if I don't get in there with a bottle fast and I don't know if I do or I don't. I think I do but I can't tell ahead. Maybe I just watch it till it settles down. All I know is everybody else is just sitting around. That's what people do. Sit around. Stay out of it. Most people don't even vote.

You get the idea Carole Lane didn't have to be a celebrity to sit at my bar on a club soda.

"You can have a Jolly Giant or a Coke. We'll charge it off to decorating."

"Oh Stiffy you're such a doll but I'm not going to sit here unless I pay the rent. If you'd do this for me—" and she told me about this yogurt I never heard of before.

"I couldn't serve anything like that. They'd take away my license."

"What's more important, your license or my figure?"

"Depends on where you sit."

"Exactly."

We set her up this special frapped yogurt drink. Take my word for it. Frapped it with a couple banana slices. Gave it the name El Bandito and did it up with vodka so if anybody asked What's she drinking? it wouldn't set any precedents making us an ice cream store.

After we had it on the card awhile Jimmy Perse noticed it.

"Should be Bandido with two d's."

"Whatever you say, Jimmy. Next time we print the card."

"Why would you serve a beverage like that in your establishment? Is there no law against pornography in this town?"

I explained it was in honor of Carole.

"In that case make it La Bandida. La as in lalala. Dida."

"Whatever you say, Jimmy."

You order a La Bandida to this day at Stiffy's you get Carole's set-up with two ounces of vodka. I wouldn't say it was a hot number. Not something anybody going into business has to know how to mix although some of my customers tell me they show bars here and there how to make it. Customer brought in a cook book once for me to autograph had this La Bandida as the specialty of our house. Must cost us heavy business from strangers looking to get a drink in New York who happen to know that book. I go with Jimmy on that—a bar that had a specialty like that, it would have to be the only one open for me to go in there. I don't think of it as a specialty, it's just something we do.

I was in Boston and I went into the Ritz with some friends who told the bartender who I was. The next thing I knew he set up this pink bubble bath in front of me compliments of the house. He didn't even have to look it up.

"We have people asking for it all the time" he lied. "We put maraschino in for the color. We call it El Bandito Ritz. How come you spell yours that cockeyed way?"

I don't know why I listened to that Jimmy Perse.

"Ignorance" I said.

I smoked that Kodak Kent, I drank that El Bandito Ritz. Certain things you have to do in this world.

5

Allen McGarvey, tired of having his ear banged about subscriptions, stopping at the bar on his way out to talk to Who is that gorgeous redhead? was a whole celebrity scene even if they saw it wrong. He was talking to me, not her. Nobody with sense would figure he took that detour across the room to ask the bartender a dumb question but that was it.

"What's good Stiffy?"

"You're asking me what's good. That's what everybody wants to know from you. From me Chivas is good."

He signed me off. "No time. What do you like in the market these days?"

Some joke him asking me that. The man didn't fool me, he was stalling to be near Carole. Carole gave him a break. She leaned around and asked him—

"Did you do that to Harbor Oil today?"

"All the ills of mankind are laid on me."

You see he didn't answer the question.

"What would you think of reaching inside your pocket, taking out a copy of your Market Letter and letting me just scan it while you take a real short one. I'll give it right back." She acted it out so it would be easy for him to understand.

"It could be dangerous."

"I just got back from India. I have all my shots."

Frank came up behind them in time to hear Carole's bid for the Letter and joined the party. He put in his two cents.

"Wait. It's coming out with filter tips next month."

You could hear the razz in his voice. McGarvey looked at him like he was tapioca. Not much fun in that man. Not used to being butt in on.

"Yes. Filters. See you, Stiffy. Good evening, Mrs Lane." He took in Greg Wyman who came with Frank. "See you, Wyman."

And shavings on your shoes, fella, for Frank.

Out he went. You could hear it around the room That's Al McGarvey. You didn't have to say The Wall Street guy.

Now Carole took up Frank. "Our hero. I hear you went back into Harbor just in time to get out. Why don't you talk to him, Greg?"

"What am I going to tell him? Stocks go up and down?"

"Chase him out of your office. You have Al McGarvey throwing money at you. You don't need Frank."

"We can use it all. We're not proud."

Frank said "I've been right all along on Harbor. That's a good stock. My timing is off, that's all."

"Ah, timing. You walk into an elevator shaft when there is no elevator and you say your timing is off.''

''We all make mistakes'' Gleason said.

''We all don't make nothing but mistakes.''

''That's true'' Gleason admitted. ''Take me, I win some and I lose some. But when I lose it's a beaut.''

Greg nodded his head, glum. Human weakness all around and he only gets three percent out of it each way.

Carole kept after Frank like she was his seat belt he didn't put on. ''I don't know where you get your information. You could have gone into Time Inc today with McGarvey and had five points.''

She didn't know about tomorrow yet when it turned out the market had the wrong Time.

Did that wave the old red flag. Frank had a hard day at the office and he had to listen to this. His nose got big. His lips bulged. His eyes revved up and went around the room. ''McGarvey! McGarvey! I heard what McGarvey said. Those were sheep out there.'' He said Sheep like you wouldn't want to be one, no sir.

''Okay okay okay. Peace. All the same the stock went up. And Lorillard too. That's his stock.''

''Oh come on. How do you know it's McGarvey's stock?''

''Well it is.''

''How do you know?''

''It's in the Letter.''

''How do you know it's in the Letter?''

''Everybody knows.''

''Everybody knows.''

''Well they do. It was in the Times.''

''Did you see it in the Times?''

''Somebody said it was in the Times.''

If you listen to that conversation it tells you something about dealing with a woman. A man your age is going live with women the rest of his life one way or another and you better learn you can't just take up things with a woman like with a man. Listen to the logical way Frank argued trying to get at the facts. One two three. I'm real high on Carole but you have to grant she said things there she didn't know anything about. Hearsay things. They just happened to add up by accident to her being right, the same way you can be right in the lottery. You're right but that doesn't make you right. That isn't a system you can bet on like science or logic. A man wouldn't risk stock market money on that, only lottery tickets. No question about it Frank was wrong and Carole was right but that's not the point. Women have a mind set to think What all the time, they don't have the routes to think Why. That's how you can tell if a man has a female nature, if you get into an argument with him and he can't handle Why.

It works the other way too. You get a woman who can talk Why with you and you better keep an eye on her going both ways. Frank, if he keeps pushing Why on her, pretty soon she'd see he has her in a corner and she'd say she's had enough of that discussion, she doesn't want to talk any more about it, change the subject.

"Okay okay I don't want to talk about it any more."

See what I mean? You can't deal too logically with a woman. It upsets them. How they get the right answers is a mystery. The fact is Time was up, and if Frank never heard of Harbor Oil that day he would be better off but that's not the point.

Anyhow, Frank Doelger was somebody I thought was one of the smarter traders around and he put on a show like that while I was looking at him. Sure of himself too so you want to go along with his ideas, like you ask Where is City Hall and he tells you left right right left right and there it is. Penn Station.

"This time I've got it right." Slammed his hand down on the table it would have raised a blister on a catcher's mitt.

"Don't do it Frank."

"Don't do what?"

"Whatever it is. I hear Harbor Oil again, Frank. You have to stop that. You have so much going for you and you do these things."

Me, I'da just said to the man It's your money, but Mrs New York Cool was taking on this grown man for a project even if he was fifteen twenty years younger. Going save him. Had that concerned look. Had that You fell and hurt yourself look. Signing on as sister, momma, pal, lover, and he's got a devil's look on his face.

"I hear you, no more Harbor Oil. Tomorrow we clear the deck and we go into—" he gave it a tada "Swimsuit Corporation of the USA."

Everybody took it for a lousy joke. They didn't give him anything back. He had to push. "I mean it. I've made a decision. I'm going into Swimsuit."

He made it sound serious enough so Carole had to say something to find out what he was talking about.

"You could use a good psychiatrist. Do you realize that I see the books and if I wasn't loyal to Sy I would be glad to sell all the Swimsuit I own and put it in pale blue chips?"

"I'm not talking about the stock. Anybody can see I'm not Greg's number one stock picker. Even I can see that. I have an offer from Swimsuit to go in as vice president for sales."

It didn't take long for Carole to pass that through Be serious to You're not kidding? and Do you really mean it? and signal she believed by putting her arms around him for a momma-size smooch. Almost tipped her hat off, she had to break away to grab it.

Then she tells him, after all this time egging him on to take a job with her company—she tells him she has to fix it up with Sy Simon. He's only the president.

"You mean I don't have a job?"

"You have the job. We need you. I'll take care of Sy. Can you come in tomorrow morning around eleven?"

"I'll be there."

She made a fist and punched him. "Frank, I'm so happy I could scream." She made a small tight one, like you let out of the neck of balloon.

"I don't know that I think too much of this" Greg said "losing a good customer like Frank."

I felt a little bit the same way, losing Frank. I should have been glad for him, and for Carole having her way on that, but I felt a little bit down. As though he was getting away from me. He wasn't that big a friend of mine then, more of a customer, so I had no right to that feeling, but there it was. I guess even then, that early, it was coming to me from the stratosphere, that something was going on between Frank Doelger and me.

"I won't let you down" Frank said to Greg. "I'll stop in now and then and make a few mistakes."

"I feel better already" Greg said.

Eight

STRINKS

1

MALCOLM MAY tell you I'm a long way getting to the point. Tell him the point doesn't mean a thing unless you have something to hold onto it with. Like on a pencil you can't use just the point.

Now you have something to hold onto, who we were, how we all got into this Swimsuit Corp thing.

Edna and I took some lectures they had Sunday afternoons at the 92nd Street Y dealing with books. One book we had was about a bridge falling in South America. One of those places down there. That was the point, the bridge went down. Happened right at the beginning so we could have closed the book and gone home, but there would be nothing to hold onto that event with and we would forget all about it. Small number of people involved, five six. Small bridge. Small country.

The rest of the book was about how those people all happened to be on that bridge at that time instead of five six different places. Didn't have anything to do with the bridge going down, nothing about the bridge inspectors and the mayor taking from the contractors, the usual reasons. Never mentioned. This book was about the people getting to the bridge, their life stories.

Would be the same stories if the bridge held up and they got across except you can't beat a bridge going down with everybody for a way to end a story. That's something you can hold on to. The the fact is the bridge would have come down the same no matter who was on it even if those particular people being on it made that bridge going down more interesting than any number of other bridges going down with even more people. Like they say, getting there is half the fun. A whole lot more than half for those particular people. Yeah.

If I had it to do I would stick to the point of why it went down instead of who was on it.

On the Swimsuit deal, if it wasn't these particular people it wouldn't be this particular event. Take away any one of us, not only wouldn't it happen that particular way it wouldn't happen at all.

Tell that to Malcolm if he gives you any trouble.

Now we got everybody in position we can get to the point, the merger.

I know as much about Swimsuit Corp as anybody including Sy. Probably as much as everybody put together after working on the Case for Harvard with those two kids Dean Dunn sent down. Man they were into everything. Made everybody remember who said what when, who controlled the stock yesterday, who had it today. They wrote it up for the class of 1970. You could look it up at the B School. All I had to do was say what I knew and take questions.

Start with these two fellas Samuel P. Simon and Joseph McD. Lane sitting down at the same table for lunch in the cafeteria at the Dallas Show. Jammed, no place else to sit. Nine tenths of what goes on in this world is just plain luck, good or bad. Mind if I sit here with you? Sit right down. If some other seat was open nearer the cashier McD would have sat there and we wouldn't have any part of this event but Edna playing the piano at Stiffy's Wall Street Uptown Bar. People going on their ways and no bridge there at all.

Sy and McD knew each other but not that much, weren't even sure of each other's names till they passed their eyes down the lapel to the Exhibitor badges.

"Winsome of California, that is some line. Do you live out there Joe?"

Listen the way he said that, like he was cooling out after singing in the synagog. Sy had me out to the bra mitzver of his niece where I heard it. They don't do much on hymns with beginnings and sign-offs like we do at Second Zion. Could be the latest Last Wave Jazz, begins anywhere and ends where they say. They do mostly solos, people out of the congregation taking turns going up.

Most of the singing you can't find the tune at all, you get the impression they're dummying words as they go. You know how people sing along on a song they never heard before and don't want you to know? Say verse number two of The Star Spangled Banner. The name of that verse out to be

Don't know where I'm at
Don't know where I'm going

Ole Burl Ives type song. That whole verse is like when you go into And the rockets red glare. Do we go up or do we go down on that next? Do we wait two or do we come right in and how loud? What words you suppose come here after this about the foe's Holy Ghost? Inkadinkadoo. When you're faking along like that it's a joyful feeling to land where you know what's coming next. Hey, June after moon and Hey right there on middle E. You're not going get anything as easy as that in The Star Spangled Banner but you always got wave and brave. You come out strong on that, want everybody to know they've been singing those particular words all your life. Then back mumbling.

You can leave that out if you want. I don't want those good buddies giving Malcolm a hard time about sponsoring communist writings. There are worse songs than Star Spangled Banner. Ima Sumac sings them all the time.

That was my impression of what was going on there at this little girl's bra mitzver. Sy went up and did a turn and you could hear how being exposed to that religious type singing slipped him into the way he talked basically. That's my theory. Could be because I didn't know the language. Fact is he didn't either, he told me later, just learned to make the sounds and give it the feeling. I was getting the hang of it myself. If they'd called me up you couldn't tell me from a visiting rabbi from Ethiopia. I had on the beanie. I could do a little E minor scat and pass okay. This little girl they had the event for, she was going talk just like Uncle Sy.

"My home is Evanston outside Chicago. I have the midwest. How about you? You live in New York, Sam?"

"Where else? I come out here to see a few stores. That Chicago must be a territory for a line like yours. Do you have the department stores?"

"Oh yes indeed I do. There are no house accounts in any territory I cover. Sam, if anybody ever tried to do that to me I'd be gone in ten minutes."

By that Sy understood somebody was trying. Sy's middle initial P stood for Potsdammer, and he knew that who would be trying was his second cousin Gary Potsdammer, head man at Winsome. Sy didn't know if he wanted to get into that now with a fella just sat down with a sandwich two minutes ago. Bastard cousin Gary Potsdammer would be the first to see there was no use paying a salesman ten percent to go in and do nothing but pick up the order when that's all he got to break the door down in the first place. Winsome was a real strong house. Big stores planned to buy it no matter what. Styles could be a little off, they still bought. Easier to do business that way than starting over every year with Okay who's on first? So let's talk to that Lane about that big commission he's drawing down. Let's take the majors into the house. Tell him the factsa life.

I know all about those factsa life. I had to study up on that. Doing business with big stores they tell you to chip in for their advertising. You wait three months to get paid and you give them an extra two percent discount for you waiting. You mark down goods so they can celebrate their anniversaries. Yeah you pay for their party. They tell you something comes in damaged you make it good on their sayso. Some little store tells you the same thing you tell them to shove it, take it up with the truck company. You keep a warehouse of inventory so they can show nothing but samples. That way they don't have to pay the rent, you pay it. You build their displays and you pay their sales girls. They rent you their windows. How about that, rent you the windows.

The real factsa life is that no store bigger than you can see from one end to the other knows how to make a living even with all that extra. There's nothing for the stockholders till they get to the financials from you paying your charge account late. That's the last thing they want, you paying up your charge on time. All that other stuff they do is just getting ready to to charge you the interest. I know all about that. I looked into it when we took in Financials Unlimited. That's called Economy of Scale.

You wind up doing so much business and losing so much money with these stores you call in the man in the territory and tell him you can't afford his commissions. Gary's going take care of those accounts himself over the telephone. But don't you worry, McD—this frees you up to put in more time with those little bastard accounts that do all this complaining about damaged goods and so on. You can build them up. All you have to do is spend a little more time out there away from home. Yeah. At that point Lane would go out and get himself another line.

Sy had a pretty good picture of all that happening because no matter what cousin Gary did it came out in Sy's mind That's exactly what that prick Gary would do. Some people affect you like that. No way they can do anything right. I'm that way with presidents of the United States. They can lay a wreath on a grave and I say Yeah they killed him, now they got the photo opportunity. Gary was from the Potsdammer branch that went west carrying their minority stock in the old family business on Long Island, the old American Notions and Worms Company that Sy built up into Swimsuit Corporation of the USA.

One day Sy noticed this bank in Texas was voting nine percent of his stock and cousin Gary wasn't voting any. 200,000 shares disappearing from one account and 200,000 showing up in another, you naturally assume that's the same 200. He called up cousin Gary to tell him they were going public and, by the way, he noticed about the stock. He assumes Gary gave it to the bank to hold in some trust? Hey Gary?

"I sold it" Gary said.

That threw Sy, not that there had been any great friendship. With some people, family doesn't mean a thing, just somebody else thinking he has the franchise to walk in the office without knocking and telling you he needs to borrow from you because somebody you hardly knew married somebody you didn't know at all and spermed out this cousin. Gary always gave Sy the feeling he didn't want to be too close because Simons never knew how to make money the way Potsdammers did so Simons might want to borrow.

"Why didn't you offer it to me? I would have taken it up."

"You didn't ask."

"You didn't say it was available."

No comment there. Leaving it to Sy to talk. That type guy.

"Do you mind telling me who it is? I would like to get on a personal basis with him like between you and me. All I have is the name of the bank holding the stock."

"If he wants you to know who he is he'll tell you."

"Okay cousin. See you at somebody's funeral." Maybe yours if everything works out okay.

He didn't know if he wanted to get into that right now with Lane in the cafeteria. If he thought Gary was a prick, Lane probably thought so too. Hard to avoid thinking it. So here'd be a man you just met having a poor opinion about you on account of your cousin. Let it go for later if there was a later. I never knew Lane. By the time I knew Carole he was dead fooling around in a little airplane, learning to fly.

"Sam, I was looking at your line in Josey's last week. That's beautiful merchandise." So they back and forthed, telling each other who they sell, McD asking how long Sy was in business and if he traveled anybody. Sy telling him he'd just laid on enough capacity to cover the country but he was still doing all the selling himself from the showroom and at a few road shows and he was spread thin. Shouldn't be out there at all, ought to be inside keeping up the quality, where they got their reputation.

Two guys looking at each other, liking each other's style, seeing if there's a con in it somewhere. Is this Lane for real or some flasher Winsome is easing out, big talker looking for a place to start complaining. Is this Simon one of those 7th Avenue characters who happened to cut two good lines back to back and from now on it's Tell them anything.

We're talking 1938, an Irishman and a Jew and it wasn't the movies. We had Father Coughlin then, the biggest thing on radio since the piano player on Dr Strasska's tooth paste program, people were talking about him becoming president of the United States. This can be a crazy country on a rainy day. I figure one out of three is available for any nut head comes along even in sunshine. Some day we're going go crazy here and try to get out of it tomorrow and there won't be tomorrow. This Coughlin was preaching that Hitler was all right with him.

These two white guys sat there over their tuna fish looking at each other with their blood. Like black and white look at each other. Is this guy okay? Never mind about the line and the accounts, is this guy okay as a guy?

"When you come east sometime look me up. Maybe we can have lunch together. I could show you what we do."

"I'll do that, Sam."

"My friends call me Sy."

"Glad to know you, Sy. We'll be seeing each other."

Lane didn't mention that his friends called him McD. His mother called him his whole name Joseph and made a big point of it so Carole never called him anything but Joseph for the sake of harmony in the family. People have these hangups about names. One day they're going give everybody the next number like in the Supermarket, get it over with. You see.

"Your boss Gary Potsdammer is a distant cousin of mine. Don't hold it against me."

"I know some people don't like Gary. I always found he'd do exactly what he said he would."

That's better than nothing. Left open though whether the things he said he was going do were suitable.

2

That was one sweet partnership. McD got the business and Sy delivered the goods. In a couple three years they had their pick of accounts, and McD was dating Carole, the new redhead model Sy's wife found modelling fur coats at Bergdorff's.

Comes the war, this fresh-married fella with one eye that looked off, and the other fella with the stiff knee and the kid who was going be in one of those iron lungs like living in a hot water tank from then on, they had no place in the service, but McD came up with a contract for hammocks. According to the two guys from the B School Swimsuit Corp in three years made 942,171 canvas hammocks. There must be SS hammocks in the original cartons in the basement of every building in DC. Wouldn't surprise me to pick up a paper tomorrow and see a big ad for them by some Army and Navy Surplus.

They made 334,860 swim suits the same three years. Couldn't get fabric or labor for any more. The stores treated those suits like subscriptions to McGarvey's Market Letter. Psst. Just got a dozen SS suits in. Get down here before noon and I'll have one put away for you. People would buy them didn't want them, just to stay in good with the store, be in place for the next favor.

Lane came up with the idea to put on shows in the stores like art exhibits.

"I don't know about that" Sy said.

"If we had a good designer and gave him a free hand we would be the talk of the Industry."

Industry wasn't a word that appealed to Sy. Sounded like something you stamped out but what were you going do, that's how they talked these days. The most you could say for Industry was it was better than Racket.

"Do we need a designer on our own payroll? Haven't we got designs?"

They hired Orloff Chandelier away from Little Miss Missy and told him there wasn't anything too far-out to cut a sample of. You tell a designer anything like that and he comes in early and stays late working off his dreams. Wasn't any outlandish thing Orloff could think of that McD didn't say Give it a whirl, we can make it landish with our reputation. Sy would say Not for us, then he'd make it with loving care and say Not bad.

SS put out creations you would say looked like your grandmomma in a bustle dress. Bathing suits with bows. High collars. They made suits from materials that melted like sugar if you put them in the water. One season they got their hands on a truckload of gold lamé.

What does the war effort need with gold lamé? Are you going make tank covers with it? SS did a whole line with that gold lamé, eight pounds per suit. It would take pontoons to float Gertrude Ederle in a suit like that.

Jesus kid. You don't know Al McGarvey, you don't know Gertrude Ederle. It doesn't make any difference, hasn't a thing to do with what Malcolm wants you to write about. Look it up under F, First Woman To Swim The English Channel. For your own satisfaction. A man can't know too much and you never know what little thing you know turns out to be important. That's what science is, adding up a little this and a little that.

Gertrude Ederle. Chunky woman wearing goggles about the time the fella with the pipe was prime minister of England. Dawes. I was always interested to know if she had on a bathing suit. Pictures showed her with this inch of black grease all over, you couldn't tell.

McD sent these classy outfits around the country and they put on the shows. Filled up the store windows on 5th Avenue. Got free pages in magazines with the models made mean-looking by starvation. Standing there spread-legged not giving a damn where ConEd guys were working. Ready for a shootout on account of a couple buttons and bows. Sold everything before they got the boxes open.

That gave McD his big idea to put a pink Sold sticker on the skirt. Just a little joke at the time like putting the tiger in the tank and blanking out the eye in the shirt ad. Not ideas you fuss over first, like is it better with a lion than a tiger. Should we take the fella's eye or give him braces on his teeth. Ideas of that quality aren't thought up, they're just there when you open your mouth. Hey show a tiger coming out that tank. Put a Floyd Gibbons on his eye. Sew a pink Sold sticker on it.

In no time at all women couldn't stand it till they were seen in these bathing suits with the Sold sticker. Patented it. Won a big law suit from Winsome when Gary tried copying it.

You had a swim suit with a pink dot, you had the best. You had a Caddy. Yeah let's say it, you had a Pinkasso.

3

Joseph McD. Lane didn't have a full enough plate, he had to go up in that airplane. It was a hard landing on everybody. Him. Carole. Sy. The corporation. Big loss for the corporation, a man like McD going out.

Sy went into a decline. Didn't want to do anything different. Kept cutting the same styles, might change a bow from here to there or change a color but basically doing the same things. Same as leaving the furniture where it was and the clothes hanging in the closet if some dear one passes on. Won't work. Gets to be like an automobile going uphill telling you in your foot it wants to change gear even if you can gas the speed up to where it was before. Hard thing for a businessman to think about switching from the gear he's used to till things in there go *rump rump rump* and he has to ask the bank for a boost. That's one thing I keep pushing on the boards I'm on. Are we coasting along or are we out front? Are our people afraid to make mistakes? Anybody doesn't make mistakes isn't doing.

Carole always told herself she didn't know about business, and what you tell yourself turns out to be how it is. Style, though, she knew style. Had her foot on the style pedal and felt things heading for a stall unless Sy got the message to change gear. Salesman try to tell him, he'd put on his moose uniform with the antlers and tell them Get on out there and Sell like McD used to. Carole try to tell him, he patted her hand.

"Bikinis, is that our niche? Is that why we're number one? Following fads? If we do bikinis we get one season out of it and bingo! our character is gone."

"It isn't only bikinis. It's the whole last season look."

Oh my, that thunderstruck him. "You couldn't say it better. The last season look. What a headline! Reliability. Quality. Tradition. THE LAST SEASON LOOK! Call the agency."

The agency came in for another bloomer party in Palm Beach and Sy made The Times. "SPORTSWEAR EXEC SAYS NO WOMAN WOULD PAY A REAL PRICE FOR SOMETHING SHE COULD MAKE OUT OF AN OLD NECKTIE."

Carole looked around for help. Saw this Lord & Taylor guy killing himself at Greg Wyman's and started working on him to come on over to her shop. Coming from Lord & Taylor with that confident face he'd have to be listened to even if he hadn't been the swimsuit buyer. Matter of fact he did corsets for them. All Frank would need was a little steer from her what to push and how to handle Sy.

"Don't lose any momentum. Whatever else happens you have to get us bikinis."

"Show me pictures of what I want."

She showed him Winsome's ads.

"It will be a pleasure."

4

Out around Lloyd's Neck on the Island Swimsuit Corp had a test beach where they saw how the creations looked up against real sand. They owned it going way back when Sy's granddaddy had the fishing worm business and then the bait shop leading on to putting in a few bathing suits for the tourists. They did okay and hired out the suits to be made by natives. That's how the business got started, a little notions store with this specialty of worms because of the location. In McD's time they expensed the beach up with cabanas and fake palm trees, made it a location for picture-taking. Two three of those movies you saw after the war with the troops landing on Tararara happened on the SS test beach on Long Island. Where the two mile condo is now.

"Take the line to the beach" Sy said. "We'll show our new vice president how we do things around here."

Nice way to do a day's work. Everybody into that back to nature feeling with shoes off. Wearing the porthole sunglasses and the straw hats with the manana fringe.

Carole thought things are so nice it might be a good idea to have a talk with Frank to be sure nothing was spoiled. She'd been watching how he went about things. Frank had kind of a sudden way. You know, like a busy waiter coming out of the kitchen. She was seeing a picture of him suddenly busting out Bikinis I want bikinis. Couldn't do that with Sy. He owned the business. You had to proceed a little.

It would be best if the whole project didn't blow up right there on the beach with Sy having a huge heartburn that this corset buyer was telling him how to do swimsuits. She pulled Frank away from the picnic spread to have a little talk behind the cabana about how to shape up for a talk with Sy.

"Sy is a reasonable and wonderful man. Once he develops confidence in you he will do anything in the world you say. Take it slow."

That was a little different from what she said before, which was get it done fast. Didn't make any difference. If first she said slow he wouldn't hear her anyhow. Frank didn't know slow.

"I know about five things, including The world is round. Another is Slow is too late. If I get talked out of that I might as well stay home."

"All right, not slow but not too fast. Remember we're an old well-established firm. We have nine salesmen out there and they need a godfather. Don't get bumped off."

"You'll get your bikinis."

Just like Joseph. All that confidence. Carole loved it.

I didn't know this was going on except what I heard at the bar. I had no particular interest in it. That SS wasn't one of my stocks. That was all being arranged for me to come in at the right time. Weird isn't it, all these arrangements going on in the world and a certain time it's your turn to come along and fit in like you're a particular part on the Ford assembly line. Did you ever stop to think that could be how it is?

So they're out on the beach. Orloff and Carole work out of the cabana with the girls, send them out one at a time with a hands-on to set up a bustle or pick up a shoulder strap. Girls go out, show off, trudge through the sand to the fake palm tree to get their picture taken. Stand there with a hand on your hip looking mean. No telling who may see your picture and want you for a cover. I mean mean, like when momma told us You take that dissatisfied look from your face right this minute or I'll give you a reason.

Yeah, real nice way to work, with your shoes and socks off and your feet in the warm sand. Shirt sleeves. Shirt tails hanging out. The buckeye sunglasses and the hats with the manana fringe. Back to nature.

Easel there with a sign the photographer was supposed to get into his shots—

WATERSIDE WEAR WITH THE EXCLUSIVE PINK DOT

Kept blowing off. Sy got tired seeing people keep putting it back up and went over and put holes in it with a ballpoint and tied it to the easel with dental floss. Have to do all the thinking around here. No wonder I'm the boss.

Went back to his director chairs in the shade of a fake palm tree. He showed Frank the dental floss and gave him some advice.

"Don't leave home without it."

Okay, I never said I knew all about everything. I'm giving you that from Sy Simon. He knows more about running a business than I do, except my own business. I'm only into the big picture on these other businesses.

Rose had a chair too. Any kind of emergency, Sy said Rose! and she took care of it. Little rusty-haired woman with arthritis knuckles and complicated glasses, you wonder how she could see with them. Type that learned everything in night school. Came in with Sy's daddy. Got paid in the low thousands. If she said she's going leave they'd double her to stay. Only she'd never say that till it was time to retire and the new girl was broken in.

Sy bought office supplies from her brother who couldn't make a living if he didn't have four sisters who told whoever did the buying where they worked He's my brother.

Would have been a scandal in the government or some big public company, nepotistical type thing, but what real guy wouldn't do it for somebody whose sister worked for his daddy? Rose knew Sy would take care of her old age if he didn't go bankrupt. Even if he did.

They don't do it like that any more. The people you can tell your troubles to today, they're always one step down from anybody who can do anything about it, and you can't get to those people. That's why they hire those other people to tell your troubles to.

Sy was Master of Ceremonies. He told Frank what act they're in, and the girls came out and did their turn.

"And now our El Chateau. Taken from an original at the Louver. Notice the riffles on the ruffles. This is La Deuce, named for the divine Eleanor. Notice the double French hip. Here's one we'll have to limit cutting on because the firm that makes these velours is backed up three years with orders from the finest furniture maker in Portugal. Renoir. Is that something?"

Hoot de toot toot. Every model that came out Carole made a little move for Frank showing him what's wrong. Scissors sign for a bow to come off. Made a little face like the sun was getting to her when she flipped a collar. Frank didn't say a word, could hardly believe girls with figures like these would want to show up on the beach in all that astrofogastro. Carole was right. There had to be some changes made.

"So what do you say?" Sy wanted to know. "Is that a line or is that a line?"

Being fair to Carole, Frank went what for him was the diplomatic route.

"Do women swim in those suits?"

Sy showed the Waterside Wear poster to Frank in case he missed it. "Who swims? Low end customers swim. Our customer shows up, gets a tan and goes back to the cabana. She wouldn't be caught dead swimming. She is strictly waterside. If she wants to get wet she takes a shower. We had a survey taken. An older woman with money in the bank is a profile of our customer."

"I don't know, I see a lot of high end women swimming."

"Breast stroking."

"That's an older woman."

"Okay, an older woman here and there but mainly a woman in the water is somebody's daughter on an allowance. Not our customer. We sell mothers. When they get their own charge accounts they want the Pink Dots."

"Winsome sells bunches of high priced swim suits."

Winsome was a name you didn't mention around Sy.

"You don't have to worry about Winsome. Do you know what they call their creations? Products. Would anybody you had to think two minutes about in the fashion business call what they do products? Forget Winsome."

"I'd like to but I went around to the Buying Offices before I came to work. They all said Winsome is moving in on us at the top of the line."

"When you inspire our sales force the way McD Lane used to they will move out."

Carole read in Sy's face Small Craft Warning flying. Frank got up and began pacing amongst the models standing around waiting for the Dismiss, poking at the bows and the bustles and the sailor collars and the buttons and other garbanzo. Kicking up sand. He picked up a shears sticking up from Orloff's work basket.

"Underneath all this spinach I can see styles. Look." Began cutting bows off the Renoir like Carole signalled and a few more he thought of himself. "Simplified. Isn't that better?"

Out came the moose uniform. "Young man—"

"I just want to make a point." Snatched off a row of bells running under the boobs of the Belles of St. Mary's. "Changes the whole feeling."

"Young man—"

Carole saw everything was going fall apart.

"He doesn't mean this minute" she said.

"Don't I though" Frank said. "We have two weeks to have a line ready before the market opens."

You want to get an idea of Sy Simon take a look at his hands. Man his size with hands like that. Lindbergh the aviator had a Frenchman friend by the name of Dr Carl Something, one of their top surgeons. To keep in practice he kept a match box and some string in his pocket and when he wasn't operating he'd tie knots with one hand inside the box. I don't know if it was one of our American safety match boxes or one of those dinky boxes they sell you in France. Either way, that's a hell of a trick to do in your pocket with one hand. Okay, maybe even harder with two but that's not the point, I'm telling you about Sy's hands. Here was a fella had hands you knew could do something highly refined even if you don't know what it was. The way Frank was going on about these beautiful creations offended a man with hands like that. He put on his antlers.

"Young man you have to have a lot of money to talk to the boss this way. Young man no more free lance designing. Hand over those shears young man."

He started up off his seat to make it happen. Frank had no objection. He was done with that part, made his point. He handed over the shears and dipped in behind the neck of Marietta, a Las Vegas model they had, and peeked. He read out

"DRY CLEAN DO NOT WASH. What kind of tsimmis is swim suits you can't get wet? These labels have to go."

You throw something ethnic at a Jewish person, he'll pick it up no matter what else he's doing. I appreciate that. You say to me Collard greens give you cancer, it takes me awhile to hear the cancer part. Collard greens are mine. Everybody's got cancer. Sy hung up there halfway off the chair. How did this fella get to tsimmis? Maybe on his mother's side?

"Who is tsimmis to you?"

"I don't know, you hear it around. Is it something I shouldn't say in front of ladies?"

"Tsimmis you eat. It is made out of sweet potatoes and carrots and stew meat and a slice of mattress. Now young man you know more about tsimmis than you know about waterside wear. See if you can get used to this, Mr Tsimmis. Every department store in the country has a four foot picture of General MacArthur in the stock room with big letters WE SHALL RETURN. Not to Swimsuit Corporation of the USA they won't. Over my dead body young man. Positively no creation goes from us without the label lockstitched in so when they try to return it because it shrank you can show them the marks where the label was cut out. "

"I'm not talking about labels. I'm talking about fabrics that don't need them."

"Without the label every five units we ship we'll get six back. This is a rich man you brought us?" he appealed to Carole. "He's personally paying for the returns?"

"We can talk about the labels later" Carole said.

"Sure" Frank said. "Let's talk about bikinis. Where are the bikinis?"

I read somewhere you can hold your breath for seven minutes if you have to, like underwater with an octopus hanging on your ankle. One is more like it. While Frank was going around with the shears Orloff set a world record for holding his breath no matter what the Guinness was to that day. Seeing these terrible things Frank was doing to his artwork that was a sure pop for nine pages in Vogue, he couldn't get organized to breathe till Frank said the magic word. Bikini. Orloff let out the world record breath.

"Vendal! Beginis? Strinks?"

Frank put it to him. "You don't think you can be in business without strinks do you?"

Orloff looked to Sy to save the company.

"Mr Zimon!"

Sy saw everything was hopeless and no use aggravating an ulcer trying to educate a lunatic in the fine points of waterside wear.

"No bikinis young man. There is no room on a bikini to put McD Lane's Sold dot. Nice try. You have excellent ideas young man but they are not for this firm."

Carole had to jump in. "Sy. Listen to him. He's right."

Seems easy for Carole to say now. Took guts at the time. Profiles In Courage type thing. Here was Joseph's partner, a fella Joseph would have walked on fire for, standing up for Joseph's ideas and being told he had to turn around on a dime—had to be done in two weeks to head off trouble that could be three four years down the road. Might not be there at all if a strong experienced guy like Sy stood his ground and let those other firms lose their positions and their mark-ups selling strinks. People always predicting all kinds of things based on a little bit going on now. Get into next year, you find out only about ten percent of it happened. Was it up to an ex-model who had a lotta money in the bank on account of Joseph and Sy to tell Sy he was wrong and the corset buyer was right?

"How can he be right? On a bikini there is no place to put the dot. How can he be right?"

Frank stepped up to bat again. "Paste the dot on her can. Do you mind?" He took the shears back from Sy. He cut a pretty good circle the size of a dime out of a swatch lying there from his sneak attack on La Renoir. "We'll package it in a neat little bag with that new glue that sticks your fingers together."

Marietta was wearing a suit that if you cut off the skirt there wasn't too much left. Frank did that. Took the trademark, looked around for glue or scotch tape but the best he had was his hand. Good enough. Socked the label to Marietta and held it there.

"Hey that's real cute" Marietta said.

"This gompany is vinished." Orloff walked down to the water looking for a safe place to drown himself.

4

Nice day out there on the water, a few boats. Sy looked up from the aggravation, noticed a fishing yacht going by. Fella on the forward deck with glasses aimed at the SS party. Fella in the steering well had a camera up, maybe stealing pictures for another Tararara epic. Sy had a different idea. He got up there in his manana hat and his porthole glasses and stood there like a statue looking at them so they knew he saw them.

"Friends from Winsome stealing a look at our line. That prick Gary Potsdammer." He hollered "Tell Gary Potsdammer to screw himself."

They went on along the shore around the point, those fellas making believe they were taking pictures of the landscape features for a movie but Sy knew they were faking it.

"I hope they got an eyeful. It's the last look anybody gets at these numbers. Rose! Tell everybody to pack it up, let's get out of here."

"Pack it up everybody. Mr S says we're finished."

"Tell Carole and Orloff and Vice President Tsimmis we're going straight back to the show room. Call my wife, tell her we're working late tonight, we have to get the whole line re-designed in two weeks." He unloaded on Carole. "Why didn't you tell me we should have bikinis? You know what you say goes.''

She wouldn't say I told you ten times. ''I told you nine times'' she said. ''But I didn't come from Lord & Taylor.''

In Sy's car on the ride back Orloff decided he would rather not look for a new job. He zaw pozzibiliteez.

''Ve can geeve on ze heeps these levish look.''

That grabbed Carole. Sounded like something exciting going on at a beach you couldn't say but looked great in a headline. Seen on the beach at Pltltlsk. Vrbdloskscz. Brand new fashion scene. Bring it up at lunch with Johnnie Women's Wear. See how it played with Verbena. Get the Ambassador to the opening at Bloomie's. What country?

''What's a Slavish look, Orloff?''

''Levish. Levish. On ze heeps ve roll ze cloth many times over. Ve use vor dimes as much goods as nezezzar. Levish.''

''With you all the way.''

5

For the the next six months, while they were turning Swimsuit around on strinks and the Tribute to Poland series and the new slogan Get In The Swim, I worked on my Lorillard. I kept buying and the stock kept going up and I bought on the margin. The more it went up, the more margin, the more I bought.

I don't mean it went straight up. Every stock has an off day now and then and I kept moving up my stops so if a real drop came along I'd be out with a real piece of my profits, but Lorillard never gave up more than a point or two. It wasn't long before I had plenty of leeway so even a few points off didn't shake me.

I dabbled a little on other things too. Things Frank put me into. I used to see Frank all the time at the bar. I would run into him now and then at Wyman's too, but he didn't hang out there as much as before. I couldn't get over being bugged by the way he was in and out of Lorillard and Harbor when I did the opposite and I did better than he did.

When I had a chance I would ask him how he was doing. He wasn't like me, he always let you know what he owned. If he picked a stock he took it into his family. Give him the least opening and he'd show it to you like somebody shows you pictures of his kids. People don't show you pictures unless they think the kids are fully equipped and going make it. With Frank you just opened the door a crack and he shoved in his stock ideas.

I kept an eye on the stocks he said he was in or unloading but it never made particular sense. He won some and he lost some like everybody. Maybe lost more, but I couldn't tell how much he had invested in each.

I tried an experiment on him. Instead of only following his stocks in my head I thought I'd see what happened if I went against him with real money. In that way I would have a more real feeling. I took it up with him in the bar one day.

"You're a savvy guy" I said. "What do you like these days?"

"Oh I'm not much of a trader these days."

"Well you have ideas. I see you studying the books. What do you like right now? What are you doing with your real money?"

You ask and people will tell you the damnedest things. Being in your line of work you must know that. He warmed up. Opened his wallet. Took out the pictures. Now that you asked type of thing.

"Oh I like GE and Nax Pictures. I like a couple of chemicals right now. Emco. Monsanto."

"Liking is one thing. What are you buying? Are you selling anything?"

"Right now?"

"Yeah. With your own money. I think you know what to do with money."

"You know I'm not the smartest investor around."

"You may have had a bad run for awhile but I think basically you know what you're doing. What are you active in right now?"

"I'm not too active right now. I just bought a little GE and Harbor Oil."

"You're back in Harbor again?"

"I'm always in and out of Harbor. I'll get it right some day."

"I betcha."

"I've been buying a little Swimsuit. We're going to make that company go, you watch."

"I betcha. Is all you do on the buy side?"

"I got out of Zenith. I began to think about one product companies. We're a one product company and we're going to change that. We have to get into robes. Maybe blouses. The thing is to do business in more seasons and spread the risks."

"You got it" I said. "I'm in a one product business too. Booze. I'm giving that thought."

"You're diversified. You sell piano music too."

Yeah. Well I heard all I needed. I had some free margin on my Lorillard profits. I bought a hundred shares of what he was selling, Zenith. Then I did something I never did before. I sold shares short I didn't own. I went short a hundred each GE and Harbor and Swimsuit. I battled my conscience on selling Swimsuit short, going against my friends. But hell it was an experiment, only a hundred shares, just to see what happened.

Greg put the orders through. When he finished he hung a heavy look on me and said "You're ordered. You're short GE and SS and HoHo. You're long Zenith."

"Yeah" I said.

He didn't say another word. Signalled me all right he could see I was doing something peculiar with Frank but Greg would never put himself into your business unless he was asked. The commissions were good enough for him. Kept that heavy look on me till somebody stuck his head in the door and brought up new business.

In the next couple weeks I made money on every one of those trades Frank gave me. I didn't make big money on every one, but money is money. Didn't lose on any either.

I didn't take my eyes off Lorillard, the main game. I put in all my cash. I margined all the law allowed. I took an advance on my profit share at the bar. Yeah I was living dangerous. One thing I never did though, I never put Edna into that stock. The stock market wasn't a subject she had any interest in. She had a load of money from her piece of the bar and record royalties and Dill put her in special things he knew about. Slow things. New York bonds. Pennsylvania Railroad. Westinghouse. Steel. Vault Bank things you keep twenty years and there has to be a time they come up out of the water at a price you can sell without apologizing. Not for me. Nothing to make you glow there.

She did notice the checking account we kept together was lower than she'd been used to looking at. There was mostly her part left in there.

"Where's all that money going?"

"It isn't going. It's being saved in the stock market."

"Are you buying a lot of those stocks?"

"Not too many. Mostly one."

"Couldn't you lose? You work for what you've got."

"I'm watching it."

"It takes a lot of your time hanging over there at Greg Wyman's. Doesn't seem like real work. Don't you quit on it sometime, like when a game ends?"

I never thought before about quitting. I just thought about doing. Well yeah, I thought, that's a good idea. Have a place to stop and look around, see where I am. See what it looked like in real money you could spend in a store.

I picked out a number and made up my mind. When I got to that number I was going review everything and consider if it's time to do something else. The number I picked was $250,000 because you could say that a way that would blow the ever-living top off your skull if you grew up on 138th Street. You could say A quarter of a million dollars. Whooee. Did you ever hear of a number like that?

I'm talking clear. I'm talking after tax. In the bank.

That's the number I'm talking about. $24,000 of my own hard-earned money was what I put in one time or other. The rest the market gave me. A quarter of a million dollars!

I watched it moving up toward the number 63 that I had in view and when it got there I multiplied it out to be sure I was right, and that was it. A quarter of a million clear for Arsdur U. Stiff after the margin clerk. After the IRS. And don't forget New York State and the mayor.

First thing next morning I went up to Wyman's to ask Greg what people did when they had that much on top. Whooee. You ever hear anything like that before? A quarter of a million dollars from just having a glow.

Who was coming out of Greg's office but Frank Doelger.

I was still in that experiment seeing how I made out going against his ideas. If he's trading I want to know.

"Look who's here" I said. "Bet a million Doelger."

"We're having a little lull and I ducked in to do a little business. Do me a favor, Stiffy" he said, dropping his voice down to deep secrecy between him and me. "Coast on over to the library table. Bunschli's over there. I could swear he had the Value Line open to our page. Now what the hell would that gang be interested in my company for. See if you can get a quick look."

Easy done. Coasted over. Threw his sleeve on the page as soon as he saw my shadow coming but I could see he was in the Apparels. In the S's. "Hi there Mr B. Just want to take a quick look at—oh I see you're using it. No hurry. I'll get to it later."

"You could be right" I told Frank.

"Thanks. Those bastards." I thought he might tip me another couple stocks but he got away too fast.

7

"I'm thinking I'll cash in that Lorillard" I told Greg.

"Are you in a hurry to pay the tax?"

"Not specially but it seems it might be time."

Wyman used to keep the order slips he was working on in a line across the top of his blotter. My eyes wandered over there, thinking what a nice pattern was made by the pink Sells and the blue Buys tucked into the brown leather lip.

Couldn't help noticing the last one in the line was Frank's pink for a hundred HO.

Right before it was a blue for 500 LL. Same customer number.

Made my mind up then and there what to do. More like something from the outside made my mind up for me. Got the glow. Seeing Frank do the opposite of me on Lorillard inspired me.

"Yeah I got my mind made up. Don't have to think about it. Sell all that Lorillard at the market. Close out my short on Harbor and buy me 10,000 long. Get my feet wet."

Glowing. Candled like an egg. This time going after my first million. Million dollars. $1,000,000. How does that sound? Maybe doesn't sound like that much now but I'm talking about when it was.

"I want you to do something for me, Greg. Anytime Frank trades I want you to do the opposite in my account. I'll sign any paper you want. You do it."

He folded his arms and sat back in his swivel. Hung that heavy look on me like before.

"I can't do that, Stiffy. What Frank does has to be a private matter as far as I'm concerned. You understand that."

Yeah, I could see that. I acted on the spur. It gave Greg Wyman more credit with me, knowing he did things the right way.

Nine

THE WALL STREET CROWD

1

BEFORE YOU could blink it was all over the market that Allen McGarvey the First Kazoo of Wall Street was tooting SS in the Letter and had a syndicate going after the stock.

Could be only a stock play for points. Could be for control. Could be to merge it into Ole Miss Airline he was going after at the same time and then merge on into Near Miss Airline and cast out uneconomicals by the routes like Heard on Wall Street said was in his mind. Looking at it that way, it made good sense. Fill off-time for the Swimsuit models with stewardess bits. Economy of scale.

No use asking him the reason, he said he had nothing to say, then he disappeared from his usual haunts and well-known watering places. The columns went looking the same place you'd look, the dictionary. If you don't know a thing there's always words. Demographics. Marketing. Projections. Cash flow. Any time a writer found a word he put it in a column and the stock was up that day. Synergism. You think about that word. That's some word, man. That's some word to have with you if you're into merger activities. My theory was Carole's legs.

Take the famous war they had over Helen of Troy, upstate town in Greece. The form doesn't say she went to Athens U and came out with big marks. It was her looks. Scale that back to just legs you could have a fella going after this little company to have access. Reasonable. If you don't think that's possible you should be writing about something that hasn't to do with people. Whatever that is. Rocks. If people are in it there isn't a thing too nutty. They had this prime minister in England used to dress up in funny clothes and go down to the redlight district and talk to the girls. Asked them if they didn't think it would be better to clean up their act and come on uptown and get into church work. I'm not talking about some rummy. This is Goldstein, the prime minister, the one they called Israeli.

Over at Swimsuit they didn't know what to think. Sy and Carole had their stock in the company moving up after it sat around the last couple years going nowhere. Business was good, what with the bikinis and all, but not that good. Well thank you, Al McGarvey.

I closed out my little hundred share short. Only time Frank ever steered me wrong. I don't think he bought that stock at all when he said he did, just had it in mind. He wasn't a buyer till he heard McGarvey for sure was a buyer and by then I was already out.

Pretty soon they all began to count. Put all their stock together and they had 12%. That left 88% floating and somebody taking a bite of it every day. I explained how that worked to Edna. We were sitting around the apartment Sunday afternoon just talking about things. She said

"You mean McGarvey can buy that company and Sy and Carole can't do a thing about it? Their own company?"

"That's how it works."

"I never heard of such a thing."

"That's how it is. You better believe it. It can be a funny world." I told her about Goldstein's bag. She said I'd have to show her that in a book.

I said I'd get a book and do that.

"I never heard of buying a company the owner didn't want to sell. If I thought I married a man who believed that I'd go into church work myself."

"There's a lot you never heard of. You never heard of Prime Minister Goldstein."

"I heard of him, I just never heard of him getting dressed up and talking to the girls."

"Now you heard."

"How about you? You made all that money on Kent cigarettes. How about you buying some of that stock and helping them out so McGarvey can't get it?"

"I can't do that."

"Isn't your money as green as McGarvey's?"

"Well yeah but that isn't the thing of it. I have a system. I can't go outside the system."

Saying that made me feel so damn dumb I wish I hadn't. I could have just told her Okay and bought a few shares and lost a few bucks and let it go at that. Now I had to tell her the system.

"I can only buy when Frank sells. I sell when he buys."

"You have some contract with him?"

"You could say that."

"I surely can. Would I be saying the truth? What kind of contract are you talking about?"

How am I going say it. I got a contract with things as they are. I have to do things the way they work. I don't know why it works that way but it isn't up to me to do it some other way. That way I could be a big loser. I don't understand about gravity either but I'm not walking off the roof of any buildings till I see somebody else getting away with it.

I told her about him selling Lorillard when I bought it and buying when I sold. I told her how I missed out on selling Harbor Oil by not doing it right away when I knew he phoned a buy order in from the bar that day. How I was in Harbor again now that he sold and I was making money. I told her about my experiment and how it worked out. I had a personal financial advisor and it didn't cost me a cent of fee for first quality advice. Had to pay deep attention.

"It's like The Man Up There put Frank and me on a seesaw. I'm supposed to stay on till I get the sign to get off. The basic thing about the market is for every seller there's a buyer and I latched on to the one I'm supposed to be working with. I got a feeling all the big winners found that same thing out but they aint saying."

Did I feel dumb. At least I didn't say anything about candled eggs and glowing in the dark.

She looked up at me from where she was sitting at the piano to see if I was in my usual reliable condition. She could see I wasn't into anything peculiar. She didn't know anything about the stock market anyhow except what I told her so she had to believe. She went back to working on arranging Puttin On The Ritz into Everybody Loves My Baby. That's something Edna has her fun with, bringing different songs together.

"Hey that's pretty good what you're doing there."

"I did that last night but you weren't listening."

"Yeah I was, I heard you."

"No you've been off in the woods somewhere since you got into this stock market. I played that last night and I looked for you to see how you liked it and you were looking off in space thinking about the stock market."

"I heard you. I'm just getting around to saying it now."

She kept going deeper into the arrangement, throwing her jaw to the side like she does when it's specially great. Nothing like being deep into something like that. Glowing. Yeah. Not only herself, makes you feel it too, like you're in there with her.

"Okay" she said coming off the song, "if that's how the stock market works. Just the same it seems to me you ought to be able to help your friends out."

"You know me, honey, I'll do what I can. Do me a favor and don't say anything to anybody about this, especially Dill. Bankers trend to go by the book. They don't always see why some things work as a matter of practical experience."

"I'm going to ask Dill to put some of mine into Carole's stock."

"It's your money. I'm not telling you where to spend it. Dill knows about those things. Just don't mention to him about Frank and me on the seesaw."

2

Frank Doelger wasn't stupid, you know. He wasn't a great stock picker but he could figure things out. I wouldn't even say he wasn't a great stock picker, he just wasn't too good on timing. A lot of people see real good how to do things but see it at the wrong time or show up with the wrong tool. Something like that. Plumbers are famous for that. Take Napoleon. Nobody saw better how to beat the Russians than Napoleon. Only he never should have tried it in the winter. If you had it to do though who would you rather make up a plan to take care of the Russians, Napoleon or or one of those presidents we get? The main thing is you would want to call up the weather number first. Any damn fool knows that. You have to be real bright like Napoleon not to know that.

As soon as the rumor hit, Frank knew the ball was coming at him, and if it wasn't right into his glove he might have to go to the right or he might have to go to the left but it was up to him to be there. Sy had no stock sense. That put it up to Frank to do the main thinking like McD Lane did when they went public. McD did all that for Sy. That's what got Carole into the market.

Most natural thing in the world would be for Sy to call his accountant and his lawyer and ask them what he should do, and neither one would have any idea more than the mailman but it would cost a hundred an hour and make Sy think something was going on. What would be going on was the fee meter clicking off that hundred and Al McGarvey taking his company away from him.

Frank knew how to run one of those takeover parties. He'd read all about them. Carole came back from Wyman's with the rumor that it was definite, it was in McGarvey's Letter. He took her right into Sy's office to get cracking.

Sy was on the phone already with a reporter who wanted to catch the next edition in fifteen minutes. He had to have that story right now. That's freedom of the press. That's their freedom to press you to do what they want when they want. The Lakers have the same freedom with the full court press on the fast break. Newspapers need that so they can do enough columns of words for the ads to shine out. It's the ads they're after. Only you kid reporters right out of school are into freedom. Now don't get people after me for beating on this and that amendment. The way it works out, the world we got makes even newspapers look good. It makes even tv look good, if you can see that. Otherwise all we got is politicians and spokesmen of one kind or other.

"I heard of McGarvey" Sy was saying in the phone. "I think I heard of him. Who is he? . . . A position? Personally I never talked to him about taking a position in this company, no. He may have talked to my foreman. If he can sew we can always use a good man with a needle but he should ask through the union . . . How would he be an owner? I'm the owner and I'm not selling . . . Fine. I'm glad he is buying our stock. He is buying stock in a good company . . . No I don't know what you are talking about. You may have a wrong number. What number are you calling?" He held the phone away from his face and asked Frank "What's going on?"

Frank took the phone, talked the fella down and told Rose to shut it off, they would be back from the coast tomorrow.

"So what's all that about?"

Some people if they know something, there is no way you're going find it out except piece by piece. No matter what you ask, these people are going show up at a hard time and say You asked the wrong question. These are the Sinners of Omission the Bible speaks of.

Then you have people who if you ask them a question you don't get any answer till they think through What's in it for me? These are the Sinners on Commission.

Then you have Frank. You ask Frank a question, you get all the answer there is. You may even get a little extra if you don't know any more about the stock market than Sy did and you have to be told about buy-outs and buy-backs, insiders, stockholder rights and disclosure. Moving on over to stockholder lists, attorney fees, accountant fees, war chests, pre-emptives, warrants, convertibles, ten days notice and hardtops. We had greenmail under a different name. Isn't anything on earth that hasn't already been had under another name. We called it blackmail.

Sy was glad he only had to hear that stuff, didn't have to understand it. He hit the jackpot with this Frank Doelger all right. Not only did he have good ideas about bikinis, he was a financial genius.

"You're the general on this. Just keep me posted."

That was a job Frank never had before. Felt good. Knew how to do these things. Knew how to run these wars. Talked some more. Told himself Watch it man, Don't overreact, Don't get into a sweat. Don't basically do the right thing at the wrong time. You know better. Have a game plan and stick to it. Gave himself the same motto Uncle Cuz Foss gave me. Think.

Carole may have had her doubts about Frank being in charge of anything that had to do with stocks but he blew on by with that breezy language. At five o'clock when Rose came in and asked Do you want me to stay? Sy waved her home and an hour later they all decided to have dinner together. Frank was still talking and had a way to go. Sy put in the kind of question the kid asked about the naked queen on a horse.

"How do you know it's McNally? Did you ever think it might be that lame-brain cousin of mine Gary Potsdammer wanting to buy back in now that we're doing so good?"

"It could be both of them in cahoots. It wouldn't make any difference, you have to go through the same drill."

"It might make a difference" Sy said. "Whatsisname might come up with a price I couldn't resist. But Winsome, they can't have it. Isn't that right Carole?"

"Nobody can have it" she said.

As far as she was concerned, the right dollars and she wouldn't care. It wasn't all that important to her to be working on the new lines and jollying the visiting buyers. Wouldn't kill her a bit to play year round golf between the Island and Boca. She could like doing something in an ad agency, whatever they did there. Take charge of fashion pictures. Tell clients the factsa life on department stores. No problem. She had an open offer from Bernbach. Another way to do it was she could go into a buying office and do beachwear. No problem. She could sit on a stool at Stiffy's and drink Bandidas. Good for our image. She had the offer. Sy though when he wasn't working hard he ate. Without the business he would get fat. He would have lunch with his wife who annoyed the hell out of him. He wouldn't move up to President of the Sportswear Association after going through all those chairs. He'd be out the game just when he had it all together with the robe company and the second factory in Idaho and the bikinis. It was more for Sy than for herself she said No sir, nobody was going take that company away from them.

"You heard what the lady said. Nobody can have it" Sy told Frank. "You're the general."

"The company is going to have to buy up some of its stock."

"You're the general."

Next day Frank is in the bar telling me he is a buyer, they're all buyers and anybody who wants that stock is in a war and he doesn't care who knows.

"We pledged our lives, our fortunes and our sacred honor on the company" is what he said. I thought that was pretty good. I never forgot that. The sacred honor part is the best. "To hell with McGarvey and Gary Potsdammer" he said. "Hit that Canadian again."

That was it. If he was stretched in Swimsuit stock, he wouldn't be dabbling back in Harbor Oil. The thing for me to do was to hang in there on HO and let the horses run.

3

Frank got the stockholder list. After Sy and Carole, nobody else had as much as a percent except the jag at that bank in Texas. The rest was in the hands of a zillion stockholders, 5,424 if you want the exact number. Frank could read on the tape every share that changed hands. Best idea was to pick up some stock, not too much to get into a bidding war. Get set to go into action if the opposition ran an ad asking for proxies.

He got a yellow pad from Rose and wrote it down. 2,012,000 shares out at today's price $18 = $63,000,000. Looked at it. Knew something was wrong. Crossed out the 63 and put in 36. Frank had good ideas but he wasn't the best on numbers. Anyhow it isn't that you don't make any mistakes that says how good you are, it's how you get back in the game. Ask Malcolm how he'd like that for one of his Sayings. No charge.

Not bad. Million shares for control. Pick up another two three hundred thou to add on to what Sy and Carole had and no unfriendly would stand much chance without that Texas bank stock. Had to keep that Texas stock on the front burner. Something else to figure in was if the opposition went after the stock with both hands it wouldn't stay there at $18. Might go to $25-$30 say. Take extra bucks to stay in the game.

He wrote on the yellow pad At $20 may need up to $10M and Texas. At 35 may need $20M. Could margin.

If you have any trouble with those numbers, come back to me. Margin is if you have a dollar's worth of stock you can borrow enough from your broker to buy another dollar's worth on a phone call. Then you have $2 worth. If that stock doubles you have $4 worth. You give the broker back the dollar you borrowed from him, you still got $3 worth of stock. You tripled on your own dollar. If you didn't borrow on the margin you would only doubled. There's all kinds of hardships in this world. The other drawback is if the stock goes down instead of up, you're losing on two shares instead of only one, and halfway down you're out of business.

I knew about margin. I learned about it on Lorillard and I was in heavy on Harbor. Great thing for the aspirin business. When you read in the paper margin buying is going up, put your money in one of those Sominex type stocks, what they call sleepers.

Carole told him he could have $50,000 from her. That was stock market money she had with Greg Wyman. Everything else she had was in company stock she already had from Joseph.

Sy was in the same boat. He had only a loose hundred grand. Frank figured to put in fifty grand himself.

"That leaves us only $19,800,000 shy. Not bad" Frank said, thinking double all those numbers and double all the stock they already owned with the margin. "What about the bank?"

"You mean Texas?"

"I mean our own bank."

"They loaned us the limit when we added the Idaho factory. All we have left is the seasonal line. We need that to carry us until receivables start coming in."

"All of it?"

"You've never seen Sy in the condition he gets in if he can't earn a discount."

He wrote Receivables on the yellow pad. He went into Melvin Goodfriend the bookkeeper's office and had a talk. Melvin worked up some figures for the new general. Frank wrote on the yellow pad, page 4, Receivables $6,000,000 immediate to 30 days. Wrote on the page the numbers he needed from the other pages and threw them away. You notice people who do numbers best aren't writing them down on paper all the time like he did.

Next day he took a plane to Groody Texas, went into Groody National Bank, met Timmons Groody president. Groody Texas looking man. Used to hearing people out. Hearing people out was the way to fill the day in Groody, not like New York where there's no time, you got to get a taxi and stall out in traffic. Groody wanted to know all about how the company was doing, what was going on in New York, what was going on in Washington. Bought Frank lunch at the Groody golf club, introduced him around. Took him around to meet Groody Timmons of Timmons Dry Goods who told him they liked SS a whole lot and would give them the corner window right on Groody at Timmons if they kept up deliveries.

The banker couldn't say who he held that stock for of course. Confidential. But after talking to the storekeeper Frank had a pretty good idea the Groodys were in it together. The banker told Frank You have the votes as long as you folks keep doing things right. He gave Frank the bank's proxy to stick in his pocket and take along home for the Annual Meeting coming up next month. Frank told him he hoped he never sold but if he ever thought of it to be sure to offer it first to the company. "Don't thank a thang about it," Groody told him. Friends. Pals.

He set Frank up so high he could have come home first class with all that leg room just by holding his arms out and taking a deep breath. Back at the ranch, Frank checked out Timmons Dry Goods.

"You ever hear of Groody Texas?" Frank asked me. "That is nowhere. That is one street as long as a block from 5th to 6th surrounded by dust and 10,000 copies of the Eyeful Tower. On that street is a store that does more business on our Pink Dots than

Nieman-Marcus and I didn't even know we had it on our books. They have $20,000 fur coats in a window that's all grayed out from sand scratches. It is like looking through your windshield in a rainstorm to see these $20,000 fur coats. The light is from a couple of tin cake plates any New York store would have sold off for a dollar each in 1930. If you had a little news store with a show window like that you would ask the landlord to replace it, and here they own 10% per cent of our company. I'm glad they like the product."

Timmons Dry Goods of Groody Texas. I knew I knew that store but I didn't know why I knew it. Maybe read it going by in a column. Tried in my head to see it on a page in the Journal. One of those things you know you know and can't bring up. I kept saying to myself Timmons Dry Goods in Groody Texas, trying bring it up. It went farther in like things do when you try too hard.

4

After the first fast five points SS settled down to bobbing around that price. Volume cooled. Your basic takeover story ends that way, drifting off the financial page, people getting interested in new events.

Now is the time, Frank told Sy, while things are quiet. One day not too far off that stock was going be bid up a whole lot higher. Let McGarvey pay top dollar. Margin's the thing. Give your stock to the broker and we'll borrow conservatively against it and buy more stock.

Conservative borrowing to Sy was about like slightly dry water.

Frank talked to him like you explain to a kid there is nothing to it to hold your breath and put your head into the pool. You can't drown in the school pool. No way. Nothing to be afraid of. Leave go of your nose and duck your head in.

"You can't lose. The broker has a dollar's worth of stock for every 50¢ he lends you. You don't think that stock can go down 50% do you?"

"It's been there."

"Not when you had sales like these. Without McGarvey buying

it's still worth every cent of $25. Wait till you tell the annual meeting we made 60¢ this quarter.''

Sy said I don't know and shook his head and said that wasn't his idea of conservative, but okay, general. Three o'clock in the morning he got up to do something about his indigestion and it hit him they were talking about breathing money for his kid in the iron lung in the next room. Sy couldn't wait to get in the next morning to tell Frank to forget it about buying any stock on margin but he had to wait because Frank wasn't there. Instead there was an Urgent from Rose on his desk Call Vincent Spinal first.

''He is the specialist on your stock at the New York Stock Exchange. He needs you fast. Do you want me to get him?''

Spinal came on so calm you could have gone to sleep in his lap. ''Good morning, Mr. Simon. I don't have much time to talk'' said it like he had all morning. ''Do you want to sell some of your stock or know anybody who does? We have more buy orders in our book than we can find stock for. We'll have to go to a pretty high price to open unless we can find sellers. I'll give them some short but I can't do it all. Do you want to let a few thousand go?''

Up to that point Sy was ready to say Oh am I glad you called, tell me how to get out of a margin deal. Anybody who wants that margin stock can have it. I don't know what I'm doing with it. Don't know what I was thinking. Spinal gave him a different outlook of his options. Price was going up.

''Oh'' Sy said. ''Well. You're asking me a question I wasn't ready for. I don't know. We're buyers, you know, we're not sellers. We think we have a great little company here.''

''I don't blame you. I just thought I would try. It looks to me like we will open around 24.''

''I'm sorry I can't help you out.''

Frank came in at ten-thirty grinning from here to here.

''We're looking good. Bought you on the opening at 24. You made a half million bucks and you haven't even had lunch.''

They battled two weeks for that stock. The SS crowd threw in everything they had including the Employes Investment Club that went for a round lot order, a hundred shares at $29, the biggest play the Club ever made. That was some meeting they had deciding to do that. They had Greg Wyman in for dinner as guest speaker on "Diversify Or Die" and when he left they heard from the Investment Committee.

"Are you people out of your minds?" Donuts from shipping called for an up and down answer on that. "Do you know what three grand is? Why put three grand in one lousy stock?"

Groaning from receiving took the punt and brought it back. "Is it worse than two lousy stocks?"

"Did you guys ever hear about diversification? Didn't you guys hear what our speaker tonight said about diversification?"

"The chair would like to say" the chair said "that diversification doesn't mean you have to diversify every time you buy a stock. We have other stocks."

Mary Lou from bookkeeping scored. "We have a committee. We elected them. Now we're all experts all of a sudden. I move we accept the recommendation to buy 100 shares of Swimsuit Corporation of the USA a New York corporation from available funds at up to $29 a share. In US funds. Good till cancelled. Make that at up to 29 1/8th."

"It isn't legal to buy stock in a company you work for" Donuts said. "I happen to know that."

"The chair would like to say that we checked that out and it's okay."

"You would like to say it but did you do it? You checked it with who?"

That market kept going up till the Swimsuit crowd loaded up good, then turned around and went down. Not bang down, just drifting. You don't drift up. When nothing much is happening, then what is happening is your particular stock going down. There isn't a river in the world you can drift up in. They have a place out in Arizona, one of those states out there. Must be Nevada, hottest place I was ever in. Vegas. You think twice about even looking out the window. We got an air-condition car and a driver and asked him to drive us around and show us the sights. One of the places he took us had a permanent miracle advertised for the tourists. Turn off your engine and let go your brakes and you'll see your automobile coast uphill. We did that. Paid two dollars for the experience.

To tell the truth it did seem to happen. We travelled along a couple hundred yards, all the time uphill according to how the bearings looked around us. They said they had a magnetic mountain in the neighborhood. Those are just words to make you think you know something you don't. All that heat, things waved in the air like underwater. That had to be one of those tropical illusions. You shut off your engine and there's only one way that car's going go. Down. That's nature. The only thing that acts contrary to nature is people.

This market I'm talking about started drifting down toward the margin of that SS crowd. Looked to Sy like ice coming down on the Titanic. Didn't like losing the same two dollars on every point going down he made going up. He should have followed his first idea and asked Spinal to take the margin off his hands.

"Sell that margin stock off" he told Frank.

"You can't do that. If you put sell orders into a market like this you tip the price down. That's exactly how those people are reading the market. They see stock out there bought at high prices by nervous holders ready to sell at the first excuse."

"You're looking at a nervous holder. Look. Front. Look. Left profile. Look. Right profile. Nervous holder. Get me out of that margin stock."

"There's only one buyer. You don't want to hand him a bargain, do you? The thing for you to do now is to put more of your stock into the margin account. It will give you a deeper cushion. You will feel more comfortable."

"All the margin. Sell it right away."

It was Sy's money. The best Frank could do was ask for a week to ease the stock into the market.

"A week." Sy drilled him with his fingers. "Five business days. No discounts after five business days."

Rose heard everything. Her money was in AT&T and ConEd but her eyes and ears were in the office. She walked in on Melvin Goodfriend and asked him if Mr S knew what was going on with the receivables.

"I presume so. He said Frank was the general."

"To be on the safe side you better check with Mr S."

"I don't see why I should bother him."

"I'll tell him if you don't."

She watched Melvin into Sy's office. When she heard Sy say "He did WHAT?" she knew that next came "ROSE GET FRANK IN HERE."

"He's at lunch with Kaufmann's. He should be back soon."

"THE MINUTE HE COMES IN—"

"Right away" she told Frank when he sailed in. Gave him just enough of a look to let him know the subject was not Congratulations on that nice deal with Kaufmann's. At the same time when he asked her what's up she said she didn't know. She didn't work for Frank. She worked for Mr S. Who she basically worked for was Mr S's daddy who died twenty years ago. He was the one who gave her time off to go to night school without taking it off her pay. He was the one who gave her brother the office supply deal.

Sy closed the door when Frank went in. Rose didn't hear a word. That meant Mr S was the way he settled down after blowing his top. Quiet. This is how it is. This is the way it has to be. Save your breath. You could change him when he was in a furor but once he settled into a groove Save your breath. My momma had a phrase. She'd say of somebody He looked like death warmed over. That's how Frank looked coming out the door when it opened, and Sy after him finishing the lecture.

"I had enough of it with stock markets. Sell every last one of those margin stocks no matter what. I mean tomorrow."

"It will collapse the market. I'm telling you the truth."

"Tomorrow young man."

"You're handing the company to McGarvey."

"It would serve him right."

"I'm gone for the day" Frank told Rose and kept on going.

Frank had told Melvin Goodfriend to forget about paying bills on time and picking up the discounts. Take those checks coming in from May Company and Marshall Field and Bloomingdale's and all those accounts and turn them into checks for Wyman and Company. Every loose dollar the company had was in the stock market. Margined.

Sy said "Rose, I'm a self made man. Sometimes I think I made a mistake."

5

I remember it was Lent and there was a flu scare and it was raining a pisser for a change and it was a Monday night so we were dark on the music. Could have closed the bar anytime after ten o'clock, nobody would notice, but your hours are on the door. Edna and I were to the movies. Had the taxi drop us to have a drink with Sid, keep him company, let him know we felt sorry for him on a night like that. Like they say in Poland, Solidarity.

Only people in the place were those two characters who ran with McGarvey. Bunschli and the other fella with the vest. You could hardly be sure who they were Sid had the place so dark. We had those light control switches you can turn up to broad daylight and down to off. Trying to get the place looking busier under the conditions he had, Sid had been playing the lights and decided the best was pretty damn dark except for the backlight behind the bar. Everybody else in a cave. Probably no better one way than another but it pleased Sid.

"We've been busier than this. Frank Doelger and Carole Lane just went out" he said as though I was holding him responsible for rain, Lent and the flu epidemic.

"What are they doing around on a night like this?"

"Sounded to me like Carole was trying to keep him from jumping off a bridge."

"You mean really?" Edna asked him.

"Maybe only climb up on the rail. He and Sy had a great big go round that left blood on the floor. From what I picked up, Sy told him he had to sell a jag of Swimsuit stock tomorrow." He breathed this at us confidentially to keep it away from McGarvey's two clowns.

What's going on now? Was I getting a signal? Was I supposed to go into Swimsuit? Lighten out and pay the capital gains on HO? That HO was doing good and I'd have to sell some if I was going in Swimsuit too. Maybe Frank wasn't going sell his own personal stock, only the company's. How did that change the rules? The system was getting overloaded.

The door opened and Al McGarvey came in stamping his feet dry, swishing rain off his hat on the carpet. Sloughed his coat off on a chair, no use bothering with the checkroom in conditions like these. Real wet like he walked up from the Battery.

"What are you doing out on a night like this?"

"Catching cold" he said.

He saw those two at the table and they saw him but none of them made a move. Kind of strange. Like they thought they might know each other but didn't. Did a little something with their eyes. McGarvey sat down at the bar alongside me, and Sid broke out the Chivas.

"If you hadn't been here it would be like finding the door locked at home." He saw I was near the bottom on mine. "Take your next one with me. You too Eddie" he said leaning around me.

"Thank you" she said. "If you two are going to sit here boozing it I'll take mine to the piano."

Tucked in his handkerchief pocket he had a cigar case made from one a those expensive skins that looked like the animal died of measles. Ostrich. Elephant looks like he died of old age but he wouldn't if they made his skin up into something—lions would have found him first and ate him. You have to shoot him to get the skin before the lions. Had an ivory latch. You don't think when you admire something like that, they killed this big living animal to get that piece of skin and that bone chip.

You think of things like that and you can't do anything in this world. You can't eat an apple because of the bacterials. Just because bacterials are small doesn't mean they don't have their own ways, their own religion and the same rights as a whale. Small people have the same rights as tall people. Where do you draw the line on how small doesn't count any more? If you don't believe in elephant skin cigar cases, okay then you can't eat apples either. I love arguments like that. Arguments where people show you you have to be consistent. I don't believe in being consistent. I believe you should use common sense, that's why you have it, to use it. I'm against elephant skin cigar cases and that's it. You're entitled to your opinion on the bacterials in apples. I eat them.

McGarvey offered me a cigar and I passed. Eat it all night if I smoke a cigar that late.

He took one out and put it in my hand. Good black Cuban cigar, would taste like candy. I don't know what trouble we made for the Cubans shutting off their cigars. Sure made plenty for ourselves. If you smoke their cigars, the Russians will have missiles there in no time. I can't use consistent-type people like that.

"For tomorrow" he said.

Lit up his own like he'd been waiting to do it all day.

"Whoosh" he said.

Edna began on Got It Bad.

"That's a good song" he said.

Door opened again and an embrulla flew in aimed right at us, closing as it came to show Carole in a high collar coat and a Cossack type hat. Black boots. Scene from a Russian movie. She shook out and opened her coat, didn't take it off, threw it open saying this and that about the weather.

Sid said "If I knew you were coming back I'd have sent out for another tub of yogurt."

"That's all right. Put up a tonic with gin and you can pour it in." Yeah well, that was bad weather. She waved back toward Edna without looking and came around to sit next to McGarvey. She said

"I saw you coming up 5th. I had a hunch you were headed here."

"Always play your hunches" he said. You have to say something, can't just sit there.

"I want to talk to you. What is it you want out of us? Why don't you go pick on somebody your own size and leave us alone?"

Face to face like that for the first time must have torn him up. "How do you mean Leave you alone?"

"Do I have to do this piece by piece? Everything was going along fine until you butted in."

"Butted in? How do you mean Butted in?"

"I can't believe this conversation" she said to nobody in particular.

"If you mean rumors about me having an interest in your company, I'm not responsible for what people say."

"Come off it."

"No really. I don't have any stock in your company and I don't know anybody who does, except you people in the ownership. That is I assume you are a stockholder, it isn't something I would know first hand."

That is a first class you-asked-me-the-wrong-question type statement, I thought. He was into that stock some way that crept around the way he said he wasn't. Couldn't see how. The man had to be a straight up liar. That's a tough type that will look you right in the eye and lie. That's government quality.

"Come off it. Everybody knows you touted it in your Letter."

"I assure you I did no such thing."

"Oh now, Mr McGarvey."

She had one leg up on the stool, the other one stretched out to the side and her coat open to a blue velvet type dress that knew just where she was. Eyeballing him to find out what was the truth. Close encounter of the first kind. Must have looked real good to him, wanted to dive in, swim around.

"Mrs Lane—Carole—I'd appreciate it if you called me Al—would it make you feel any better if I swore on my mother's name that your company was never mentioned in any letter I wrote? I never recommended that anybody buy your stock. I don't own one share and I undertake that I never will. On my mother's name."

Now that threw her. Threw me too. On his mother's name.

"I don't know what to say."

"You could say you believed me. If you would want me to I will say it to the press tomorrow."

I wouldn't say she believed him or she didn't right then, but if a man lays it out flat like that, what are you going say if you want that man on your side? You can't say Stick it.

"I didn't expect this. You would do that? What can I say? That would be wonderful."

"I'll make a statement the first thing tomorrow morning."

"I apologize if I've misjudged you. You have a fierce reputation, you know."

Now it's in the air there should be some kind of reward. He's done a nice thing for her. She's looking at him in a friendly way. Here could be a nice guy and she's given him a hard time.

Lucky I'm there. People don't listen to what comes out of their own mouths, and what just came out of McGarvey's had trouble written all over it. I stuck my two cents in, something I don't usually do. At the bar I'm a taker. The customer's the giver.

"Whoa on that talking to the papers. If you do that the stock is going fall right out of bed. Who's going buy any SS tomorrow if it's all over the market Allen McGarvey won't touch it? Is Frank going buy it all up? Is the company going take it?"

Carole put that in the grinder. Didn't like what came out.

"Oh Lord—" she said.

"I'm afraid that what Stiffy says is as usual well-taken" McGarvey said.

She grabbed his arm to hold him back from going into the press room to talk to the reporters. "Of course. How dumb can I get? Please don't say a word. Just leave it there. Sleep late, don't get up until the market closes. Be unavailable."

He closed his hand down on hers to make the bargain. First contact he ever made with her. Maybe smelled her going by, something like that, but first skin on skin.

"Anything you say, Carole."

"Thanks for bringing that up, Stiffy. I am so sorry I misjudged you, Al. I better go home before I do any damage."

As long as I was so popular I had still a better idea. "Hey, Al, why don't you buy some of that stock as a friend of the management? That would be good news under that stock."

A real genius of an idea, I don't mind saying. It went into Carole's grinder and came out a whole lot faster and looked a whole lot better than the last one.

"Wouldn't that be great? Would you do that, Al?"

His face worked the odds and in general did what you would expect of the Wall Street Whiz getting ready for a big deal. Came out negative.

"I couldn't do that. I just swore on my mother's name I wouldn't do it. You wouldn't respect me if I broke my word."

"Yes I would" she said. "This is a special case."

"I couldn't. I really couldn't. If your word is no good on Wall Street you aren't worth anything. Another double there, Sid. The market is based on good faith. You can't tamper with that. There would be no bottom then."

"You couldn't take a small position and make it known?"

"Not in the circumstances. I'm afraid not. It's a matter of principle. I regret that I deposed on my mother's name, but having done so I have no choice but to honor my pledge."

"I think you're putting me on. I really think so."

"No I wouldn't do that."

"I can't believe what I'm hearing. If you're playing around with us that would be contemptible."

That was a hard word. Got him off balance, hit him hard, considering how things had been going so good between them only a few seconds before.

"I wish you didn't think that."

"I wish I didn't myself but that's how it comes out. I don't know what to think. You're on the level that you haven't been buying our stock?"

He held up three fingers. "On my honor." Silly looking thing, grown-up man getting a few grays over the ears, swearing like a boy scout. Finally got to Carole that she had to believe him and it left her as bad off as before.

"Sheeee-it" she said. "If you're not the buyer it must be—"she cut off before she said Gary Potsdammer. "Sheeee-it."

"Could I see you home?"

"Thank you. No." He heard she meant No all right.

He reached for her tab.

"Thank you. No." She signed.

She closed her coat and closed him out. Set the wet Russian hat back on her head and opened the embrulla the least bit to be ready to shoot it out as soon as she got through the door. Only two blocks to go. Like always she left the drink without touching it. Couldn't see much of her legs under the shiny raincoat, but what he could see McGarvey looked at before he turned back to the bar, put his head down reading the dents and scratches.

The two honchos decided they had enough too. They brought their check over and paid up. Stopped behind McGarvey. Bunschli said to the back of the great man's head

"You still have time to explain, Allen. Once I pass through that door—" McGarvey was going let him pass but he hung on. "I cannot tell you how disappointing it is to be displaced as Standby Numero Dos by a Harvard man. Really, Allen."

"I've explained you were not displaced. You lost nothing. Both you and Henry are Number Two."

"The bond of trust is shattered. There can be only one number two at a time." They're talking to the back of his head and he's talking to the bottles.

"If you hadn't looked in my briefcase you would be just as happy now as you were this morning. If you choose to make yourself unhappy it is not my fault. Would you like to be Number One?"

"Would Kissinger stay two?"

"That would depend on whether you looked in my briefcase again, wouldn't it."

The other fella said "The meat on which this here our Caesar feeds is boloney. Let's go."

They went into that damn miserable night. I told Sid and the waiters to go, Edna and I would close it down with the customer.

6

That man had been out in the rain a long time. You could smell wet wool coming off his clothes. The combing of his back hair where it was thick down to his collar came apart, all the set was out of it. A big man, hanging over that Chivas like he was a fortune teller. French cuffs soggy.

"What's good, Stiffy?"

Everytime he saw me he asked that question, like you say hello, only you don't say hello when you're already on your second double. I didn't know what he expected me to tell him.

"You got it."

"Be serious. I carry great burdens."

"I'm not too good on that but I'll give it a try. What's the problem?"

"I want to get advice for a change instead of giving it all the time. If Bunschli and Gilders had not leaned on me, they would have blown over in the first wind. Hollow men. I chose to step aside. No man should be beholden to another this way but here I am, ready to lean on you. Ironical isn't it. All I want is a little advice about the stock market."

"Allen McGarvey is going ask Stiffy Stiff for stock market advice?"

"I've been walking around in the rain for an hour thinking Who of all the people I know would I want an answer from? Stiffy, I said. By George, that Stiffy is a man whose judgment I would have confidence in. Does that surprise you?"

What's the man expect me to say? Don't surprise me a bit, the only thing surprises me is it took you all this time? Like Carole said, the man can seem like he's putting you on. Let it play out.

"Certainly I am not the first person to express confidence in your judgment. I observe the excellent way you conduct this business. I know who your partners are. I observe you at Wyman's. I am impressed."

"You're just watching me lose money."

"Ah ha ha. I don't believe that for a moment. I believe you do very very well. I am a very observant man. Tell me straight, if you had to buy one stock tomorrow, what would you buy?"

If a fella's drunk I know how to handle him. If he's only oiled so he runs easy he has to take care of himself. I didn't know how to take that man. Seemed to be on the level but it came out so cockeyed, McGarvey asking me about the stock market. Yeah. Maybe I was giving off confidence vibes. Nothing I did caused it. You tell the man in the moon how beautiful he looks, he knows it's nothing he's done, it's the sun bouncing off him. Could be good vibes bouncing off me from somewhere else. France. Could be DeGaulle's vibes. You don't know how those things work. Uncle Cuz and Dill gave me the same song about having confidence in me.

"If anybody asked me I'd tell him to see if he could get a look at McGarvey's Market Letter."

"That would be a pretty good answer but I can't use it. Look at it this way. What does the market rest on?"

I didn't know he wanted an answer but he waited around till I came up with one. I gave him one I picked up somewheres. "Some folks believe everything rests on the back of an elephant. There's this big elephant holding up the whole world. How does that appeal to you?"

Not the answer he's looking for. Well, I wasn't the one to ask in the first place.

"Confidence" he says."The market rests on confidence. And why do people act on the Market Letter?"

"That's an easy one. It's got the good stuff."

"No no no no. I marvel at your innocence. It's because they have confidence in it. It isn't what I put in, it's what they put in. Confidence is what counts."

"Okay with me. You put in the confidence and your troubles are over."

"How can I have confidence in it? I write it. I am behind the scenes. I see the chef's thumb in the soup."

Yeah everybody's jumpy about what goes on in the kitchen, but the way I figure, anything going on in my kitchen is ten times better than goes on in anybody else's. Didn't understand why McGarvey wouldn't see it the same way. I was going tell him that when he leaned over to me at a confidential distance where nobody else could hear.

"Communications with priests and bartenders are privileged. Isn't that so, Stiffy?"

"I'm playing your rules."

"There is no McGarvey Market Letter. Confidential."

"Anything you say."

"You don't believe?"

"Let's say I know better. I read about it in the paper all the time. People know people who get it. I see various people showing their Standby cards ready to lay out twenty five grand for a subscription."

"All those things, yes. But no Letter. I'll tell you something else. Confidential. There is no McGarvey."

"Oh yes there is Virginia and he had one too many double Chivases. You stopped somewhere before you got here."

Edna picked up I needed help. Closed the piano and came over. "Are you fellas going to sit her boozing all night? Everybody afraid to go out in the rain?"

"Sit down here a minute, Eddie. I've asked Stiffy for advice and he puts me off like I've had too much. I had two small Scotches. I would say that was the right amount for a friendly discussion. I told your excellent husband there is no McGarvey Market Letter. There is no McGarvey. A wiser man than I raised the question about diamonds—If you take away sparkle, hardness, color, weight, size—can you say then that it is a diamond? Take away the Market Letter. Take away the companies I never tookover and the stocks I never bought or sold—can you say there is an Al McGarvey?"

"You still got your hair."

"He's trying to talk serious and you're talking about his hair. Listen to the man" Edna said. "What's on your mind, Mr McGarvey? You're among friends. Anything we can do for you?"

Upshoot was we got a cab and took him home with us to sleep it off. Put him on the pullout couch in the piano room.

7

That's it, the famous stock market operator Al McGarvey never bought any stock all that time. Never raided any company, took one over or busted one up. Never did any of those things.

Never put out any Market Letter. Just walked around looking wise, saying he wouldn't talk. Made up rumors for those two clowns

Bunschli and Gilders to bounce off anybody who'd listen.

Hand it to him, he made up good rumors. He had good stock market ideas. Spent time studying, going over charts, looking things up. That's where he was when nobody could find him, some place he could look something up. The library on 42nd. Up at Fordham Law. Columbia Business. Register of Deeds. Smithsonian in D.C. Hanging around Wyman's. Looked in at Merrill Lynch and Bache now and then, listening to broker talk. Time wasted, if you ask me, for a man who wants to make money on Wall Street, but nothing beats information if you have to fill up a four pages of a market letter.

All that coming and going at Wyman's, he never bought a share.

"I figured one day I was going to get one sweet block order" Greg said. "When he finally called it in I knew I had it coming."

I'll tell you about that order he gave Greg Wyman.

He kept me up half the night giving his life story, getting shed of the guilt. It got down to that the man never had to work, he had all these trust funds. Idea of work never got to him. Nobody brought it up. Supposed to be work enough keeping track of investments but the trusts did all that for him.

He's standing around doing nothing but tennis and scuba diving and known to have all those investments and all kinds of people come up asking him what he thinks. They want him on the board at the hospital because they know he can write a check, then first thing you know they make him chairman of the investment committee. Big good looking fella with all the money in the world and gals standing in line and people telling him what a smart apple he is, and he gets this terrible fear. What if he says something dumb? What if he votes for bonds and they get stuck with them when the Fed raises the interest? A man with all that money and that big reputation doing that dumb thing.

He likes the idea of people bowing down all right, but the idea that he might blow it is too much. He clams up. No committees. Mystery man. Study up on things, put out a few words in a way nobody can come back and hang you with. Work on the eagle look. Build up the idea of still waters running deep.

I'm telling you what the man told me. The man must know.

In Egypt they had this Spink. An Egyptian would ask the Spink what were the odds that the next man coming down the road was his old man. We had this at the 92nd Street Y. The Spink wouldn't say this odds or that, he'd tell a story you could figure out any way you wanted. If what you decided went against you, you just naturally knew you were the dummy, you didn't get it right. Couldn't be the Spink that was wrong.

"Oh yes" Jimmy Perse told me when I gave him my idea of the kinda person McGarvey was. "A branch of the Spink family came over to this country and settled down south with William Penn and the crackers in Philadelphia. In the odds business too, same as on the other side. They put out the Sporting News newspaper."

I happen to know that's true, I used to read their paper. Another branch of the family got into boxing. I know them, they're the dark branch, you can see the Egyptian in them. Leon Spink is a customer of mine when he's in town. Might be a relative of Leon Bean, I don't know. I never knew Bean.

I know how the Spink thing works. People ask me if the interest is going higher. I don't answer right off. Give the other fella the idea he was the first to think up that deep question. Puts him in the game. Makes him think he's smart too, so he doesn't have to care so much what I think. He can even forget he asked me. He can get to feel a little spinky himself. Could make a move I tell them, could make a move. Easy thing to get talking that way. I'm not going tell a man who may already be worried enough about it How the hell do I know if the interest is going higher. If it got out Arsdur U. Stiff didn't know, there might be a panic.

McGarvey was a worse case than me. I'm not in any hurry to let people know if I made a mistake but I don't carry it so far I wouldn't give Greg Wyman an order because the stock might go down and embarrass me in Greg's eyes. Hell, he gets the commissions. Anyhow, I don't buy stocks thinking they'll go down. That's the wrong attitude.

Coming up on that rainy night he decided he was a gutless wonder. Turned on to that by finding himself scared by the likes of Bunschli and that other fella taking a look in his brief case and finding out the way he did things. Scared of what they would say. Scared of Carole turning him down. Scared of Wyman seeing he didn't have good stock ideas. Getting too old for that fear. Life going on by and he knows he's faking it. Can't keep that up. Get out while you got your hair.

Don't walk around in the rain feeling sorry for yourself. Do something drastic to show you aint going be like this any more.

How about asking Carole Lane out? How about practicing for that by buying some stock? That's it, first thing in the morning buy some stock, then get on the horn to Carole Lane.

Only question was Which stock? leading on to him walking around in the rain running stocks through his head till he got the idea Stiffy was his man for advice. Ask me. All I knew was Frank was wrong. Am I going say Go ask Frank Doelger and do the opposite? Might not work for him like it did for me. He might not be connected the same way.

It used up a lotta his nerve asking Carole to walk her home, and she turned him down just like he knew she would. Lucky he had it so fixed in his mind he was going ask me for a stock tip it didn't knock it out of him when she said No. A more superstitious type man might say it wasn't his day, let it go and take a new start next week. Nothing a man with a resolution is looking for as much as an excuse to get out of it.

"I'm taking a nap" Edna said. "You better too if you want to be any good tomorrow. Sleep good and Stiffy will make you one of his breakfasts and you surely will be a new man. He can cook you into the best frame of mind you ever had. Then if you're looking for a way to spend your money you can buy some of that Swimsuit stock and help out your friends. Get Stiffy to do that with you. Good night for now."

"I'll think very seriously about that. What do you think of that, Stiffy?"

"I'm not thinking about it at all except the going to sleep part and then breakfast."

Didn't want to have this discussion on what stock to buy with

Edna's spotlight on me looking for Swimsuit. She took it up in bed anyhow but all I said was it was up to him, how would me telling him what to do free him up to act on his own ideas.

"He can practise on that later on. Right now he can practise buying what Carole would like. You too. I don't understand you at all, not helping your friends out."

Edna's a good sleeper so that didn't last too long and she went out.

Didn't seem too much time passed when I heard him up and around the kitchen banging the coffee machine around. I thought The man can't sleep, I'll get up with him. I showered and I set up one beautiful breakfast with panned trout a fishing friend of Sid dropped off and my sourdough muffins. I do trout with capers.

He did the shower and came out freshened up and got into breakfast, holding up different stocks to examine for one to buy. The man knew more about stocks than Merrill Lynch Pierce Fenner Smith and Beane too. I know you don't know about Beane. Beane was before Smith, that's all you need to know, has nothing to do with these events. Malcolm knows who Beane was. Leon Bean. Dropped the e off the end, changed his whole personality. He quit brokering and went into fishing boots. Built a big catalog business with people who do capers with trout. That's the whole story. I don't want to take any more questions on that.

"Okay" I told him, "so what you have to do is pick a stock and phone in the order. People do it all the time."

"What if the stock goes down?"

"You can afford it. I got stocks that go down." They're the ones I was short on. They're supposed to go down.

"Doesn't it bother you when Greg knows you made a mistake?"

"No way."

"You mean you don't care what people think?"

"Well yeah, I care but I don't let it tie me up that much. That's what goes on in their heads. I got my own life."

"That's certainly interesting. Where do you draw the line? What if A.J. McGarvey is known to have bought a stock that's a loser? Won't people laugh?"

"I don't think people would pay the least attention. You're not running for president. They don't even pay attention to that. If they laugh, the thing to do is laugh with them, like it's a So what? Most things are so what.''

''By George.''

''I'll get an order in on that at the opening. What's the symbol?''

''How's that?''

The man had no humor in him.

Well back to Swimsuit. Did I think he should buy Swimsuit?

Where I wanted him was in Harbor Oil with me. Big buyer. Have it known at the right time. Up goes the price and I take the pot. I had to go easy on that, bearing in mind Edna's wishes.

''I'm not encouraging you in or encouraging you out. That's strictly up to you.''

''Do you own any Swimsuit?''

''I don't say I do or I don't. Either way doesn't say it isn't a good company and I wouldn't ever own it. I might own it tomorrow. That has nothing to do with you.''

''I would like to do it out of respect for Carole's wishes.''

''That's up to you whether you going do it out of respect for her wishes or my wishes or your wishes or your momma's wishes.''

''I swore on my mother's name.''

''You did that, yeah. I'm not looking for trouble with your momma. That's strictly up to you.''

''What do you think about Lorillard?''

''What I know is in the newspapers.''

''I think you know more than that. Do you own any?''

I didn't want to mislead him on that. I told him I was a seller for personal reason. He didn't like the idea I sold even though I said that was nothing against the company.

What did I think about General Motors?

That was before they sold me that lemon-flavored Nova so I had nothing special against them but I told him I thought they were all missing out on small jobs you could get around the city in. I mentioned Volkswagen the German car. He thought so too but he was watching the Japanese. What did I think of this Mitsubishi crowd making automobiles? That wasn't even the sixties we were in then and Al McGarvey was thinking Japanese automobiles. I don't even think the Japanese were thinking automobiles at the time, they were still driving around in ginrickies.

"What about Harbor Oil? I happen to know you're interested in Harbor Oil" he said.

"How would you know that?"

"I happen to know. Do you like it at today's price?"

"It could be okay. What I think isn't the subject."

He began talking about Harbor Oil and he knew more than I knew about that company. He knew they didn't know how to find oil but they had land all over hell and gone and must have reserves they weren't telling anybody about. They had reserves around L.A. and Colorado and Canada and even in New York. The man just liked to find out things.

Told me about a day he took a boat along the Island to see if they had any signs of development on their land there, any rigs or anything.

"It's in the Potsdammer Tract. There wasn't a sign of anything going on except a beach party. Clowns wearing goggles and manana hats. They waved us off."

"That's a great name for a movie" I told him. "The Potsdammer Tract."

Man, I was shaking. I knew so much now I didn't know how much it was.

In the annual reports oil companies and mining outfits send their stockholders they have these drawings of locations and what the geologics look like when you frammis down below the delusion formations. Gives the stockholders confidence they aren't reading nursery rhymes. Real places. Real holes in the ground. Kind of stuff I wouldn't even read in a barber chair, just pass my eyes across. Just the same your eyes are open and those pictures leak in. I could see as clear as if I studied it for ten minutes POTSDAMMER TRACT written over one of those drawings in the Harbor Oil report.

My head flipped on to the back page where they list the directors. Flipped to it without me even thinking. There on the list was GROODY TIMMONS. Underneath was the line giving his credits.

Timmons Drygoods Company.

It hit me that Swimsuit didn't own that test beach at all, it had been sold off in that big tract by whoever—Sy's daddy probably, before Sy was born. They just kept using it. Didn't know any better, like you play in an empty lot until some day somebody comes in with a bulldozer. Miles of Long Island, all belonging to Harbor Oil. Wham-o!

Oil on Long Island. Real estate on Long Island. Did that Frank Doelger know how to pick stocks!

"I'm not telling you what to buy. You can keep asking all day and the market will open and close without you. You know ten times as much about stocks as I do. The market opens in five minutes. Pick up the phone."

"You're in Harbor Oil. I know you are."

"Say I'm in it, what's that to you? Pick up the phone and give Greg whatever order you want if you're going in." Just to show you how fair I was about it, the last thing I said was "Don't forget you were thinking about Swimsuit. Your momma might forgive you. I don't know how strong your family feelings are."

He picked it up and looked at it like he never saw a phone. I told him the Murray Hill. Meanwhile my insides are jumping up and down with Harbor Oil. Man, oil on Long Island. Real estate on Long Island. Finish up here, man, and let me get on with my business.

He dialed in. Listened with his face screwed up. Eyes popped up when he got an answer.

"Mr Wyman please . . . This is Allen McGarvey." Put his hand over the mouthpiece. "I got the research director. He must be a new man. Sounds Oriental."

"Hang in there."

"Good morning, Wyman . . . Yes . . . Yes . . . I'd like to give you an order . . . Yes . . . That's kind of you to say . . . I'd like to buy 100 . . . Yes" Put his hand over the mouthpiece. "He wants to know of what?"

"Good question."

"What should I tell him? You're not in Swimsuit are you? I know you're not."

"What I aint in has nothing to do with you. That's between you and your momma."

He went back into the phone. "Let's say . . . ah Harbor Oil. That's it. HO. Harbor Oil."

Good thinking, man. Covered the phone. "He wants to know what price."

"Tell him."

"Tell him what?"

"Tell him what it's worth to you. If you know you want it give him a market order." Get on with it man, get on with it. Get done and let me get outa here. Go little glow worm.

"But I wouldn't know how much that is until it's bought."

"That's how it works. You may miss a big eighth."

"Oh my." Back into the phone. "That is a market order . . . Right. Harbor Oil . . . Right. I appreciate that. Thank you . . . Oh wait Wait WAIT!—"

Too late, the other side was off. He hung up and began scrambling to redial, did it wrong, checked the number out with me, dialed it again, full of groans and nerves and naturally got a busy.

I asked What's the trouble? while he was breaking up the dial again and pieced it out of him. Small misunderstanding—

"He confirmed me for 100,000 shares. I told him 100. Jesus Lord. 100,000. You know I said 100, Stiffy. You heard me. He confirmed 100,000." Spinning that dial like Wheel of Fortune.

"You don't think he expects an order for 100 shares from Allen J. McGarvey do you?"

"What do you mean Of course? That's $3,000,000. THREE MILLION DOLLARS."

"Big deal. Don't you have THREE MILLION DOLLARS?"

Challenged him. Manhood took over. Man of steel. Lenin. Put the phone back on the cradle. I'm in, he said. I took the phone and dialed and got through.

"Is that you Lee Wu? This is Stiffy. Tell Greg if anybody finds out Al McGarvey bought Harbor Oil I'll personally kill him. Get that Buy slip off your blotter. Okay? . . . Thanks a bunch. I'm on my way down to see you."

One thing I absolutely didn't want out today was any word that McGarvey was a buyer. I had my own buying to do and I wasn't interested in paying any more than I had to. Going be expensive enough with that $3,000,000 no-limit order in the market.

Ten

NO BOX LUNCH

1

NO DOUBT about it I was in way over my head but you can't name a project of any size where that isn't so of whoever is in it. Some people are too dumb to know when they're over and other people whistle going by the graveyard to let you know they have no concern, they have this problem in hand, but we're all in way over. You're out there with outdated charts in shoal water. Average man just wants to stay afloat anyhow. I had an idea where I wanted to go but it was way out there.

I started picking up Harbor Oil stock looking to be a millionaire. Wouldn't that make it plain to everybody I wasn't getting by only on account of Edna? I was way past that on paper, got used to the million faster than a quarter. Like Uncle Cuz said, there's no such thing as enough money. Trying to be a big fish in a pond before. Now here I was in the middle of the Atlantic Ocean like Ederle headed for Ireland.

Had a big investor with me. Ace in the hole. Show Al McGarvey at the right time, up goes the price, take the pot. Only there was this mudflat out there, you could see a brown shadow under the water where Bunschli and that other fella were going blow the whistle on the Market Letter and raise questions. I left Al with Edna still sleeping and told him to sit tight till he heard from me or Greg.

I had a plan to beat the Market Letter problem. I went down to talk to Greg. He's a man who sees things and you can trust him. I told him the whole A to Z. Got the reaction you would expect. The man was staked down in red ant country.

"Holy sweat it went by in four lots. 100,000 at 30 and change. How the hell am I going to break an order like that? Is he good for the order? Holy sweat."

"He's good if he doesn't have heart failure first. My opinion is he's loaded. If you want handmoney I'm vouching he gets it here in the hour."

"Jesus how does that play at the Hanover Bank? I've got Stiffy Stiff vouching for Allen J. McGarvey. I've got to talk to him. Where is he?"

"He's at my place at the Western with Edna. Before you call him you want to think about the Market Letter. Bunschli and that other fella will kill him in the newspapers."

"What's that got to do with me?"

"That man's a good customer of yours now, you owe him something. He didn't give this order to Merrill Lynch, he gave it to you. When you get him, why don't you ask him to have lunch and talk over him doing a Market Letter for Wyman and Company? Be the making of your business."

While he was getting that through his head the phone rang. He started the Ah so Wu bit but me sitting there changed his mind. "Ah so. Greg Wyman here. . . . Hello Mr McGarvey. I was just going to call you. We got your hundred Harbor Oil. 35,000 at 30 1/8th and 65 at a quarter. The market now is a quarter to a half. Thank you very much . . . You can send it over if you want to but you don't think I'm worrying about it, do you?"

He began listening real hard. He reached for a Buy slip and wrote on it 100,000 SS market.

He listened twice as hard as before and reached for a Sell slip and wrote on it 100,000 HO market.

Said it back real slow this time to get the confirm while he looked at me over the top of his Ben Franklin glasses like he was dealing with lunatics.

"If you are going out of the position this fast maybe you ought to get your check over" he told Al. "Do you want me to call you when we're made?''

''Let me have that phone'' I said and grabbed it. ''Al, do you know what you're doing? What would your mother say?''

''I talked it over with Edna. Wait a minute, she wants to talk to you.'' She came on strong.

''Stiffy, you leave Al alone. He made the right decision. He's helping his friends. You do your thing and let him do his.''

''I just wanted him to be sure. It costs money going in and out of stock like that.''

''He's got money. He's got friends too. Some people forget their friends when it comes to money. You leave him do his thing.''

Some people. That's me. ''Sure. I just wanted to be sure.''

''If you're not sure now you never will be.''

''Good thinking, Edna. Got to run. Catch you for dinner.''

Pitiful. I could use him in Harbor Oil and he's out there in Swimsuit. Pitiful. I should never left him alone with her bleeding to death about what those bad people were doing to Carole. Should have taken him with me and hid him in my back office. When I do something dumb I'm not the last to see it.

Greg was battling those red ants. ''I have to get these orders to the floor. I have to think things over. Jesus a $9,000,000 rip-rap.''

''Up to you. Just think about those newspaper guys looking for him. You and Al could sit right here and work it out to do a Market Letter. Have lunch. Have something sent in. Chop suey.''

''Ah so. Let me get the orders in.''

Greg made a couple three hundred thousand cash just sitting there making a phone call. That was before everybody thought to negotiate this and that. From that day Wyman went first class, put a door on the office, bought a seat on the Exchange, bought the building he was in and cleaned it up, threw out the Baltic Trading companies. That was a milestone happened to him. Bigger even than Wu.

I couldn't wait for any of that, not even him getting back to McGarvey on the Market Letter. I had to get over to Dill. If I didn't have McGarvey I needed Vault Bank.

I had the annual reports from SS and HO with me and I tore out the figure pages from Standard & Poor. Yeah I did that, tore them out.

You can't act up to the best that's in you every last time, you have to do what the condition needs and make it good to the Lord some other way. I don't believe for a minute He expects us to know what the best thing is every last time. We're the only living thing He let have common sense. Probably doesn't know Himself if it's best to leave the page in the book for some one who could do without it or me taking it to show Dill. You don't go into an important meeting without a paper to give people confidence you did your homework. People believe more in paper than they do in you. Who knows if I don't have the page Dill might not spring and it would turn out I couldn't give them a thermometer, let alone say that hospital.

He went through the annuals and the S&P grunting hn hn hn while I laid it out. Checked out the maps. He skied, knew what a mountain five miles from Aspen was that showed on a Harbor map. It helped he had a place on the Island and knew what waterfront was. Ranch as big as Brazil south of L.A. All that land in there on the statement at cost. Bought before they knew anything to do with land but dig worms and grow potatoes.

"Today's the day to get movering" I told Dill. "$3,000,000 worth of stock went out on a market order. Prices will be soft."

He sprang. He got on the phone, asked the lawyers to come over, had Casey running in vice presidents. Put one of them on the phone to a fella in Texas who knew his way around there. Fred Lebrand came by in twenty minutes. Nothing happens till Fred sees the figures.

His idea was buy the Groody bank too, eat the whole damn pie. Never saw him like a deal better than that.

"All right, you have a $40,000,000 line" Dill said.

Fred said to put the orders through Pat Barnes. "His trader will get us those eighths and quarters on the floor. We don't want to lose anything on the floor."

I was sorry to have to cut out a partner but I had other responsibilities. I told them the trades had to go through Wyman and Company. Greg Wyman had been in on this from the beginning.

"You mean that crappy little broker in the attic on Madison?"

"That's the one, Fred" I said. Jiu jitsu. I'm not going argue about what he called him, he knew who he was.

Dill said "We have a day's work to do, don't spend it shovelling shit on the road. Split the orders between Pat and this other broker hn?" That's the deal I said, and took it back to Greg who had Al in with him having egg rolls sent over from the Mandarin. You don't have $200,000,000 trusts and take-out from Nedick's.

Al decided right there that the first big story in the first copy of the new McGarvey Letter was going be the good prospects of the Swimsuit Corp of the U.S.A. Market share. Bikinis. New factory. Lay it all on the table. Disclose how much he owned. Begin life over.

Pleasure seeing a man with confidence he's using his powers.

"Great idea" I told him. "Can't miss. Make your momma proud."

Then over to the bar. Looked around for somebody to give the straight of it to. Beevo Nolan, Kilgallen's chief runner there loading up. If you want to watch somebody being confidential, you keep your eye on me sitting down head to head with Beevo.

"Beevo, this is real. You can't mention my name but I happen to know Al McGarvey was the big seller in Harbor Oil today. This is not one of your hypes, Beevo. I bet if you ask him he'll admit it. He's over with Greg Wyman. Only a block from here. Dorothy will love it. Just don't mention my name."

"I don't know where you chaps hear all that" Al told Beevo "but I would be less than truthful if I didn't say you have it right."

Dorothy led with the item next day. I gave it to two o'clock for everybody and his brother to throw stock at the market before I told Greg and Barnes Okay start buying, take every share they'll give you, just don't walk on each other's feet bidding against each other. Work it out.

I don't know if I had what they call Insider Information. All I knew nobody else knew was I was a buyer. Who'd care about that compared to McGarvey being a seller? I just played the cards I had. We bought a big jag of that oil stock real cheap before it got back into an expensive mood.

2

When Swimsuit Corp had its Annual Meeting the next week everything was done as far as I was concerned. Well almost. As Yogi says, we hadn't heard the fat lady sing yet. They had the meeting in that theater they have off the lobby in the Barbizon, not the ladies' Barbizon, the other one with the little alley lobby leading in from Central Park South that Trump bought. The officers and directors sat in a row on the stage yakking back and forth with attorneys and accountants. Musical chairs. Ear secrets.

Even with McGarvey in with them they didn't have enough stock, the other fellas picked theirs up too fast and you couldn't buy any bigger than hundreds any more. It wasn't cousin Gary Potsdammer, it was the Groodys like I figured. Sy didn't even know till he saw it in the Journal in the barber shop that Groody Bank filed it represented more than 50%.

A lotta percent. Well okay it was his friend Groody and not Garry the Prick. Sy knew it was more stock than a friend should buy up without telling him but he had Groody's proxy.

He had it as long as it took him to go from the barber's to the Barbizon where he found Groody revoked and had his own slate in mind for directors. That gave Sy a little different slant on friendship.

A half hour after the meeting was to start Sy still hadn't called it to order, get on with it. He knew his company was going down the drain.

Looking around for who was doing all that proxying you couldn't miss the chubby guy rippled into his rodeo gabardine. Shoelace tie. Tattooed boots. Sitting off to the side with his lawyers from Moot Root and Loot. The Texas guy was Groody the banker. Groody went up to Sy with a buddy smile and a handshake.

"Glad to mate you, Mr Salmon. This is gonna be a rail fraindly thang" Groody told him. "Don't you be one bit concerned. Soon as this mating is over we'll sit down rail fraindly and settle this thang. Noss to say you again too, Mr Dowlger."

"Glad to have you here" Sy said.

"I'll be down to see you in Texas one of these days" Frank said.

Might bring a shotgun.

''You do that. Give us some notice and we'll get in a game of gowf. Yall be good now.''

Went back to Moot Root and Loot.

Gordon knew the lawyers. Eased himself over and passed the time. I don't know how lawyers who are supposed to defend you to the death can get along that well with people there to kill you. Gordon came back and sat down with Counsellor Bragdon and me. Since Uncle Cuz brought Bragdon in, we'd spent time together. Good man. Had an office in the back of a real estate company on 7th Avenue and a shelf of thirty books and that's all he needed. He was my personal lawyer on this.

''They say they have it'' Gordon said ''and I don't doubt it but they don't have it of record.''

''Either way I would adjourn'' Bragdon said and Gordon got up and yakked at Sy's lawyer and they went to Sy and yakked and finally Sy nodded his head like you do when you decide that's it and he picked up the gavel. When he stood up you knew he was boss of the meeting. Tall fella of comfortable weight and gray hair puffed over his ears by a good barber. Gray pinstripe with a straightup square Hickey-Freeman shoulder. Blue shirt with a white pin collar. Regimental tie. French cuffs shot out an inch.

''The meeting will please come to order please. Please. Please. The meeting will please come to order. Please. Ladies gentlemen and stockholders the twenty-third annual meeting of the Swimsuit Corporation of the USA will please come to order. Thank you. Will the people talking in the back please take their seats. Thank you. Ladies and gentlemen you are aware of certain rumors about our stock and have been pleasantly surprised by the way the price has been going up. It's some compliment to the progress of our business. Enjoy. Speaking for those of us in the management, we don't intend to sell the historic percentages of ownership we have held in this fine firm—'' That's what his lawyer figured he could say that would still leave him a loophole for that margin stock they bought and then sold. That was extra over the historical. ''However ladies and gentlemen there has been very big trading in our stock since the date of record to qualify voters for this meeting. So much in fact that we don't know if the stockholders here really own the company. We need time to study the situation. On the advice of our lawyers therefore I declare this meeting adjourned for two weeks, the 24th, same time, same place. Thank you.'' Down came the gavel. One of the Oots was on his feet. Also a lady waving her glasses.

''Objection'' Oot hollered.

''Don't talk to them, you adjourned it'' Mr Bragdon mumbled in his vest. Like the Harbor Oil people, we were off to the side so we could conference in private.

''I am outraged'' the lady said.

''Don't talk to her. Walk away from there'' Mr Bragdon told himself, sending his wishes through the air to Sy.

''The meeting has been adjourned'' Sy said.

''That's it. You got it. You're adjourned. Get off that platform '' Mr Bragdon mumbled.

''You can adjourn him'' the lady said putting the finger on Oot ''but you can't adjourn me. Is there to be no lunch? I bought stock in this company thinking it was first class. But no lunch? Not even sandwiches? Every first class company does something about lunch for the stockholders.''

That was the truth then but companies caught on that people were buying one share to get the lunch dividend. You starve to death now if you depend on the company you own to feed you. Except my companies, we treat you right.

''Yes, Mrs Davis'' Sy said. ''Glad to see you here. We made a judgment that being in the heart of this great city with so many fine restaurants, the stockholders might prefer to make their own luncheon arrangements this year.''

She was out in the aisle now with the floor mike. Should have shut the power off when they journed. She knew how to handle the mike, how to push the switch. Kept her face in it. People who don't know move in and out.

''You call that judgment? It took judgment to decide against lunch? No wonder you adjourned the meeting early. Guilt. You lose my vote, Mr Simon, and the vote of many other loyal stockholders you have insulted. Not even a chicken salad sandwich and a cup of tea.'' Pretty good applause around the house.

''Now Mrs Davis—''

''Get off the stage'' Mr Bragdon wished on Sy. ''You're adjourned. Get away from there. Go down and hold her hand.''

''I voted at Pennsylvania Railroad yesterday and they served a nice lunch on real china. Progressive companies do that. Swimsuit Corporation of the USA doesn't serve even a box lunch. If other companies adopt such a policy it will be the end of free enterprise as we know it. I for one will not be at the adjourned meeting and I will revoke my proxy unless you can assure us that we will have at least a nice box lunch.''

Applause all around now except a couple fellas saying Sit down already. Here's a quarter, go out and buy a hot dog.

''We will look into that, Mrs Davis. We will do that. I thank you for bringing it up. We will give it thought.''

Oot was still hollering objections but Sy had a full plate. Wouldn't look at him. Mr Bragdon's wishes reached him and he came down to lay the Land O'Lakes on Davis. That proved the meeting was over, nobody was up there to catch the flak. I went up and slid into his seat next to Carole.

She looked so damn sad, like the world was ending and there was nothing for her to do but watch it go. Carole was into that age when the details may not be what they used to but the whole effect is as good as ever, maybe better. Same as with pictures. If you look at an Italian picture those crackles don't count against it at all. Wouldn't be as good a picture without it because lasting is part of it.

I always had a special feeling for that woman and I wanted her to know I was doing something for her in this deal. Wanted to tell her everything was going turn out okay but who was I to say that? I was undercover, couldn't show my cards. Lotta money riding on this thing. I wasn't any flapmouth letting people in who don't have to know.

''Tough on Sy'' she said. ''He loves the business.''

''Everything's going turn out okay'' I said. Didn't mean anything for me to say that.

"I wish I could believe it. What are you doing here?"

She didn't think of me as a holder, I was just a guy who did a little something in the market.

"I got Edna's stock to vote. You're looking at a proxy. I'll bet you never saw a real living proxy before. You can tell by the teeth." I showed her.

"I'll remember. Thank Edna for the votes."

It added up, Edna was known to have star money from records, and when she did a performance now and then it might get into the papers that she had five six grand for the gig. Like they say, she was a credible name. Not me.

"I got to tell you you look great" I said. "If my wife was anybody but Edna I'd be making all kinds of trouble for you. Don't you worry about a thing. This stock thing is under control."

Starting to flap my mouth. Shut up.

"If you say something I'm supposed to pay attention. Al McGarvey says you're the smartest guy around."

"Yeah well" I said. "There's no way that can be true, but hang in there. You're not losing any money on the deal at these prices."

"It isn't the money, it's the business. What's Sy going to do without the business?"

"They can't run your business with oil guys from Texas. You'll get contracts."

"That isn't the same thing."

Yeah well. That's what I thought too. "Hang in there."

3

I walked out with Mr Bragdon. You couldn't tell if anything bothered him, he always had the look. Could have been his feet. Clown feet. Kids called him Snowshoe. He would take a step and set his heel down and the rest of the foot would be like looking around for the best place to land.

With feet like that a boy wouldn't be anything in sports and the girls would laugh at him. The average kid would see he was adding up to zero and he'd quit even thinking about amounting to anything, but if you had a kid like Marcus Bragdon he'd say I got time on my hands to hit the books, see what that does. Skinny man in big clothes. He could have turned around inside his suits without getting out. Best damn lawyer anywhere and he had only thirty books on a shelf in back of the real estate office.

Something was bothering him. "I want to know Why does that Texas crowd want to own a New York bathing suit company?"

"Investment. They read the SS statement, they like the bottom line, they say What the hell. Investors don't care about the company, it's the figures."

"That's the best theory you can come up with?"

"I had a private theory for about ten minutes it had something to do with property on Long Island but I can't see how that can be." I told him about the Potsdammer Tract and the test beach. "But if they already own it they don't have to buy Swimsuit to get it."

He snow-shoed along. "I've been looking for a theory of this case different from I want and You can't have. Did you ever hear about adverse possession?"

I never had any of those I knew about.

Did you ever hear of Squatter's Rights?"

"I get an A on that one. You move into a place and there's no way they can get you out. It's yours. Oh hey—"

"There's more to it but that will do for now. Does Gordon's office know about the test beach?"

"They may know it's there but I don't think they know about the Potsdammer Tract. They never mentioned it. I never heard anybody but Al McGarvey say anything about the Potsdammer Tract."

"Could you get that Annual Report over to me today?"

4

A week before the journed meeting Groody got 62% of the Swimsuit stock recorded on the books and asked Sy to meet and work it out in a fraindly way.

Sy shut down the showroom and turned it into a big office to make room for his accountants and Mitch's team of lawyers and Dill's people and Counsellor Bragdon and the Texans. Mitch was on the inside of things by then on account of the Vault bank connection on Harbor Oil. He was showing Edna's and Al McGarvey's Swimsuit shares.

I didn't want to be in there. Didn't feel it was done yet.

We had the stock yeah. But I didn't feel it was done. Enough people there looking after my interests. I was learning to delegate. You have to delegate if you move in those circles.

When Groody and the Oots and a couple more came in and saw all those people with Sy they backed off and looked at their tickets to be sure they hadn't got to the Polo Grounds by mistake.

Groody made his little speech about how he could see they would all get along fraindly and Oot took over.

Oot said they were there to settle a price to take up the rest of the stock. Said his people liked the way the corporation was going, they had no complaints. They'd give Sy a good contract to run the Swimsuit division. Promised not to fire anybody. Basic thing they were there for was offering a good price for the rest of the stock they didn't have.

Good price yeah if it was a swimsuit company.

How about if it was an oil company with two miles of waterfront in the Potsdammer Tract?

How about if there wasn't any oil there but it was a real estate company with all that sand beach on Long Island?

"That isn't your waterfront, that's our waterfront." Oot had an engineer there laying out the maps. "The Potsdammer Tract" the engineer showed us. "All this is owned by Harbor Oil Company. It includes the beach as you see. Your people are squatters."

The map was the same one that was in the Annual Report. They were all set for the adverse possession bit and thought they would blow on by. Might have to act generous and offer a better price for the minority stock to get rid of the nuisance but that would be it.

It turned out that squatters wasn't their problem. We didn't even have to use adverse possession. Swimsuit owned the beach all along.

Mr Bragdon looked it up. The map was wrong. The words said where the boundaries went but seventy five years ago somebody drew a straight line down the beach instead of jig-sawing out two miles for Swimsuit, and that was the map in Harbor Oil's safe. Two miles only as deep as a football field didn't make that much difference seventy five years ago if you were from Texas and you were buying twenty miles as deep as a county. Mr Bragdon passed the paper with the magic words on it to Mitch Gordon. We weren't into the Swimsuit side of the deal. Harbor Oil was our subject.

Gordon started in about the lines but Sy butt in.

"Who's squatters? My father told me that when he sold off the Potsdammer Tract he held out two miles of beach, and if my father said it, that's how it is. We pay the taxes. Would we be getting tax bills on property we don't own? You got a bad map there."

"Sir, we ah not that kind of people" Groody said, reaching for his card and his dueling pistol and looking around for his second.

Gordon wanted out of the duel. Always have them too damn early in the morning for a New Yorker. You go straight from Elaine's and your hand isn't all that steady.

"Mr Groody" he buttered him "we respect that you have made an honest mistake but it is a mistake, and the record will support us. Maybe we don't even have to go that far. No minority stock is being offered to you gentleman here at any price. Now do you mind my changing the subject and asking whose proxies you hold?"

Oot said "That is an improper question. Groody Bank is the holder of record."

"You might as well disclose" Gordon said. "If your principal is Harbor Oil, the majority stock of Harbor Oil has passed to new ownership that will show on the books of your transfer agent tomorrow morning. I am advised that the new Harbor ownership will not want to displace the present Swimsuit Corporation directors but they may wish to replace the Harbor Oil directors."

"How's that fraind?"

You can see we did a Jiu Jitsu on them. They wanted Swimsuit, we let them have it. Good way to keep their money occupied. Then we took Harbor and got Swimsuit on the side. Considering they were blind-sided they behaved like real sports.

"Jest assuming that what you infarm us checks out" Groody said "who would your praincipal be?"

Gordon looked at Mr Bragdon and got the highsign it was okay to say.

"Mr Arsdur U. Stiff."

"Stiff? I never heard the nime." He asked Oot "Did you ever hear that nime?"

"The only Stiff I know runs a bar on Madison Avenue."

Hey, that was fun time. Wished I was there.

Mr Bragdon telephoned over before the meeting broke up to say how things stood. Said he thought there would be no contest. The Texas people knew if Vault bank was in the deal it would be what Mitch said. They were talking now about selling out their minority interest in Harbor to us at a fair price. Mr Bragdon asked how did I feel about taking up the Harbor Oil stock they still owned?

I said I wasn't feeling yet. I'd wait for the journed Swimsuit meeting to settle everything out. Then I'd see.

"You don't have to be in any hurry" he said.

Frank was who I was leery of. He was sitting on his Swimsuit shares but now he knew Harbor was going control Swimsuit. Who knew what he might do in the next two days if he got turned loose at Wyman's. He could swear off Harbor like he said but he could swear on again. I couldn't see what that would do to me but I knew it was something. I thought of having a few of the boys kidnap him for two days but then it wouldn't look good if it got out that a millionaire had people kidnapped. Wouldn't do a thing for the race image either.

I had two days to sit out and I wasn't going go against nature. Frank was out of Harbor and I was in and I was going down that road all the way but I was looking for a red light.

I didn't even like the idea of Frank high-balling into the bar before anybody else saying Goddam he never heard anything anything like it.

"You are some poker face. Doing all this wheeling and dealing in Harbor Oil and nobody knew a thing."

Didn't want to discuss it. "Yeah well. I had some luck."

"You had to pick the stock to have luck with. You know that was always one of my favorite stocks. I was always in and out."

"Yeah well you're not doing bad with Swimsuit. We're going eat off the same plate from now on."

Frank had eyes like police car lights. They went around and flashed on you and went around and flashed again. I got the full flash this time staying on me. Almost needed dark glasses when Frank put the full vision on you.

"I get as much kick out of you making a killing like that in Harbor as if I did it myself. I mean it. Just like I did it myself."

"You were an influence. You aimed me at that stock. The first I heard of that stock was from you."

"That makes me feel even better. I should feel lousy because I got out and you stayed in but I feel great."

"You got the right feeling. You fellas get to keep your company. We'll work it out that way."

"But a killing in Harbor Oil is something else. I've been in and out of that stock trying to find the time for a killing and I never made it. It was the first stock I ever owned. I'll never forget, I bought 300 shares right after the war for a dollar and a half a share and I put it in my shirt drawer and it's still there."

Now why did the man have to say anything like that?

"You mean you still have it?"

"My lucky stock."

"Come on, Frank. Only people from Massachusetts—places like that—keep stock that long. You must have sold."

"No I never sold. I was in and out of that stock but I never sold my lucky stock in the drawer. Not bad either. It must be worth $10,000 today."

"All that time. You sold it and forgot."

"Not me. It's under my shirts."

I reached over the bar and grabbed him by the coat. People had to figure we're in a disagreement, I was going sock him. "Listen, Frank, I got to know. Are you just talking or do you have that stock?"

"I've got it. What's the federal case?"

"I just have to know, I have to be sure. A certificate that old I might want it for a souvenir, something like that." Sounded nutty even to me, you can imagine how it sounded to him. He eased my hand off his lapel and made me an offer.

"Walk over to my place and I'll show you."

Stupid damn situation, right? "Okay, we'll do that." You'd think he'd be scared to be alone with me carrying on like that.

We walked over to his place and we went into his apartment and he opened the second drawer down of a big maple chest. He dug under a pile of shirts and took out a black leather folder. Inside was this crackly stock certificate with The Harbor Oil Corporation A Texas Corporation and so on printed in red. 300 shares like he said. I felt absolutely pitiful. All that money I was making, those companies I was taking over, all the margin I had out, and all the time I was being set up for a crash.

"Yeah you have it." I admired the date. "April 8, 1946. That's a date missing from my collection. I'll give you $50 a share for it. How about it?"

"I couldn't do that. It's my lucky stock."

Damn superstitious knucklehead.

"Make it a hundred. 30,000 Americans Soldiers. Sign where it says and I'll write you a check right now. April 8th 1946 is a date I have to have for my collection no matter what. Here, I'll write you a check." I opened up my pen to encourage action.

"That's some fat price" he said.

"Right on. I like a deal where both sides are happy." I opened my check book and wrote down the date. Move it along. His eyes started going around the room his usual way when he is only half with you. "No I can't do that. I don't need the money and it would break my lucky chain. Thank you, no."

I pushed him some more and raised the price but money was no part of it. I lost him right there.

5

I had to think and add things up. I was in the same shape as Al McGarvey that night he was walking around in the rain looking for answers. I went back home.

I heard Edna playing piano and I went on back to the bedroom. Lay down and looked at the ceiling. What could go wrong? Something was going wrong. Frank and me on the same side of the seesaw. Government come after Harbor on a tax case. Law suit for them spilling oil, they would have to dig up Texas to get it off the environment. Something. I got up and went in the music room. Edna was noodling on Birdland.

We had a little rough-edge between us the last couple weeks on account of the Swimsuit situation, especially after she thought I was trying get McGarvey off the deal. I had it planned to let it all out tonight and explain I was helping in my own way. I didn't want to live another day with her taking an unfavorable attitude to me.

''Edna'' I was going say ''Here's what I've been doing to take care of our friends.'' Tonight was the the night for me to tell her everything was okay and now I didn't know if it was or it wasn't. That damn fool Frank Doelger with the stock in his shirt drawer. The Lord was trying tell me something.

I didn't know what to think and didn't want to talk about it. Just looked in on her. If you're going look in on her if you feel good, you're sure going look in on her if you're low or trebled.

''Come on over here a minute'' she said, shifting to the high side of the bench and showing me the bass side. ''I was hoping you'd come in. I must have wished you home. Sit down here a minute.'' The keyboard was in my lap, the bench was made for her. ''Play Blue Skies a minute.''

That's one song I play pretty good. Not too many black keys. I gave it my A minor E seven vamp to get set and went into it. She came in over me playing Birdland. ''Stay on Blue Skies. Stay on it. You're good on that'' she said.

We had a ball dueting those two songs into each other. Edna had a million ideas and I got a few myself if I sayso. I forgot all about

Swimsuit and Harbor Oil and Frank for a half hour while we did that. I did it for the tune. I did it for the comp chords. Basie stops. Lefthand walking chords I didn't know I could do because I always went at the piano with two hands and when you get down to it I'm only good enough to do one hand at a time. You cut back on one hand it makes the other one stronger. After that you put them both together. That's what practising is, I never did that. When I sat down to play a song I went at the whole thing the way it played in my head, only it was a long long distance call from my head out to my fingers. Most of what my head sent out didn't get through. Edna playing along beside me was part of what I was doing. Blew my mind I was connected to anything that good. When we quit we put our arms around each other like kids.

"You sit still" I said. "I'll put some dinner together. I don't see eating out tonight."

"I can do a salad" she said. Edna puts a hard-boiled egg in a green salad and a little mustard in the dressing. With a sweet and sour sauce I made for the ham slice I found in the refridge we ate pretty good.

"It's a celebration" I told her when we sat down. "We saved Swimsuit for Carole and the gang today."

I said it without intending, like you walk along and you trip. I was going sleep on it overnight. Think what might still go wrong. Let it come to her some other way. She has a banker, let him tell her. I might not even be in the game myself when I bottom-lined it on Frank holding that stock. Think. But you're sitting there and you're in a mood, feeling so good from playing the piano together, and it tripped out. I usually don't have that big a mouth.

Soon as I said it I saw floating on the wall like a movie Frank sitting in front of me on the ground end of the seesaw and Groody riding high. Fear went through me like you pulled a chain and it flushed. Edna didn't see the movie. She was as pleased as I ever saw her on anything.

"You did that?" she said. "You put your money in with Al and me? I knew you would do that for your friends. That's the man I love."

"Yeah well. You might have to find another reason to love me, honey. What I told you is confidential, you can't tell anybody because it isn't all set. There's a problem and I want you to understand it's serious. Frank is holding that oil stock and I didn't know it. If he's in—well I don't know."

"What do you mean you don't know?"

"I mean I know. Frank and me being teamed on the see-saw is no small idea. It could be the whole ballgame."

"I never heard such superstition."

"That's what you say. I'm telling you it's nature. It's how it is. It's like gravity. You can't tell me anybody knows a thing about gravity but there it is. A good man can jump six seven feet but he can't hang there, he's got to come down. That's the rules you play by. We wouldn't even be in the discussion if Frank didn't tip me onto Harbor Oil. Swimsuit just came into it. Now he's tipping me out. That's where I come down."

She studied me like she saw me for the first time, those Indian eyes. Made her little whistling moves with her lips.

"You're still playing twosies with Frank? How can a man like you put yourself in another man's power? Answer me that."

"I'm not in his power. It's the opposite. I'm not doing a thing for him. He's doing it for me."

"He's doing as much for you as those cigarette ashes do for Jimmy Perse. Things go on the same time without being connected except on your sayso."

"Yeah well. You know. I can't just talk my way past this."

"You worked it out. You figured how to get the oil company. You figured how to save Swimsuit for your friends. Now you say it isn't going to happen because you see a picture on the wall of you and Frank on a seesaw?"

"I didn't say it wasn't going happen. I said I got to work it out."

I was feeling heavy pressure. We were sitting at the kitchen table. I got up and took out a bowl and broke four eggs and separated the yellows for a custard. Nothing cools me down better than cooking up something.

"What are you making now?"

"I have an idea for a little custard dessert with strawberries. A dab of brandy."

"You want to get away from talking this over, that's what you want to do."

"I can talk when I'm cooking."

"What you want to do is run a restaurant."

"I wouldn't mind. That's what I started out to do before the bar."

I whipped the eggs and put in a dab of sugar and salt and thought about the seesaw and the restaurant and big chocolate cookies. Talked out of my restaurant idea by Dill. Talked off the seesaw by Edna if I let her.

"Frank had that stock all that time you didn't know. What difference did it make? Tell me that."

"I don't know. It gave me the confidence."

"It gave it to you. Now you got it. It's yours. Are you going to give it back?"

Kept working on the eggs. Decided on sherry instead of brandy. Beat it in. Tasted it. Good like I expected.

"Here taste this" I gave her a dab on the end of the spoon. She took it without putting her mind to it. Still arguing with me in her head. Mad looking. "How does that taste?"

"Fattening. Are you going to let a man you say yourself doesn't know which way is up decide for you? Have you got more confidence in him than in yourself?"

I have to close my mind when I taste, have to listen to it. Was there enough sugar. How it went together. If I was deaf I don't think I could taste anything right.

"What are you going to do? Answer me that."

Okay, the sugar part was okay. I had something good going there. I put down the spoon and gave Edna my attention.

"Okay Edna, what I'm going do is send a check to some Pittsburgh charity organization. You tell me which one. I'm going mark it in the name of Moonrow Fargason. That shows my appreciation for him sending you to me. It's going be a big check. Then he's going be on their list like you're on Planned Parenthood and they're going be after him the rest of his life. The phone's going ring as soon as he sits down to dinner 'Hello there Fargason. We got this special drive we need our special friends on.' They're going put him on everybody's list to get a dinnertime call and I bet he's a man won't want to give up a dime for anything like that. That makes you and me even with with that sonofabitch Moonrow Fargason. Now right after I cook this up we get to the Swimsuit problem."

6

At the journed meeting they elected me chairman. I said I'd do it if Sy and Carole and Frank hung in there. They had the options to buy up the Swimsuit stock from Harbor Oil anytime they wanted. I didn't know anything about swimsuits I just knew the big picture. Is everybody happy?

Mrs Davis waved her glasses and brought up again about lunch.

"That's taken care of" Sy said. "If you will all go down one floor to the dining room you will find a beautiful spread. When you get to the dessert, you will be interested to know that it was made by our new chairman Mr Arsdur Stiff who is, I have learned, a world-class chef in addition to his other talents."

"The new dining room at Stiffy's on Madison Avenue will be open in two months" I put in, taking advantage of the advertising. "We'll be happy to welcome you folks."

"I move the stockholders give the new chairman a round of applause" Mrs Davis said.

She came up after the meeting and we got acquainted. Nice lady, just wanted her chicken sandwich rights. We fed the stockholders a shrimp salad in a tomato and fresh garden asparagus and a French horn roll and my dessert, and after lunch I sat down at her table like we were friends from way back.

"Well Adele how did you like the lunch?"

"Excellent. It was much better than General Dynamics where I voted yesterday. They served chicken sandwiches and they were dry."

"How did you like my dessert?"

"I didn't want to say anything. It was delicious but too many calories. You have a lot of stockholders who are turned off by an insensitive thing like that. But it was good. I have to say it was good."

I told her my wife said the same thing. As a matter of fact I looked it up and it isn't half as many calories as a piece of apple pie. I found out later what I invented was an Italian dessert they call zaboloney that had already been invented except for the strawberries but I didn't know it at the time. People in the same line of work come up with the same answers without copying each other. It's natural.

We keep it on the menu under Chef's Diet Custard with strawberries. We still put out thirty forty a day. Thousand, that is. I don't know why they call it zabaloney, there's no meat in it. The only meat dessert I know is mincemeat pie.

Al McGarvey overlooked the dessert in his inside story. Even so he took first prize from the financial writers for the best story of the year. Doubling his trusts wouldn't do as much for that man's happiness as giving him that prize.

Yeah I gotta say it was better than if he got Carole. Once he got used to real work everything else shook down into place next to that. You don't know who your real woman is till you know what your real work is. That's the kind of thing you hear me say you want to watch out for. They went out together a couple times. That was as far as she wanted to go. Okay, those things happen. He was working. He met another girl and liked her even more. That's how things go once you get into the world and move around. Everybody can't get the one woman he thought of like me. You got to have a little luck for that.

7

Harbor Oil was a money-making fool. We put in that two mile long condo on the Island. That's in the Guinness. Water view from every room. We put the fountains in for the people in the back. We put in the shopping center. We did the resort in Colorado. We did 24,000 condos on the ranch in California and have space left waiting on a new idea. When the Arabs gave us the high oil prices we found out we had oil and gas in a lot of those little sections Groody picked up and never did anything with.

The real money didn't start for another year. After I opened the dining room I saved a regular table for eight in the back for any partners who dropped in for lunch. On this particular day we had all the seats filled and they all ordered Stiffy's Diet Custard for dessert and they began to kid me about how good it was.

Dill said "If you franchised this you could sell a dozen or two."

Greg said "Stiffy's McEgg McCustard. How does that grab you?"

"Ah so" I said.

"McColonel McStiff" Mitch Gordon said. "Grow a beard. Go around the country and Mcpeddle the McCustard."

"You do it, you have the dignity" I told Sy. "You can have the recipe. While you're at it, do something with my lemon baked beans."

"Stop kidding around" Freddy Lebrand said. "Get out of this chickenshit one-meal-at-a-time-bit. Franchise is the way to go."

Hand it to Freddy Lebrand. He can be a mean sonofabitch but he knows where money is. He turned off the jokes, and first thing you know we were into franchises. I sent in the recipes and Freddy sent in the accountants. Every new Stiffy's we open Malcolm sends a big balloon and I give my speech on how to take care of customers.

If you want to know what money is, forget oil companies and real estate and go into franchises. Seems only a day after we started that they had my picture on the cover of Forbes Magazine. IS THIS MAN THE RICHEST OF THE RICH? I don't have to tell you anything more about that, it's all been printed.

You just be sure to say Edna and me are still in the same place at the Western and still walk over here every day doing what we always did. She plays piano. I run a damn good eating place. All that other is extra.

We got it all under Arsdur U. Stiff and Company Inc. Some fellas came in trying to sell me the idea to change the name to AUSCO.

They jiggered the letters around and came up with the line The USA CO. They'd do that for me for $2,000,000 dollars, including four sizes of envelopes. Good deal, usually only includes three. I squinched up my eyes and told them I'd think it over.

We don't even own an automobile, never did after that Nova General Motors hung on me. The checks go into the foundations and they push it out. If I'd known about jobs like that when I was a kid, getting paid big numbers for giving money away, I might have developed a strategy to get into that line of work. They don't tell you about jobs like that. Hard to fire a man for not giving somebody else's money away away fast enough. All the average man would need would be a little warning and he'd speed up. No shortage of places to put it. There's a big difference between who has money and who can use a little. If money was a natural thing like water it would level out, wouldn't it? Wouldn't need anybody special to spread it around.

When I say something like that keep your eye on it. Malcolm can put it in with his Sayings if he wants, but you keep your eye on it. Just because Arsdur Stiff says it doesn't make it so. You have to see for yourself if money is natural or it isn't and if it should level or it shouldn't and all that. My name on it doesn't give it any more sense than if a hundred and ten year old Zulu taxi driver said it in his native tongue. Doesn't give it any more sense than the president of the United States' name on a joke makes it funnier than you saying it. Man, do you realize they laughed hard when Gerald Ford told a joke? That's what you want to keep in mind. That's nothing against Gerald Ford.

The basic thing is Edna likes to play piano and I like to cook and we worked it out that way. Wouldn't make all that much difference to us if we did it in Groody Texas if we could make a living at it and had the same quality friends.

We were talking about that with Carole and Sy a couple weeks ago. We went out there for Sy's birthday, his ninetieth. He doesn't come into town any more. Can't walk too good. Diabetes. We got a foundation working on that. Carole must be toward eighty. What they call Upper Middle Age. You have to be a hundred to be old under the new rules. We were sitting around the pool and I told Carole

"When I first knew you I was sure you had your eye on Frank Doelger and wanted to get together with him. What Carole wants I figured Carole gets."

"You thought what?" she said.

"Yeah. Frank. I thought you two would get together."

"I thought you could add better than that. I did want to get him into the business. I thought we needed somebody like him and I was right. But personally I was waiting around for Sy."

"They surely do make you wait around" Edna said. "This one took forever."

Yeah but when I got the zap I moved.

The only zap I ever had that didn't work out was that one where my KGB followed the Dow. That's the opportunity you could say I never did anything with. Not that I need it, but it bothers me that it's in there and I can't use it. Like your tonsils or appendix. What's the damn thing for?

I get a new KGB every year on my checkup. Keep it in my wallet. Take it out now and then. Look at it. Anytime I meet anybody I think might have a new slant on it I show it to him like you show a picture of a missing kid, maybe somebody saw him somewhere.

Here. You got any ideas?